# LIGHT RAID

CYNTHIA FELICE AND CONNIE WILLIS

ACE BOOKS, NEW YORK

LIGHT RAID

An Ace Book
Published by The Berkley Publishing Group
200 Madison Avenue, New York, New York 10016

Copyright © 1989 by Connie Willis and Cynthia Felice.

Book design by Ernie Haim

First Edition: May 1989

Library of Congress Cataloging-in-Publication Data

Willis, Connie.
  Light raid / by Connie Willis & Cynthia Felice.
    p.  cm.
  ISBN 0-441-48311-9 : $17.95 ($24.95 Can.)
  I. Felice, Cynthia.  II. Title.
PS3573.I45652L48  1989
813'.54—dc19                                            88-30853
                                                            CIP

Printed in the United States of America

10  9  8  7  6  5  4  3  2  1

# LIGHT RAID

To Bob,
who never lost faith in us

# LIGHT RAID

# HOMELESS CHICKS TAKEN UNDER WING OF LOCAL PATRIOT

Ella Ponsonby has opened her home and her heart to the frightened, lonely children evacuated from Denver Springs in the continuing unpleasantness. The adorable waifs, made homeless by the threat of light raids, adore kind Mrs. Ponsonby. "She's a saint," says a fifteen-year-old lucky enough to have been taken under her wing. "She's like a mother to us."

"I'm just glad to do my bit for the Red Cross," Mrs. Ponsonby says wistfully. "I love all my chicks like they was me own."

Mrs. Ponsonby retired to neutral Victoria three years ago, just before the Western States allies joined the Commonwealth in the war against Quebec.

"At first I just opened my home to the children of friends back in the Western States," recalled Mrs. Ponsonby, a retired Hellene of Hydra Corp in Denver Springs, "but then I heard the Red Cross had many lonely and helpless refugee children, and that's when I opened my home to total strangers."

(Caring Mrs. Ponsonby outside her home, which she turned into a shelter for homeless waifs, Screen 2. How to adopt a waif for the duration, Red Cross, Screen 279.)

# CHAPTER ONE

When the mail rang, I didn't exactly race to answer it. In the first place, I was in the middle of diping Verity Ann and to stop would have meant starting all over again. Since I had already reached the stage where I had my knee on her stomach and was yelling, "Just wait till Mrs. Ponsonby gets home. I'll tell her you were a naughty, naughty girl," I thought I'd better finish the job.

In the second place, the mailboy kept delivering government handouts and neutrality guidelines just so he could flirt with whoever answered the door. He had already delivered today's real mail, a letter from Mrs. Ponsonby's sister in Yellowknife, and had spent half an hour talking to fifteen-year-old Chilkie. Besides, if he was delivering real mail, it was probably a notice saying another evacuee was available and asking if dear, kindhearted Mrs. Ponsonby was interested, in which case I didn't want it. I couldn't silence the bell on my wrist terminal because I was using both hands to keep the baby from wriggling out of her paper dipe, which meant the only other working doorbell in the house was still ringing, too. But Chilkie was safely up another flight and out of hearing even the racket in the kitchen, so if I just ignored it maybe he would give up and go away.

He didn't, and as I made one final heroic effort and got the Velcro grips firmly fastened over Verity Ann's fat little bottom, it occurred to me that the reason for all this frantic ringing might be a letter from my father. I scooped up the baby and ran downstairs.

Six-year-old Beejum already had the door open and was telling the mailboy that Chilkie wasn't in, like I had told him to do. "Ariadne is, though, Skids. Do you want to talk to her?"

"Sure," Skids said, leering across Beejum at me. "I always want to talk to you."

"Well, I don't want to talk to you."

He shrugged. "Okay, then, where's Chilkie?"

"Her parents in Denver Springs sent for her."

"She doesn't have any . . . " Beejum said, and I grabbed for the letter and shut the door all in one motion.

"Parents," Beejum finished, sounding outraged. "You know that, Ariadne."

"Of course I know it. But how do you know Skids isn't a spy?"

"A spy?" Beejum said, his eyes lighting up.

"Careless words can lose the war," I said, and fumbled with the envelope, trying to get the silly thing open. "Why can't they use the comm like they do at home? You'd never catch them delivering the mail by hand in Denver Springs."

"Is it a letter from a spy?" Beejum said.

"No." It wasn't from my father either. I could see that without even opening it. It lacked the censorship and neutral communication stickers that were splattered all over everything that came from the Western States. It had a Victoria internal comm sticker heat-stuck to the perforation line, and there was no way it was going to come open without tearing the thin hardcopy inside.

"Why can't you Victorians do anything the simple way?" I said, struggling to keep Verity Ann balanced and get the envelope opened at the same time. "There're a lot more chances for spies to waylay a boy on a gyroscooter than to intercept a comm signal."

Beejum shrugged.

"Here," I said, handing him the hardcopy and repositioning Verity Ann. "Is Chilkie still upstairs?"

"Yeah. On the third floor. With the twins," Beejum said, solemnly examining the perforation. "They threw up."

"I suppose I'd better see if I can help her," I said, and started up the stairs. Carrying Verity Ann was like lugging around the wrong end of an energized magnet, and the prospect of the upchucking twins was almost more than I could bear. There seemed to be no limits to Mrs. Ponsonby's generosity where evacuees were concerned. She had taken the twins only a week ago, and right now she was down at the Red Cross Shelter seeing if there were any more evacuees available. I hoped there weren't. There were already nine of us, and the only one old enough to help me was Chilkie, who was not exactly in love with children.

Neither was I, and becoming less so with every passing day. Mrs. Ponsonby had been delighted to get me since I was over the usual evacuee age and that meant she could take in a lot more children and collect her Red Cross bonuses for them without doing any of the work. Mrs. Ponsonby had told the Red Cross people she needed double bonuses so she could "restore" her two-hundred-year-old wreck of a house, but she didn't spend them on any improvements I could see.

The room I shared with Beejum and the baby leaked, the voice recognition unit on the household computer didn't work, and the plumbing was a real mess. The house got its hot water and heat from a natural hot spring under the house, but the pipes were as old as the house and so heavily encrusted with minerals that there was hardly any water pressure and often no heat. Mrs. Ponsonby had gotten an extra bonus last month to fix the pipes, but she hadn't made any moves in that direction so far. When the water stopped altogether, which, according to my calculations, would happen any day now, she would be forced to do something about it. I could hardly wait.

"Here," Beejum said before I got halfway up the stairs. He was holding out the opened hardcopy to me. Verity Ann lunged for it and practically pitched over the banister.

"Thank you," I said, and took it from him. I sat down on the stairs and handed Verity Ann the comm sticker to chew on. The letter read, "My dear Ariadne, I just received a letter from your mother. Until now, I had no idea you were in Victoria. Please say you will come to luncheon today at one o'clock at the Empress Hotel to make up for my unintentional neglect of an old friend's daughter." It was signed with a neat facsimile signature that read, "Clare." And at the bottom was added, "I realize this is short notice. If you can't come, just call the Empress and leave a message for me."

Verity Ann was choking on the sticker. I smacked her on the back and caught the soggy red wad in my hand. I fumbled in my pocket for a honey teat for her, trying to think who Clare could be. I was sure I'd never heard the name before. Maybe she was someone who had worked at Hydra Corp and then married into another corporation. Or maybe this woman was writing to someone else altogether, and I was not going to get to go to lunch at the Empress at all, but instead was going to stand in front of Mrs. Ponsonby's old-fashioned hand console, trying to call up something everybody would eat for lunch, the twins wouldn't promptly cancel, and Mrs. Ponsonby wouldn't condemn as too expensive.

All of a sudden I knew I couldn't face another one of Mrs. Ponsonby's Home for Evacuated Children lunches. If this Clare woman had made a mistake, she wouldn't know it till she saw me, and if I was lucky, not until some time after we'd ordered. And I would get lunch and a little kindness and (if she really did know my mother) a chance to complain about being a full-time baby-sitter. She might even put in a good word for me about going home. Light raids or no, Denver Springs had to be better than this.

I didn't tell Chilkie I was going until I'd put Verity Ann down for her nap, changed into my best jams and sandals, and put everything I needed into my bag. Then I went into the kitchen and said casually, "Guess what I got in the mail today. An invitation to lunch."

"The mail came?" Chilkie said. "Did Skids bring it?"

I was tempted to say no. Chilkie seemed to think Skids was crazy about her, but he never missed a chance to flirt with me and probably with every other female on his route.

"Skids wanted to talk to you," Beejum said, "but . . ."

"You were upstairs," I said hastily, "and he was in a hurry. I'm going out. Tell Mrs. Ponsonby I'll be back by four."

"Four!" she said, outraged. "You can't leave me here all afternoon by myself. What about Verity Ann? What about Beejum?"

Ordinarily I would have tried to be reasonable and explain to Chilkie how badly I needed this lunch out, but I knew she'd throw a fit.

She had thrown one when I showed her the ferry pass I'd stolen from Mrs. Ponsonby, even though she knew perfectly well that it was impossible to get out of Victoria without one, and that I was determined to go home.

"You can't go off and leave me with all those brats!" she wailed.

"I won't go until you turn sixteen and you can come with me. Then we'll leave together," I'd said. When she had realized I wasn't going to run off and leave her, she'd even helped with my escape plans, though lately she was so involved with her Romeo mailboy, she wasn't much help. I'd had to do the pipes myself.

But even though I'd promised not to run off to Denver Springs before her birthday, I took my handy-dandy escape kit with me everywhere I went, including now.

"I'm just going downtown," I said patiently. "Verity Ann's asleep, and Beejum's in your room, going through the love letters Skids sent you."

She yelped and dived past me up the stairs. I checked to make sure the twins were strapped in their high chairs and out of reach of anything sharp or edible, and walked back to the foot of the stairs. "I don't know what you're getting so upset about," I yelled up at Chilkie. "He can't read yet. Goodbye."

She yelped again, and I made my getaway, nearly crashing into the mailboy as I went. "Give me a lift to the tube stop, will you, Skids?" I said.

"Sure," he said. "Where are the two of us going?"

"*We're* not going anywhere," I said, climbing onto the padded bar behind him. "*I'm* going down to the harbor."

He gave me that Romeo grin of his and peeled away from the curb, barely giving me time to throw my arms around his waist and hang on. He stopped the scooter right in front of the airlock to the vacuum tube where the magnetic levitation cars ran every few minutes. "You sure you don't want me to go with you?" he asked.

"I'm sure," I said, trying to get the pleats back in my jams with my fingers.

"You don't know what you're missing," he said, grinning, and then in the same breath, he added, "Is Chilkie still at home?"

He stomped down hard on the accelerator and breezed off before I could answer. I hurried through the airlock and into a waiting maglev. The airlock sealed and the car moved through the translucent tube silently. I sank into the padded seat, feeling better than I had in months.

When I'd first gotten to Victoria, I'd been hopping mad at Mother and Dad for sending me to a strange country, away from home and company, in the middle of a war. They hadn't sent me at the start of the war, which was when everybody was getting killed in laser-light raids they didn't have any warning of. I had been working with Mother on important war work then, the GEM biot project, as an apprentice biologist, waiting the last months till my sixteenth birthday so I could get full researcher status, and nobody had seemed at all concerned about my being lased.

Then, suddenly, right before my birthday, I'd been packed off to adamantly neutral Vancouver Island because Denver Springs was "too dangerous." Well, Victoria wasn't all that safe either, what with babies throwing up right and left and Mrs. Ponsonby cutting our lunches down to malnutrition levels, and pretty soon I was so mad at Mrs. Ponsonby I stopped being angry with Mother and Dad.

The tabloids helped soften my attitude toward them, too. If you could believe the reports on the terminals at every street corner, Denver Springs was taking a real beating. Quebec had really stepped up their light raids, though according to the tabloids only on military and commercial targets. But Hydra Corp was a commercial target, wasn't it? And there were rumors of something I found even scarier than batellite attacks: drought. Maybe my parents had known more than they were telling when they sent me away so abruptly.

I didn't stop being mad at Mrs. Ponsonby, but there wasn't much I could do about her, so I concentrated on getting back home. I wrote pleading letters to Dad and reasonable ones to Mother. Dad's letters back to me were sympathetic but firm. They contained explanations of why I couldn't come home that had been lined out by the censors. I imagined all kinds of terrible things in the blank spaces.

Mother had no patience with my homesickness. She had come to Hydra Corp from Quebec at fifteen, an orphan and refugee, had married my father by the time she was sixteen, and had never looked back once. "I spent my time trying to fit into my new situation, to make friends of my co-workers and new family instead of weeping over the family I'd lost. I suggest you try to do the same," she wrote.

Of course she hadn't been homesick. She'd had to escape from Quebec after the takeover, and besides, she'd had my father and all of Hydra Corp to help her fit in.

Mother's letters had convinced me of one thing. She would never send for me unless I had a better reason for wanting to come home than homesickness. I had tried to give her that reason by setting up a laboratory in Mrs. Ponsonby's basement laundry room. It was totally private since Mrs. Ponsonby would never think of doing the laundry herself.

Unbeknownst to anybody, I had brought some live GEM biots and an assortment of experimental hydra with me. I had some wild idea of making a breakthrough in the GEM research that was giving Mother such fits, and coming home in triumph. There was nothing wrong with the little genetically engineered memory chips except that they wouldn't replicate. I tried everything I could think of in my limited lab, including putting some of them in the freezer, an experiment which resulted in Mrs. Ponsonby's dumping them down the sink because she thought they were leftovers. Nothing worked, so I quit fiddling with them and started working on something more practical: an escape plan.

The hydra I'd brought were easier to grow. The little water-pumping and cleansing organisms are the bread and butter of Hydra Corp, for they make arid Denver Springs into the lush oasis it is by tapping water tables too far down for the best mechanical pumps to reach. But the hydra can be adapted for lots of other purposes. For one thing, you can dry up springs as well as tap them by merely strengthening the hydra's cell walls. Hydra Corp did it all the time, to cap water sources that were too polluted for even the hydra to clean, and even to convince nonpaying customers to settle their bills. They could also stop up Mrs. Ponsonby's plumbing so that she would get in trouble with the Red Cross and lose her license to keep evacuees. So I had worked on mutating the hydra and putting them down the pipes; even with the mineral crusting already there, I figured it would take a while.

What worked promptly was a nifty little mutation that had the consistency of putty and the color of skin. It would cover up my evacuation tattoo when the time came to get out of Victoria.

And then Dad's letters stopped coming. He had never written all that regularly, but always more than once a week, and I hadn't heard from him in over a month. Mother's letters had always come once a month and practically on the same day (I figured she had me on her terminal calendar: form letter and fill in the blanks). I had gotten six letters from her in the past month, and not one of them mentioned Dad. Her letters had never been chatty, but now they were totally without news, vague in a way that was disturbing. The tabloids had daily stories of terrible city-leveling light raids and sabotage, but she didn't mention them or her research or anything. It was as if the letters were written in a vacuum. As if, I thought as I got off the maglev, she were trying to keep something from me.

I stopped short. That was the real reason I was trotting down to the harbor in silk jams to meet somebody I didn't know. I had been trying this whole month to convince myself Dad was too busy to write and Mother was only being her usual businesslike self, but I hadn't bought it. Mother was keeping something from me, and I was going to find out from this Clare person what it was.

I walked across the street to the Empress Hotel. It's a massive building, almost a hundred years old, and it's patterned on an even older building that stood there near the head of Victoria's harbor for more than a century. The tabloids are always full of gossip items about who's staying at the Empress, and there was a gaggle of reporters in fedoras on the front steps who looked up as I walked past and then down again since it was obvious I wasn't anybody. The doorman didn't even bother to look up and neither did the desk clerks in the huge lobby.

I didn't know where I was going. I knew from the tabloids that high tea was served in the lobby, but they also talked about a dining room and a bar, and something called a garden cafe. I could see several middle-aged ladies sitting alone at tables on the terrace, but none of them looked at all interested in my arrival, and I had a feeling I would be stopped short by the management if I went up to one of them uninvited. So I hesitated, biting my lip, and looking very much like an evacuee. It must have been a snap for Clare to find me.

"Ariadne," said a voice from behind me.

"Mother! What in the world are you . . ." I said, wheeling around. "I mean . . . I thought . . ." For one wild moment there I had been sure it was Mother saying my name, but of course it wasn't. It was simply an accident of voice, the fact that I had been thinking so much about Mother on the way down here. "You must be Clare," I said lamely.

"Yes," she said. She had blond, straight hair and blue eyes. "I thought we'd have lunch in the Garden Cafe. It's a little old-fashioned, but still very nice." She nodded to a waiter hovering nearby, and he led us to a table.

Very nice was hardly the word. Real cloth tablecloths and stainless-steel silverware, real china plates. The waiter handed us menus instead of bringing up a terminal. The menus were cards printed by an old-fashioned impact printer. Lines were drawn through two of the entrees, and there was a disclaimer about the management being able to make substitutions without notice, subject to the market, etc., which meant the tubes to the Commonwealth and the Western States had been blockaded again, or Quebec had hijacked a load of honey and sunflower seeds in one of its many "neutral country checks."

"They used to have terminals at each seating, very nice," Clare said. "The war has even touched the Empress, though not her service, I'm glad to say." She laid her menu flat on the table. "I'd suggest seafood, something caught here in the Strait. Anything else may not be available."

Clare was elegantly dressed in a skirt and fitted jacket cut from what I thought was real wool. She had on earrings and a delicate shoulder chain. She looked like one of the rich and famous whose pictures were always on the tabloids, having lunch at the Empress Hotel. Her voice, which really didn't sound that much like Mother's, had the clipped Victorian Commonwealth accent.

I said, "Where do you know my mother from?"

"That's a long story," she said. "Let's order first and then I'll tell you all about it."

She beckoned to the waiter, and he was at her elbow instantly. Clare ordered a seafood salad, and I mumbled that I would like the same thing. After he'd disappeared, Clare said, "How are you enjoying Victoria? It's not like home and company, is it?"

"No," I said, and found myself telling her all about Mrs. Ponsonby and her baby factory. I hadn't meant to blurt everything out like that and wasn't quite sure why I had except that I really had about reached the end of my rope and that comment about home and company had made me feel she might understand what no one else in this benighted country seemed to, that I did not just miss Denver Springs, I missed Hydra Corp.

I talked for a good five minutes about Mrs. Ponsonby and the babies and Chilkie and Skids before I remembered I hadn't asked her about Dad and the funny change in Mother's letters, which was what I had come here to find out about, and I hadn't let her get a word in edgewise. At least I hadn't said anything about my trying to sabotage Mrs. Ponsonby's pipes with my biot garden, but the way things were going, I probably would the next time I opened my mouth.

I was glad when the waiter appeared at my elbow, scattering paper doilies everywhere, and filling cups with camomile and milk, making conversation impossible. Clare smiled and shrugged, and we both sat silently until he had left us alone with two heaps of what looked like canned salmon on a lettuce leaf.

"Oh, dear, the war has affected the Empress more than I'd realized," she said. "I'd hoped for fresh salmon." She picked up one of about five forks and smiled at me. "Sorry. I suppose you can get this at Mrs. Ponsonby's."

I didn't dare get started again, so I smiled back, grabbed for a fork, any fork, and dug into my salad. It *was* canned salmon. We ate in silence for a few minutes, as if she were waiting for me to start chattering again. Finally she said, "You must be thinking it was very rude of me not to have gotten in touch with you before now, but I didn't know you were here. Your mother wrote me a month ago, but I didn't get back to the island till yesterday."

A month ago was when my father stopped writing. I looked up at her, my heart starting to pound. She looked down at her lettuce. "I've been up in Yellowknife on government business for several months. Otherwise I would have contacted you sooner. It sounds like you've been very unhappy."

"I wish I were home with Mother and Dad," I said. "There's so much censoring on the tabloids I can't find out anything about Denver Springs. Did Mother say anything about how Dad was handling the light raids in her letter?"

"What?" Clare said. There it was again, something, some flicker of nervousness or tension every time we got close to the subject of my father.

"Have there been any laser raids close to Hydra Corp?" I said.

She took a sip of her tea and then looked up at me. "I only know what I see on the tabloids, I'm afraid. They didn't mention any escalation in light raids. I didn't read about any civilian raids. I'm sure your mother's fine."

She was lying. Or maybe phrasing her words so they were the literal truth, but a lie nevertheless. She had not said there weren't any civilian light raids. She had said the tabloids hadn't mentioned escalation. And she had said, "Your mother is fine." Not, "Your mother and father." The waiter came back. He removed the plates and then brought over the pastry cart. It had apparently not been hit by the blockades. I stared at the iced cakes and carob mousse for so long that Clare said, "Two of the raspberry torte." The waiter cut a hefty slice for me. I let him put the plate in front of me, wondering if he could see how shaky I was. Something was definitely wrong at home, and Clare knew about it.

Clare picked up another of the forks and said, "Why don't you come stay with me?"

"What?" I said.

"I live in a big old house on the north end of the island. I have plenty of room, and I can guarantee there are no dipes to change, no babies to take care of. I'd love the company. Please say you'll come."

If I had come to this luncheon only to confirm my fears, she had done just that. Dad hadn't written me in a month and there was something wrong about Mother's letters. She had written Clare and told her what was wrong, and it must be bad, very bad, if she had to appeal to a friend I didn't even know to take in her daughter.

I made a great show of eating my cake and drinking the rest of my lukewarm tea. Then I said, "I've written my father to ask him if I can come home. I don't think I should give you my answer till I hear from him."

She tried to smile. "You do realize you can get mail just as easily at my home?"

"Probably more easily," I said lightly. "Our mailboy, Skids, isn't very reliable. But even if I have my mail forwarded, I can't just leave Mrs. Ponsonby without anybody. She'll give all my work to poor Chilkie. I've got to give her a couple of days at least to find somebody to adopt who's old enough to change dipes."

The waiter left a chrome-plated check readout facedown on the pewter tray. Clare palmed it to check the amount, then added a tip and signed off with a four-character input. The waiter did his faster-than-light act, and we pushed back our chairs. "All right, Ariadne," Clare said. "I'll call day after tomorrow. I admire your loyalty to your friend, but . . ."

But what? Am I going to hear something in a few more days? Am I going to get a black-bordered letter handed to me by Skids?

"You're right," I said. "I can't wait forever. I'll tell Mrs. Ponsonby tonight and do my packing. You can pick me up tomorrow." I hesitated. "It's very nice of you to ask me to come stay with you."

"I'm happy to do it," Clare said, and immediately seemed more relaxed. "Can I give you a lift home?" she said at the door of the hotel. She gestured toward the old Parliament building at the head of the harbor. "My gullwing's tethered a few blocks away."

"No, thanks. I don't think it would be a good idea for you to bring me home. Mrs. Ponsonby isn't going to be very happy about this. I'd better tell her by myself. I'll take the maglev." I leaned forward and kissed her on the cheek. "Thank you so much for asking me. You don't know how much this means to me." I hurried down the steps and across to the maglev station.

I hoped I'd convinced her I intended to accept her invitation. If I hadn't, and she reacted in the wrong way to that impulsive kiss, she might call Mrs. Ponsonby's this afternoon. Even if she didn't, Mrs. Ponsonby would give me only until four on the dot to get back and start ordering supper for the children. It was already three. I waited on the platform till three cars had gone by, then went back outside to make sure Clare was gone. She was. I hurried out of the station and down to the harbor.

That last bit of conversation was the hardest thing I'd ever done.

You can get mail at my house, huh? She knew perfectly well that I was not going to get a letter from my father. That was why she had asked me to lunch and offered me her house. Because she pitied me. Because something had happened to my father. And it had something to do with a light raid.

When was she going to tell me? When we were safely at her house, at the north end of the island where there was no maglev service, where I couldn't possibly run home? Or did she and Mother plan to keep up this act of careful letters and edited conversations until the end of the war?

I didn't care what they planned. I had a plan of my own. Chilkie would never understand me abandoning her this way, but I couldn't take the risk of calling Mrs. Ponsonby's house to let her know what I was going to do. I would send her a comm message once I got home.

At the ferry station I went into the privy and locked myself in one of the cubicles. I opened my bag and pulled out the makeup plat I had stolen from Mrs. Ponsonby. I had practiced doing my face to look older until I could manage it in a couple of minutes, which paid off now. I piled my hair up on top of my head, and then pulled out the mutant hydra. I was glad I had grabbed them at the last minute. I peeled the layer of biots from between the plastic sheets and slipped it on the back of my hand. The little darlings promptly turned flesh-colored and spread out into a single opaque layer over my tattoo. I snapped higher heels onto my sandals and put on another layer of Mrs. Ponsonby's lavender lipstick. Halfway home, already, I thought, and wondered what I would find when I got there.

# Light Raid Predictions

Victoria and salmon both light raid victims, and droughts will spread to the Maritime Provinces.

"Neutral Victoria will be a batellite target before the moon is full again," predicts Mona Zinfield, psychic house painter who correctly predicted the Western States' entry into the war three years ago, "but heavy fog will prevent perfect sighting from the orbiting battle stations, and the laser beams will miss their target, destroying instead Butchart Gardens, one of the wonders of the world. "Michael Jackson fans will win the court battle that opposes his being awakened from his century-long sleep in a hyperbaric preservation chamber on what would be his one-hundred-and-fiftieth birthday, favoring instead waiting until the war is over so that Michael can live in peaceful times."

"Salmon won't run this year because the water temperature in the Strait has been raised by light raid strikes on cruisers and destroyers," says Bannerman Jones, who serves as consultant to Olympic Peninsula communities as well as owning hydrofoil rental and charter services, "but river fishing will be excellent."

(More from predictions, Screen 3. Renowned salmon fishing, Screen 4A.)

# CHAPTER TWO

As soon as I was safely across the border into the Western States, I tried Dad's ID string. It worked, and that was the best news I'd had so far. If Dad was . . . if anything had happened to him, they'd put a freeze on his account, and anybody trying to make a transaction would automatically be picked up for questioning. Not only were there no questions and no sheriffs appearing suddenly at the terminal, there wasn't so much as an identity check. That meant Dad didn't know I was coming either, but I preferred to think of it as his giving his tacit approval to my getting there as soon as possible, and bought a ticket on the overland caravan.

It took a day and a half to get home. I spent the first few hours sleeping, and then, once we crossed the Rockies into Montana, I spent a lot of time looking out the windows at what had caused the war. It was hard to believe that that endless sweep of blowing sand had ever been fields of wheat and pasture for cattle, and that people could live in places where there weren't hydra.

We made a water stop at the Billings oasis and again at Cheyenne, and I half-expected Dad to have me pulled off the caravan at one of them, but he didn't, and he wasn't there to meet me at the north end of Denver Springs when the caravan pulled into the makeshift landport they'd been using since all the shuttle flights had been grounded, which worried me even more.

The landport was outside the hydra-made oasis that encompassed most of Denver Springs, and I suppose that made some kind of sense, what with the water shortages and the dust the overlands stirred up, but gullwings were back in use and their blades prevented the dust from settling. It occurred to me that the dust could be a deliberate attempt to discourage light raids on the remaining transportation. Quebec's batellites lased anything the Western States or the Commonwealth put in the air, so atmospheric craft operated only during storms when the thick clouds absorbed the laser beam. Local ground turbulence and thick haze were a pretty effective defense against lasers, too, but it was hard on the lungs and eyes, and on my jams, which were already the worse for wear after my scramble across the border.

I was filthy by the time I got to the street shuttle that would take me downtown to the tubes. There was nothing I could do about the silk jams, but I used Mrs. Ponsonby's makeup plat to blend in most of the smudges on my face. I debated pulling the biots off because they were turning green around the edges and curling suspiciously, but decided it was too risky. Even this close to home, I could be picked up by an evac warden and find myself back in Victoria on the basis of the tattoo alone. I decided to keep my hands in my pockets when necessary.

My old student pass worked to get me into the downtown terminal. Then I realized that most of the people were not even offering passes or plastic to the attendants. When I saw that the terminal was full of light raid instructions, I figured the relaxed security at the gates was because they couldn't reasonably make people stand outside for a string check when the light raid sirens were going.

But inside, there were a lot of wardens standing around, watching the maglev cars glide in and out, and maybe watching for evacuees, too. I sidled up to a tabloid display while I waited for the southbound maglev. The header read, "Treason Suspect Refuses to Talk," and a subheading under it said, "Drought Sabotage Still a Mystery." I couldn't get the story without putting a token into the tabloid slot. I didn't have one, and anyway, here was the southbound maglev pulling in. I ran for it.

I was going to Cheyenne Heights, but that station had been crossed out on the route map inside the car. The car didn't go any farther than Black Forest. The tube had been seared between there and the Garden of the Gods where it ran aboveground in the west floodplain. I tried not to think of how long the batellite had been able to stay in a stationary orbit to do that much damage before the GTAs had driven them away.

I followed a handful of people to the stairs, feeling strangely vulnerable as I came out into the sunlight, but Woodman Valley looked the same as ever, only a narrow line of charred grass where the tube's vacuum seal had been breached. I guess I'd expected half the city to be gone, the Rockies' Rampart Range scarred and smoking.

The Rockies looked untouched, blue-green in the afternoon haze, the valley green with new spring buds where hydra thrived. In their midst were brown spots, the kind you sometimes see in a new field where the water-carrying hydra haven't finished filling in. But that couldn't be the case because the hydra in Woodman Valley had been old and strong before I was born. It might be laser damage, but even an abortive raid would have left evidence of thermal damage, like the char by the tube, and this just looked dry. This had to be the drought problem the tabloid said was sabotage.

The silhouette of buildings along the Heights was unchanged, but the polished red granite and limestone domes of the corps had been sprayed with garish metallic paint to reflect some of the laser energy. Close in, a parking lot had been scraped clear to accommodate a hodgepodge of vehicles: scooters and gullwings with homemade taxi signs painted on their fenders and fuselages, and official-looking Transit Authority stickers on the windshields.

I walked over to a scooter that didn't look like it would fall apart before we got two blocks. A woman wearing secondhand shuttle fatigues with the stripes ripped off the sleeve left a group of similarly attired people who were clustered around a drinking fountain.

"Where to?" she asked. She rocked back on her heels and looked at me, as if sizing me up.

"Cheyenne Heights."

"Where in Cheyenne Heights?"

"Seventeen Hydra Compound. Why? Have there been light raids there?"

The woman shrugged. "No more than anyplace else." She put her hands in her pockets and scrutinized me again. "You have anything to do with those tabloid reporters I took down to Hydra Corp this morning?"

"Tabloid reporters?" I said. Dad had barely tolerated satellite network reporters at Hydra Corp, but with most of the satellites blinded because of the war, tabloids were more popular than ever. Still, I couldn't imagine them being interested in Hydra Corp.

My blank look must have convinced her because she gave a half nod. "Payment up front, cash."

"Cash?" I didn't have any. I shook my head. "Thanks anyway," I said. I glanced at the mountains, saw that the sun was well on its way to catching them and falling behind. If my legs didn't give out, I might reach the house by morning.

"Wait a minute, kid. You evacuation?"

She was looking at my hand for the sticker and would not have seen it because the biots, though turning green, still hid it. So did my bag strap. "I was," I said, "but my folks just sent for me."

"Okay, hop on. I'll take payment on the other end."

The driver steered the scooter along streets I didn't recognize, and I wondered if she'd chosen the route to keep me away from the damage. "Been gone long?" she asked, turning another corner.

"Two years," I said.

"Where do your folks work?" She was watching me in the rearview mirror.

"Hydra Corp."

"What do they do?"

It was coming to me slowly that she was trying to figure out what to charge them. If I said that my mother was head of Research or even that my father was chief of Security, the fare would go up. "Dad mucks out the spoilage vats, and my mother works in the greenhouses."

"Yeah," she said. "I thought of getting an assembly line job before I lucked onto this rig. Every other damn country involved in this war has full employment, but the Western States had to let the feds get involved. Can't get anything unless you join the army, and I never did care for painting roofs." She shook her head and kept driving.

We were coming up on Space Park, an old and beautiful technology development area. Hydra had been deep-set there so that the big cottonwoods could grow in the floodplain. I saw a burned tree, then a whole row of them, standing like charred skeletons. There was starting to be a lot more damage, though most of it was neatly boarded up as if to hide it. I wondered how many boarded-up piles of rubble there were in Cheyenne Heights.

The farther we went, the more damage there was. Whole blocks were gone, the road below littered with broken glass. I saw what I thought at first were downed trees until I saw one with the streetlight attached.

"I'm surprised your folks sent for you," she said, starting up into the hills at the foot of Cheyenne Mountain. The hills and valleys made a crazy quilt of ruined blocks interspersed with silver-painted houses.

"Why?" I said, worried all over again. "Has Hydra Corp been hit?"

"No, but with all that sabotage mess . . . You say your folks are expecting you?"

"Yes."

"How long ago did you hear from them?"

I leaned forward. "A week ago," I said. "Why?"

She stopped the scooter on glass and other things that went crunch under its weight. "Because we're here, kid. Seventeen Hydra Compound."

Rubble. Blocks of granite and limestone, tiny stones that were mostly black. I got off the scooter, not believing what I saw. The lawn was gone, smooth and black where rubble didn't cover it, and someone had pounded in a sign that said, "Off Limits." There was so little left of the house that I couldn't get my bearings except for the darker line of charred stone that must have led up to the front door. The whole thing stank of smoke, though there wasn't so much as a wisp to be seen. This hadn't happened yesterday.

I turned to ask the driver if she knew when it had happened. She and the scooter were gone. And my bag. And half my life. I felt a sudden certainty that Dad and Mom were under the heap of shattered furniture and jumbled rocks, a panicky desire to dig wildly through the rubble to find their bodies.

That was not possible, of course. If there was anyone under the rubble, the sniffers and the lift-and-moves would have been here as soon as the raid was over. I knelt and touched the shattered rocks that had been our doorstep. They were cool to the touch. The raid was at least a couple of days old, and the rubble did not look like it had been disturbed, at least not by heavy equipment.

I stepped gingerly over what had been the front door and onto the crumbled remains of the living room, fighting with every step the sickening feeling that I was going to look down and see my father's hand. It was impossible to keep my bearings. Where did the living room end and the bedrooms begin?

I saw a piece of wood I thought came from the big worktable in Mom's office and then a stoneware plate, lying intact on top of pulverized rock. Okay, I thought, if this is the kitchen, then Dad's office is that way. I walked straight back, nearly to the end of the rubble, backtracked when I spotted splinters of our cedar tub, stopped behind half a door that was still standing, and began digging.

I was looking for the house computer. That would have been the first thing Dad would salvage, or rather the safety would have been. I used an unidentifiable piece of wood to pry up a big chunk of rock and expose a bundle of optical fibers. Their ends were cut, not seared, and I pulled gently on the fibers to see where they led. The resistance told me they were either attached to or caught under something, and the fibers didn't look damaged at all.

For a moment I thought Dad had come and taken the console out, and then rejected the idea. He wouldn't have taken the whole console, just the safety. No, the console, or the slag remains of it, had been stolen by looters. And how had looters dared to take things out of the house of Hellene Dares of Hydra Corp? Because he's dead, I thought numbly. That's what Clare and Mother were hiding from me.

"What in bloody hell is going on here?" I heard a man's voice say. He had an accent like Clare's. "Who are you and what are you doing here? Didn't you see the off-limits sign?"

"Yes," I said to a tall, bearded man. He wore a Grecian chlamys over a khaki uniform, but I knew he couldn't be Hydra Corp, not with a beard like that. The short red cloak had some kind of insignia on it. He was carrying power tools and a photovoltaic power pack and looked as if he knew how to use them.

I stood up. "I saw the signs," I said, more bravely than I felt. "They don't apply to me." It suddenly came to me that he must be a looter. He probably thought the cape was enough to get him by in a Hydra neighborhood. I looked around, wondering how far I'd have to run to find a working comm to report him or at least get help. This whole area was leveled, nearly to the top of the hill. "I live here, which is more than I can say for you," I said, "so you'd just better leave."

"You live here?" he said. He gestured at the rubble behind him.

"Yes. I'm keeping watch for my father. He doesn't like looters. He said he'd shoot any that he saw on sight." I didn't really think that bluff would work. He didn't look like a soldier, picking up things to pawn on leave time. He was wearing an officer's uniform, and maybe he was one, but the tools made me think he was probably a professional looter, and if he was, he'd done his research and knew this house belonged to Hellenes Dares and Medea of Hydra Corp, and that their only daughter was in Victoria.

"You'd better leave," I said. "My father is coming back in just a minute," and then it hit me. If he'd done his research as well as I thought he had and had still risked coming to loot our house in broad daylight, it was because he was sure the owners of the house wouldn't be coming back. My father was dead. I suddenly didn't care what he took.

"Go away," I said dully. "This is my house."

"Your house?" he said. "That's not possible. This house belongs to . . ." He stopped and looked hard at me. "You must be Hellene Ariadne. I'd no idea you'd be here so soon."

"It looks like I should have been here sooner," I said bitterly, but he wasn't watching me any longer. His wrist terminal was flashing a configuration of lights and was beeping softly. Did that mean he had an accomplice somewhere?

"Come on," he said, and grabbed my arm.

"Let go," I said. "You can take anything you want. Let go of me."

"This way," he said, pulling me back toward the street. "The shelter is over there." He'd dropped his tools so that he could hold on to me with two hands.

I kicked him hard, but he brought up his knee to protect himself, and I only got him in the shin.

"Will you please stop?" he said, his voice angry and loud. "There's going to be a light raid. We must get to shelter."

I couldn't get out of his grip, not by struggling. "Let me go. I have to find my father. You can't get away with this."

He held me firmly by the arms, but his voice was quiet and reasonable. "I don't know what you think I'm doing, Hellene Ariadne, but it occurs to me that the reality is something quite different. There is going to be a light raid within a matter of moments. We must get to shelter. When we do, I'll be happy to make any explanations you'd like, but right now there isn't time to answer your questions. We must hurry."

"Light raid?" I said. "I don't hear any sirens." Just then I did, the unmistakable rising wail I hadn't heard since before Victoria. I permitted myself to be hurried the half block to the shelter since I had no idea where it was, but I promised myself I'd report him to whoever else was in the shelter. There might be a comm, too, and I could call Hydra Corp and get help.

The shelter was down a manhole in the center of the street. The looter pulled up the silver-painted cover with one hand, and a cloud of miller moths erupted from the dark depths, startling him, but not enough that he let go of my arm. I swatted at the furry, fluttering creatures as he bent over to throw a switch. We were apparently in an abandoned underground maglev tube. Lights went on below, and I could see shelter signs and printed rules tacked up on the tunnel and another cloud of millers stirred up by the lights. He motioned me ahead of him.

He didn't let go of my arm until he absolutely had to, but he had to let me climb down the second half of the ladder unaided, and once at the bottom, I darted away along the side of the cables, looking for a comm or people in the tunnel ahead.

"Hellene Ariadne, there's nothing but a cul-de-sac that way," I heard him say. His voice echoed. There was nobody else in the shelter except the moths, and they wouldn't be any help. There was no comm either, and he was right about the dead end. I came to a wall and stopped. I turned around and started to look for a rock or a piece of metal that I could use to bash him with if he got too close. There wasn't anything I could use. The walls and ceiling of the tunnel were nothing but lased-out rock, not even shored up by beams. An exposed root of a hydra-fed tree poked through the ceiling and dripped water. There was a big puddle of mud underneath it and a lot of dead moths.

He started down the tunnel toward me. I backed up flat against the wall and put both hands up to ward him off. "You'd better not come any closer," I said. "My father's Hellene Dares of Hydra Corp. He'll have you in front of a laser squad if you so much as touch me."

He stopped, looking surprised and almost offended. "I assure you, Hellene, I have no intention of . . . My name is Joss Liddell. I work with your father at Hydra Corp."

"I don't believe you," I said. Now that I had had time to look at him, I certainly didn't believe him. He had reddish-brown hair and a trimmed beard, neither of which I had ever seen at Hydra Corp, and his accent was definitely Commonwealth. Maybe he wasn't a looter after all. Maybe he was a Quebecker spy. "How did you know there was going to be a raid before the sirens went off?" I said.

"I got the signal on my wrist terminal from Hydra Corp. Your father has fixed up a direct link with Civil Defense so there's no time lag. Quite ingenious, that. Civil Defense hasn't a clue he's done it."

"My father," I said eagerly, forgetting he was a spy. "Have you seen him? Is he all right. He isn't dead?"

"He's not dead," he said.

"You're sure?"

"I'm quite sure. I saw him not half an hour ago at Hydra Corp," and I knew he was telling the truth.

I shut my eyes in relief, and when I opened them, he was looking at me oddly. "I thought he was killed in the laser raid that got our house," I said. "I hadn't heard from him in over a month. That's why I came home, and when I got here I found . . . I thought you were a looter." As I said it, I realized that I no longer thought that.

"I'm not a looter," he said. "My name's Joss Liddell, and I'm equerry to His Royal Highness, Miles Essex."

Of course. The grandson of the Commonwealth's venerable King Peter. I should have recognized the insignia. Dad had written quite a bit about Essex when he had first come to Hydra Corp to help on the war research projects. Dad had liked him. Several times in his letters he'd mentioned Essex's willingness to cooperate and Dad had been especially impressed with the fact that Essex had been willing to give up all his usual titles and staff to work in the more democratic Hydra Corp, though Joss had apparently not been included in the gesture. Mother had not been as impressed. She had barely mentioned him, and when she had, she'd referred to him as "our 'helpful' ally."

There had been pictures of Miles Essex with his grandfather at Yellowknife in all the tabloids in Victoria, and after I found out he was at Hydra Corp, I'd started looking at them. I'd been surprised because he was so young and good-looking, with his fine blond hair, blue eyes, and winning smile. He had a reputation with women, too, Mrs. Ponsonby had informed me with a sniff. "I would imagine your mother is glad you're safe with me in Victoria," she had said as she handed me another baby.

If Essex was young, his equerry (whatever that was) was younger still. He looked five years older than me at the very most, in spite of his no-nonsense, middle-aged manner. He was not as striking as the prince, but I was willing to bet that his reddish-brown hair and beard had made a stir at Hydra Corp. He certainly did not have the prince's smile. He was frowning at me now, and although he had stopped looking offended, he still looked grim.

"You said my father's at Hydra Corp," I said. "That means the buildings haven't been hit."

"No. A few minor laser nicks, but that's all. They've left Hydra Corp pretty much alone," he said, and frowned more deeply. "You said your father hadn't written you in over a month."

"That's right," I said. "I knew something was wrong from my mother's letters, and I decided to come home to find out what it was."

He was frowning even more.

"Something is wrong, isn't it?"

"Yes," he said.

"What?"

"I'm not at liberty to tell you." He looked at his wrist terminal, which was flashing again. "That's the raid-over. We'll be out of this mud hole as soon as I get a confirmation from Hydra Corp. Then I shall take you to see His Royal Highness and your father."

"And you're sure my father is all right?"

He looked unhappy. "Yes. Neither he nor your mother was hurt in the laser raids that hit your house."

"Then what's wrong?"

"It's not for me to tell you. Your father should be the one to explain . . . everything to you."

The sirens abruptly sounded the steady all-clear. "I've a scooter up the street," he said, "if it wasn't knocked out by the lasers. I'll just check topside. I won't be a moment." He climbed quickly up the ladder and pushed the manhole cover aside. "It's safe to come up, Hellene Ariadne," he shouted down to me. "There've been no lasers here."

I followed him up the ladder and let him help me out onto the street. The landscape looked unchanged, though it would have been hard to distinguish any more laser damage from the rubble they'd left before, but there was a column of smoke rising farther to the north. Joss went on ahead to get the scooter, and I stood looking at the shattered mess that had been our house. Father was all right, Mother was all right, Hydra Corp hadn't been hit, yet something was wrong, and I could tell by Joss's determined refusal not to tell me anything that it must be bad.

He pulled up beside me with the scooter, and I got on behind him, bracing myself against the acceleration of the scooter and against the news that waited for me at Hydra Corp.

from the *Western States Tattler*

# Our Night of Horror— Honeymoon Blitzed by Batellite

"We never heard the sirens. It was like something out of a horror holo. A spot in the ceiling in the corner of the room blackened and spread like oil over water. Then the whole bedroom erupted into an inferno."

Nikolas Kritzis and his bride of three hours, Cleo Kritzis, had just returned from their wedding reception to the groom's newly decorated home in Cheyenne Heights. The lovely above-ground home, standing since the last century, had just been restored after being lased only days earlier. Kritzis, an employee of Hydra Corp, worked night and day to finish up before the wedding, confident that now the home was safe from another raid. "After all, lightning never strikes twice," he said. "I thought the first time was an accident. The batellites are only supposed to attack military and commercial targets. But I was wrong," he told a *Western States Tattler* reporter who witnessed Kritzis's escape from the house of flames. "My poor Cleo . . ."

(Wedding holos, Screen 17. Aluminum paint sale, Screen 17A.)

# CHAPTER THREE

**H**ydra Corp was painted a blinding silver in compliance with light raid defense requirements, but it was there, looking so solid and familiar in spite of the aluminum paint that the tears I had thought I had under control welled up again, and I scrambled off the scooter and wiped my nose on my sleeve, hoping Joss wouldn't see.

Joss had stopped at one end of the portico that fronted the building, instead of going up to the front steps. "The building's been hit once, but only nicked," he said, guiding me away from the front and up the side steps. He led me into the portico and then hesitated. "You wait here, until I call for you," he said, and pushed me gently behind a pillar. "There may be reporters."

Reporters? The taxi driver had said something about reporters being in Hydra Corp. Once we'd become involved with war work, Dad had allowed a once-a-month tabloid conference in the portico and had installed security systems that ensured they didn't get in any more often than that. He needn't have bothered. Even war work hadn't warranted anything more than occasional queries from the reporters. Hydra Corp was much too conservative for their taste.

I watched Joss approach Minerva's portico terminal. He said his name and pressed his hand so that the scanners could read his palmprint, and he was instantly surrounded by men and women in the traditional fedoras with press tickets stuck in them, which meant reporters.

"Where did you go this afternoon? To see the prisoner?"

"Is it true she's confessed to sabotage?"

"Why was Essex out at the jail all morning?"

"How much longer are you going to keep her locked up?"

"No comment," Joss said.

"Is it true there are more arrests in the works?"

"Why did your boss call Yellowknife this morning?"

"You'll have to ask him," Joss said. "He's just coming in now, I believe." He pointed at the far reaches of the tether field where a silver gullwing was settling. I could just make out the profile of a blond man at the controls, a purple chlamys visible over his right shoulder.

"Prince Essex," one of the reporters said.

The tabloid reporters bolted down the steps and out onto the silver paint. Joss motioned me. "Hurry," he hissed. "We've not got much time." Joss shoved me through the main door and hurried me along the hallway to the staging area.

"His Royal Highness will be a bit unhappy about my putting the reporters on to him, I should think," Joss said. "But it couldn't be helped. He'll be quite glad I managed to get you inside without any pictures." He pushed the door open. "Some of the employees have been rather undone by the light raids and decided Hydra Corp was safer than their homes," he said. "It's a bit of a zoo, I'm afraid."

Zoo was the right word. Luggage, folded blankets, and cardboard boxes were piled against the walls of the staging area and heaped up anywhere there was room for them, including the worktops of the terminals. Velcro lines were strung like hydra-watered vines across the middle of the room. Wadded-up bundles of clothing, pillows, and even pots and pans were stripped to them. It looked like some sort of exotic bazaar set in a jungle.

When I had left for Victoria, the staging area had been filled with banks of Minerva's consoles with techs in front of them who monitored everything from the hydra gardens in the lowest level to the cafeteria's supply of madderblend. It had taken that many techs just to handle the exception reports Minerva didn't have programs to apply against. I knew the volume of hydra orders had gone down even before I'd left for Victoria, but I wasn't prepared for this. There were maybe ten techs working at terminals amid the clutter, and twenty more cooking dinner over a makeshift solar cooker they had put together under the skylight. I recognized many of them, even Gaea, who was my age and with whom I'd been so angry because her parents hadn't sent her off to Victoria when the light raids started. She looked up from her console at me. For a second I thought she started to smile in recognition, but when she saw Joss she quickly turned back to the terminal. No one else smiled either, though I recognized almost all of them as Hydra Corp people.

"My mother permitted this?" I said to Joss. She must be absolutely furious at this invasion of Hydra Corp, or else off on another business trip, unaware of what had been done. And Dad. I couldn't even begin to imagine the security nightmares he'd be having with all these people.

"Where's my father?" I said. "I want to see him."

Joss was leading me steadily through the jungle of laundry. "I thought perhaps you might like to have a bath before you see your father. You are rather a fright, you know." He had said this quietly, reasonably, without a trace of a smile, and I couldn't help grinning at his seriousness.

I probably was a fright. My digging in the charred ruins of our house had completed the job my trip home had started. I knew what my clothes looked like, and I hated to think what my face and hair did. Probably Gaea hadn't even recognized me, but had thought I was some poor laser-struck refugee Joss had rescued.

The thought of a hot bath in Morning Glory Pool, with the mineral water up to my aching shoulders, was unbelievably tempting, but I knew once I got in the mineral pool, I'd be asleep in no time. Besides, I wanted to see my father right away. I didn't have time for a bath. I'd take a quick shower and change clothes if that was the only way to get Joss to take me to him, but no hot bath.

"I want to see my father as soon as I've had a shower," I said firmly.

"Very well. The baths are this way," he said, and I followed him, even though I knew perfectly well where the baths were. His approach to the clutter was the same as his attitude toward me. He didn't fight with the suitcases and laundry and boxes. He stepped over or under or around them without effort, avoiding trouble or emotion, occasionally even turning back to talk to me. I tried to follow his lead, but ended up whacking my shin on the corner of a baby's high chair and then nearly hanging myself on a drooping Velcro line. After that, I watched where I was going and pushed things out of my way.

The baths were at the far end of the staging area and down a short curving staircase. I considered slowing down till Joss was around the curve and then bolting for the exec offices, but those were on the opposite end of the building and upstairs from the baths. Was that why the shower had been suggested in the first place, to keep me away from my father until Joss had been given orders on what to do with me?

Joss didn't give me the chance to do more than think about ditching him. He stopped at the top of the stairs and motioned me ahead of him down into the steamy, sulfur-smelling room. The bathroom was like every place else except that the steam kept people from hanging their clothes up to dry. The stone floor was comparatively clean, and Morning Glory Pool looked the same as ever, dark blue at the center, cooler blue around the edges, steam rising in wisps from it. I had half-expected to find detergent suds from people doing their dishes in it.

They had certainly done dishes every place else. The recycler must have given out with all these extra people living here. People had been washing out clothes in the sinks, and from the looks of things, rinsing off the dishes in the showers. Someone had even hung a towel on one of the ornamental protrusions around the Minerva terminal. I stepped into one of the cedar stalls, kicked aside plasticware, took a kettle off the showerhead, and turned the shower on, hoping they hadn't given out along with the recycler.

I didn't really think they would have. Hydra's own water system tapped a thermally heated pocket in the water table, and a cold aquifer even farther down. The hydra that brought the water to the building were mature, able to increase capacity to match the company's needs over the years. Hydra Corp would have hot showers and relaxing mineral baths long after everybody else in Denver Springs.

I was right. The water came out of the tap steaming and smelling heavenly, and I suddenly realized just exactly how tired and dirty I was. I kicked off my battered sandals and pulled off my jams, which I handed over the door to Joss, and said, "These need to go into the recycler, if there still is a recycler. Is there a coverall anywhere? Or a toga?" I thought maybe he'd be dumb enough to go upstairs to get me something to wear, but he simply banged open a few lockers, talking the whole time.

"Oh, the recycler's still working. It just hasn't caught up. And it isn't as bad as you think. Only the unused laboratories have been set up for living in, and Essex didn't allow that until last Tuesday."

"Essex?" I said.

"Tuesday was when all this started. There was a batellite raid that lasted half the night. We're lucky we didn't lose more of our people. Before that, people just moved in by ones and twos to their offices and ate in the cafeteria."

A pair of clean-looking blue-green coveralls appeared over the top of the stall. I left them there and shampooed my hair. They're not your people, I thought. They're my people. Joss had been acting as if he and his Commonwealth prince owned Hydra Corp, as if anybody could come in and be accepted by a company that prided itself on having most of its people Hydra Corp born and bred, some of them second and third generation. My mother must be livid at the thought of these Common-wealthers coming and taking over.

"Is Mother away on business?" I said.

"You might say that," Joss replied.

"When will she be back?"

"Back?" Joss's voice sounded oddly hollow from outside the shower stall.

"From her trip. Is it hush-hush government stuff or something?"

"Yes," he said after a moment. "By the way, the big Tuesday raid isn't the first one that got your house. It was first hit over two weeks ago. Very selective. Burned out your house computer and set a few fires in your wiring. Most of the damage you saw today was done Tuesday. I guess the Quebeckers figured they hadn't gotten everything the first time."

"Was Dad able to save anything from the house?"

"Oh, yes, he'd already . . . he moved in here after the first raid with some things."

I could not hear him all that clearly under the water, but that did not sound like what he had intended to say first. He had told a lie about Mother's trip, too, and I wasn't willing to accept the muffling of the water for the uneasiness I kept hearing in his voice every time I mentioned my father. I was going to see my father by myself, I decided, and the sooner the better.

I rinsed off my hair and asked in rapid succession for a towel, a blowbrush, and a Velcro hairband, but Joss's locker-banging had been less productive than I'd hoped. The towel was handkerchief-sized and the blowbrush gave out after about a minute, but between them my hair was dry enough to get a band around.

I stepped into the coveralls and stripped them shut. They were a little small, but long enough in the legs, and they smelled like soap. I opened the door of the showers and let Joss hand me my sandals.

I sat down on a littered bench to strap them on. "I want to see my father now," I said, trying to strike the right balance between firmness and reason.

He didn't answer, and when I looked up, I caught him looking at my bosom. I looked down, surprised to see that I hadn't stripped the coveralls shut quite as far up as I'd thought.

"I wonder," he said, frowning. "Perhaps you should put your own clothes back on. His Royal Highness . . ."

I yanked the strips together and firmed them down. "I'll be glad to change my clothes before I see your Royal Highness. But right now I want to see my father, and he won't care what I'm wearing. These will be fine." I stood up. "I want to see my father now," I said.

"Yes, of course," he said, though he still looked doubtful. He led the way up the stairs and back through the jungle of the staging area.

"We shall have a spot of tea first," he said, leading the way past the few techs and their terminals and away from the exec office floor again. Tea and then supper and then meetings and more delays and would I get to see my father at all tonight, or even tomorrow? Joss was stalling, and the old sickening feeling of dread was returning. Something had happened to my father and they were afraid to tell me. Worse, they had done something to my father and did not want to tell me. I was not going to stick around to see what new delaying tactics the resourceful Joss could come up with. I was going to see my father right now.

I didn't have any real escape plan, but as it turned out, I didn't need one. I didn't duck far enough under a hanging line and my Velcro hairband brushed against a strip of tape and brought a teddy bear and two baby blankets down between us. Joss helped me untangle my hair from the mess, handed me the Velcro hairband, and we continued on through the staging area until we were almost opposite the stairs that led to the exec floor and nearly ready to start down the longer stairs to the cafeteria. Then I picked a nice heavy bundle of bedding hanging over Joss's head, reached up and hit it with the strip, and took off for Dad's office before Joss could get himself out of the tangle of sheets that came down over his head.

I didn't bother with a circuitous route—Joss had to have figured out by now he'd as much as told me where my father was. Only the newcomers had spilled over into the staging area, he'd said. The rest were living in their offices. And Dad had moved in after the first raid on the house.

I raced up the flight and a half to the exec floor, knowing I wouldn't have much time to talk to Dad alone before Joss came bursting in. If Essex's office were on this floor, too, Joss could contact him and have him head me off. I hoped the sheets would keep him away from his wrist terminal for at least the minute or so it would take me to get to Dad's office. If, in fact, Dad was in his office or at Hydra Corp at all and able to talk to me. If, in fact, he was not buried somewhere among that rubble that used to be my home.

I almost cried with relief at the sight of Dad's dark head above his cushioned armchair. He had swiveled the chair so he could look out the window at Pikes Peak, just like he always did, and if I ignored the suitcase in the corner (in spite of what Joss said, he hadn't saved much from the house) and the neat pile of dishes on his desk, I could almost believe it was two years ago when I was fifteen, and everything was fine.

"Dad," I said.

He didn't hear me. I walked all the way into the office. "Daddy," I said again, and this time he swiveled slightly in the chair, not so he was facing me, but so that I could see his profile. He was looking out toward the hill, behind which was the rubble that used to be our house. The sun was setting, and there was a faint red glow to the mountain mahogany shrubs, as if the whole neighborhood had burned down and was still smoldering. Dad's face was reddish from the light and I could see that he looked tired. But he was all right.

"What is it?" he said, and I realized he must not have heard me at all.

"It's me," I said. "I'm home."

He swiveled slowly to face me, and then stood up, so suddenly he set the chair moving. "When did they let you out?" he said. "Why didn't they tell me? You didn't tell them where it was, did you?"

"It's me, Daddy," I said with a sick dread. "I came home."

He took a step toward me, away from the window, and I could see that the ruddy sunset light had fooled me badly. He was not tired; he was sick. His face was thin, with lines as deep as laser scars pulling his mouth down into an expression of despair. "I couldn't find it, Medea. I've tried and tried . . . they wouldn't let me in to see you . . . I . . . so worried you'd break down and tell them . . . looked everywhere . . ."

He must be suffering from some kind of shock. The light raid. He must have been hurt in the light raid. Hurt and in shock.

"Daddy," I said loudly and firmly. "It's me, Ariadne. I've come home from Victoria."

He stopped and looked at me, moving his head a little to the side. He passed his hand over his forehead and said, "Ariadne? The light blinded me . . ." he said, sitting back down in the chair. "How did you get here? Did somebody tell you?"

"Tell me what?" I said.

"I thought you were in Victoria," he mumbled. His hands clenched and unclenched on the padded arms of the chair. "With Mrs. Ponsonby . . . shouldn't be here . . . not safe . . . didn't want you to know . . ." He put his hand up to his forehead again and started to cry.

I had been standing there, frozen with dread and worry, unable to move, but at the sight of his tears I couldn't stand it anymore. "Daddy," I said, and came around the desk to kneel beside him. "I'm home. I'll take care of you." I was crying, too. "Don't worry. Everything's going to be all right."

He didn't even hear me. His fists were still clenching and unclenching compulsively. It must surely be some sort of light raid shock. He needed medical help. I would have to get in touch with Mother immediately. "Daddy," I said, straightening out his hand and holding it against my cheek. "What's happened?"

Joss opened the door and stood in the red light from the window, out of breath. "I wanted to spare you this, Hellene Ariadne," he said, and looked genuinely sorry. "I should have told you straightaway."

"Told me what?" I said, gripping Dad's hand.

Dad was crushing my hand in his determination to make a fist, but his voice was so soft it was almost a whisper. "They've arrested your mother, Ariadne," he said, and started to cry again. "On charges of treason."

from the *Denver Springs Post-Gazette*

# Light Raids Blister Denver Springs

The third light raid in two weeks sent Cheyenne Heights residents scurrying for shelter again this afternoon. Today's raid, which lasted from 4:16 to 5:08, hit an area eight blocks square on the northern edge of Cheyenne Heights. (List of damages, addresses, Screen 9.)

"Why us?" mourned Fred Watkins, standing in the rubble of his kitchen. His house, at 1689 Happiness Way, was hit in last Tuesday's raid. "We didn't do anything to the Quebeckers."

Watkins is one of the few residents still left in Cheyenne Heights. "Most of the neighbors are living down in the maglev tubes or else they've moved into Hydra Corp. Not me. I figure it's Hydra Corp the batellites have been trying to hit. I'm staying right here. The bedroom and bathroom weren't hit."

When asked if he was worried about future raids, Watkins replied, "Not me. Everybody knows a light raid never strikes twice in the same place."

# CHAPTER FOUR

"**A**riadne," Joss said, and then made a move toward the door as if he were going to try to keep me from bolting again. But I wasn't going anywhere. I wasn't sure my legs would even hold me up if I tried to stand.

Mother. It had never once, in all my wild speculation, occurred to me that it was Mother in trouble and not Dad. Even now I found it almost impossible to believe. Mother was in trouble. She always knew exactly what she was doing. There must be some mistake.

"Oh, there's no mistake," my father said loudly, and I realized I must have spoken aloud. "Your mother's in prison right now. A spy. They're going to try her as a spy, Ariadne." He sounded as if he were going to burst into tears again, but instead he swiveled the chair almost running it into me. "What are you doing here?" he shouted at Joss. "Get out!"

Joss said quietly, "My lord Essex requests that you and your daughter join him in his offices for dinner."

"Oh, he does? Why? So he can get Ariadne to testify against her own mother at the trial? Or is there going to be a trial? Maybe you'll just put her up in front of a laser squad."

"Your mother's been interned for questioning, Ariadne," Joss said. "No charges have been filed against her, and she's not even technically under arrest. We're just . . ."

"Then why's she in jail?" Dad shouted. "Why have you got her locked up? They say she's a spy, Ariadne. Your own mother. A Quebecker spy. But they don't have any proof. Not . . ." He broke off abruptly and stood up, so fast the chair swiveled and crashed into me. "Get out!"

I was trying to pick myself up off the floor. I couldn't see Joss's face, but I heard him say, in the calm, reasonable tone he had used before, "I'm just conveying the prince's message, Hellene Dares," and I found myself suddenly, inexplicably, feeling sorry for him. Feel sorry for your father, I told myself. They've done this to him. Feel sorry for your mother. She's in jail. But all I could think of, as I pulled myself to a standing position and moved forward to put a restraining hand on Dad's arm, was Joss saying, "I wanted to spare you this," and looking like he meant it.

What a mess. Having to arrest the Research head of Hydra Corp and listen to abuse from her husband. Then in walks the daughter, who doesn't know anything and can't be told and has to be kept away from reporters and from her drunken father until he can get her to Essex. I decided to put Joss out of his misery.

"Thank you for asking us to dinner, Mr. Liddell," I said. "I'm afraid my father and I are both rather tired and—"

"Going to turn 'em down, Ariadne?" Dad said. "You can't do that, not when it's His Highness calling. It's a command performance, isn't it, Mr. Liddell?" He put a nasty emphasis on the name. "We're not invited to dinner. We're ordered, aren't we?" He lurched forward and stuck his face up close to Joss's. "Aren't we?"

"Miles Essex would like very much for you to dine with him," Joss said evenly, but he was looking at me, and I had not been wrong before. It was pity in his eyes. That settled it.

"Then we accept with pleasure," I said, my hand clamped down hard on Dad's arm to keep him from any more theatrics. "Shall we go?" I said.

"This way," Joss said, and started down the hall. There was no one to be seen in the whole upper hall. People had probably scattered like rabbits at the sound of the fight.

"You know where we're going, don't you?" Dad said loudly. "To your mother's offices. He threw her in jail and then moved in. What do you think of that?"

I didn't know what to think of any of this, but one thing was becoming increasingly clear. Any hope I had of finding out what was happening around here was going to have to come from Joss or Essex. I was glad I'd accepted the dinner invitation. Not only was Dad drunk or drugging, I was not sure which, but he was so consumed with anger and despair he was making himself believe all kinds of things that weren't true. The Commonwealth weren't occupying forces. They were our allies, the only ones the Western States had, and they had been asked to come here. I remembered that from a letter of Dad's before the censors started masking communications. Essex had been sent to work on the GEM Project, and Dad had been all in favor of it.

It took us a while to get down the hall, and by the time we made it to Mother's office, Joss was holding the door open. Dad was leaning more and more heavily on my arm, his head dropping on his chest, and I saw Joss make a move toward helping him, but I shook my head in warning, and Joss nodded.

Dad's head jerked up. "Oh, I see," he said. "You're on their side, too. My own daughter. Are you sleeping with him yet, Ariadne? You'd better be. I'd hate to see him get his information for free. Is he any good? Huh? You women are all alike, whores and traitors, all of you."

"I think that's about enough of that," Joss said firmly. He took Dad's arm.

I was flushed a mortified red that had climbed up my neck like a rash. "He's ill," I said desperately.

"He's drunk," Joss said. "You're in no shape to have dinner, sir," he said to Dad in that amazingly reasonable tone. "I think you'd best go back to your office and sleep it off."

"And where will you go? What will you do after you've gotten rid of me?" Dad said. "Go off to bed with my daughter the whore? You want to get rid of me, but I'm not going. I was invited to dinner by his high and mighty Royal Highness, and I'm going to dinner!" He lurched clumsily through the open door.

"He's sick," I said pleadingly to Joss. "You can see that, can't you? That he's sick?"

"Good evening, Hellene Dares," a deep voice said as I went through the door, and then I was facing Miles Essex. He looked just like he did on the tabloids, maybe even better, tall and distinguished, with those piercing blue eyes and the gorgeous, almost phony golden hair.

"And you must be Hellene Ariadne," he said.

Even his voice was familiar to me, a younger version of his grandfather's voice that I had heard every Monday at Mrs. Ponsonby's when I watched King Peter give his weekly "Address to Our Allies."

Essex took my hand and kissed it.

"How do you do, Your Highness?" I said, and stopped just short of curtseying.

Dad was slumped in a fragile-looking chair, looking nearly asleep. I glanced anxiously at him.

Essex was saying smoothly, "You gave us a bit of a scare, Hellene Ariadne, bolting like that. We'd no idea where you'd got to."

I suddenly remembered the tabloids had called him a ladies' man. These borrowed coveralls were far too tight. I should have taken Joss's suggestion that I wear something else. "Why is my mother in jail?" I said.

"It's rather a complicated tale, I'm afraid. Would you like a drink before dinner? Some sherry, perhaps?"

"I want—" I said.

"Drinks and dinner," Dad said from the chair. "How civilized! Have a drink, Ariadne. We have to be civilized to our enemies, don't we? But don't turn your back on him while he's mixing the drinks. I'll have an ouzo, Your High Highness." He heaved himself up out of the chair. "On second thought, I'll pour it myself."

Joss was at his elbow instantly, handing him a glass and pouring the ouzo for him from a long-necked crystal decanter. I wondered if he was trying to limit the amount of liquor in the drink. As it was, it looked like far too much, and Dad downed it at one gulp.

"Why is my mother in jail?" I said again. Essex put a glass in my hand.

"Your sherry," he said, as if I had asked for it. "Won't you sit down, Hellene?"

He motioned me toward the sofa. It was my mother's, but everything else about her office had been changed. Where the statue of Zeus had stood, there was a large china vase filled with red roses, and Minerva's terminal now sat on a spindly-legged, gilded writing desk. Next to it was a terminal I didn't recognize, one obviously from another system. Miles Essex pulled up an equally spindly chair whose back was embroidered with the royal crest.

I sat down on the edge of it, took a sip of sherry to placate everybody, and tried again. "Why is my—"

"He put her in jail so he could take over Hydra Corp," Dad said. "Medea was in his way. She wouldn't work on his precious GEM Project. She thought the drought was more important. But he"—he gestured wildly with the empty ouzo glass—"His Mighty Highness

doesn't care about Hydra Corp. He wants us to dry up and blow away."
Dad's voice had gotten louder and louder and then suddenly collapsed
almost to a whisper. "Your mother's in jail, Ariadne," he said, and I bit
my lip hard to keep from crying at the sight of what Essex had done to
my father. "And we're all having dinner. Well, I don't eat with
traitors!"

He raised his glass high above his head as if he were going to
smash it and then abruptly stooped and set it on the low table in front
of the couch. "You," he said softly, "my whoring daughter, can do
whatever you want."

He barged out, slamming the door behind him. I stood up. "I have
to go . . . help him," I said. "He's ill."

"Joss will see that he gets back to his office, Hellene Ariadne,"
Essex said. "I think you should stay and at least allow me to tell you
what's been happening here at Hydra Corp."

I hesitated. Joss started for the door. I wanted to fling down my
glass of sherry and make a dramatic exit, but I knew if I did I would
forfeit all chance of finding out what was going on. Dad wouldn't,
maybe couldn't tell me. He was calling me his whoring daughter. I
doubted very much that he'd be willing to explain everything to me.

And I had to find out, I realized as I stood there holding the sherry
glass while Joss went out of the room. I couldn't help Dad or Mother if
I didn't find out what was going on around here. Essex's story would be
biased, but it would make sense, and I could decide for myself what I
believed of it.

"All right," I said, and sat back down on the chair, feeling
suddenly exhausted. "I'll stay."

"Let me get you another bit of sherry, and we'll have a nice chat,"
Essex said, grabbing my glass and refilling it. "You look positively
done in, my dear. Joss tells me you literally ran the entire way here from
Victoria."

"Not quite," I said. I took a sip of the sherry. Until he said that,
I hadn't been doing too badly, but suddenly the strain and fatigue of the
last two days seemed to hit me all at once.

"Have you had anything to eat on this odyssey of yours, dear girl?"

I shook my head, too tired to answer. I finished my glass of sherry,
and Essex leaped up to refill it again.

"I don't think I'd better have anything more to drink on an empty
stomach," I said. My insides were starting to feel a little peculiar. So
was my head.

"Nonsense," Essex said. "A bit of sherry's just the ticket. When Joss comes back . . ."

"I'm back," Joss said.

"Oh, jolly good," Essex said. "You can fetch us a bit to eat. I think we shall dispense with a formal dinner. Ariadne's too done in. We'll just have tea, I think." He handed me my third glass of sherry.

Joss paid no attention to him. He sat down in the chair opposite me. "I've put your father to bed," he said, "and I've stuck a sleeping patch on him. I hope that's all right."

I nodded, wondering in a dim sort of way how Joss had managed to do all that without Dad hitting him. "He needs his sleep," I said. "Thank you."

"He should sleep through the night," Joss said, "but you needn't worry in any case. I've put a . . . I shall keep an eye on him."

"I think," said Essex a little too loudly, "that . . ."

Joss took the sherry glass out of my hand. "I'll go fetch you some tea," he said, but to me, not to Essex. "I think you'd best not have any more of this until you've had something to eat. I shan't want to put you to bed, too." He stood up and looked at Essex. "I should think you might want to move into the dining room, my lord," he said courteously. "This door opens on the hall."

"Excellent idea," Essex said, a little too enthusiastically, and I wondered what Joss's remark was supposed to mean. Was Dad not in bed with a sleeping patch? Was he going to barge into the room again, shouting insults?

Essex followed Joss to the door, and they had a conversation I couldn't hear except for the word "reporters," which occurred several times. It wasn't Dad they were worried about. It was those tabloid reporters I'd seen on the steps.

For the first time, it occurred to me how strange it was I hadn't heard anything about this on the tabloids in Victoria. They would surely have made hay of it—Prince Imprisons Research Head. Even if Hydra Corp wasn't big enough news in Victoria, royalty was. Somebody had put the lid on tight, and oddly, that made me more instead of less convinced that what was going on here was of incredible importance. I must make Essex tell me what was going on, and right now.

I stood up and practically fell over. I used the spindly chair to get my balance, and then Joss came over to take my arm and lead me into the room my mother had used for staff meetings. Her functional conference table and chairs had been replaced by an elegant, carved wooden table with purple velvet chairs. Joss plunked me down in one of them and said, "I shall be right back with tea."

"You should bring something to eat instead of just tea," I said. "I'm starving," but I didn't think he heard me. He was already out the door.

Essex smiled as if I'd said something funny and sat down opposite me. He looked as if he were going to start off on another round of polite nothings. I said quickly, "Why is my mother in jail?"

Essex looked uncomfortable. He glanced toward the door as if he wished Joss would come back and take over. It was all very bewildering, especially Joss's behavior toward his boss. Essex had ordered him around as if he were a butler or something, but Joss had paid no attention to him. Which meant what? Maybe I didn't understand what an equerry was. Maybe . . . I realized with a sort of hazy shock that I was letting my thoughts wander again. "Why have you put my mother in jail?" I said again, this time so loudly Essex practically jumped.

"She's not in jail, Hellene Ariadne. She's being held for questioning."

"Where?" That was the wrong question. I didn't even care where she was right now. Why couldn't I think what to ask? "Why are you holding her?" I said before he could answer.

"She's refused to work on the GEM Project. That's a project we've been working on that concerns biotic memories which—"

"I know all about the GEM Project," I said, and he looked surprised. "They were working on it before I went to Victoria. I was working in Research." I didn't think I should say anything about my continuing to work on the GEM biots in Victoria until I found out why Mother was refusing to work on the project. I wasn't even sure I should have told him I'd worked in Research before the war, though surely that was in Minerva's memory.

"What exactly did you work on?"

I tried to think what I should tell him, whether I should make something up or whether it was safer to tell the truth because of the possibility of his checking what I'd told him. Maybe I should refuse to tell him anything until I could get my thoughts in order. It must be that I was tired. I had gotten so tired I couldn't think.

While I was still trying to come up with an answer, he said, "Did you use your house computer?"

Well, of course I used our house computer. What did he think I was, an illiterate? And what kind of question was that, coming on the heels of my telling him I'd worked on the GEM Project?

"Do you know if your father installed—" he said, and Joss knocked on the door, a special knock, a signal of some kind, and came in with a tray.

"I've brought tea," he said, and shot a glance at Essex that was some kind of signal, too, though I didn't know what it meant, and I was simply too tired to figure any of it out.

Joss set a gilt tray on the table and sat down. I could see why Essex had smiled at me before. I had forgotten that tea was what the Commonwealthers called supper. Mrs. Ponsonby hadn't had tea in her lovely household. She called up soup on the kitchen terminal twice a day and didn't refer to the meals as anything in particular.

There were sandwiches on the tray and some kind of English cakes filled with a jelly that looked awful. There was baklava, too, and the bread and cheese I had been used to at Hydra Corp. Joss poured a cup of tea for me and then put hot milk into it, which tasted wonderful. He held a plate up and poised a serving fork over the food, for all the world like a butler now.

"I'll have some bread and cheese," I said, and let him serve me.

Essex sat down, looking uncomfortable. Joss served him, too, the perfect servant, and then said, almost conversationally, "We've been having a bit of a problem here at Hydra Corp. We were sent here to assist with the GEM Project last year."

I waited for Joss to try and tell me what the GEM Project was, but he didn't, and I felt foolishly pleased.

"You know how critical to the war effort an operational GEM biot would be," Joss went on. "It would make our communications systems impervious to a blast of electromagnetic pulse. If Quebec gets an EMP-proof memory biot first, they'll wipe out our defense systems and batellites and proceed to laser us to a bloody pulp. We know," he said, seemed to think better of it, and said instead, "our intelligence people tell us that Quebec's research scientists aren't even close to bringing a biot to maturity. Hydra Corp is, or it was when we came here to supervise the research and to make sure the Quebeckers didn't carry off any information. Or biots."

He stopped and looked at me. "You're not eating."

"I'm listening," I said, and hoped I wasn't blushing. I was

listening and trying to make sense of his story through the fog of fatigue and hunger that was giving my stomach flip-flops. But I was also watching Joss and thinking how really nice-looking he was. Not handsome, like Essex, but nice. Nice reddish-brown hair, nice gray eyes, and that wonderful, reasonable voice that could convince you of anything.

"You can eat and listen," he said. I took a gulp of tea and picked up the bread. Nice. He even cared about my getting enough to eat.

"When we got here, we found the GEM Project at a complete standstill. No work had been done on it for months. Hellene Medea told us there was a drought threatening Denver Springs, and that research on the project had been suspended until they could find a remedy for the water shortage. Essex at first tried to divert part of the research team back to the GEM Project, finally to bring in his own people, but he found himself stopped at every turn. Memory missing out of the Minerva, uncooperative personnel, a whole vat of the biots destroyed by a careless worker."

"Sabotage," Essex said over my shoulder. He had taken out a pipe at some point and was puffing on it. I wondered how Joss would look smoking a pipe. Nice.

"Two weeks ago your house was hit, just the house computer, nothing else," Joss said. He stopped as if he were trying to decide whether to tell me something and then went on. I couldn't tell what he'd decided. "Last Tuesday your house was hit again, completely obliterated."

"Definitely sabotage," Essex said, puffing away. "There have just been too many coincidences for it to be anything else."

"But why do you think my mother's sabotaged Hydra Corp? Lots of people work here. It could be . . ."

"Hellene Medea was born in Quebec," Essex said.

He was tamping down his pipe. I felt like knocking it out of his hand. I stood up, spilling my cup of tea, and faced him across the table. "My mother was a refugee from Quebec. A refugee!" I said. "She escaped after the takeover. She hates the Quebec government. She told me. She's the last person who'd ever be a spy. She— "

"Ariadne," Joss said. He'd stood up, too, and now he grabbed for my arm. "Ariadne," he said quietly. "Listen."

I wrenched my arm free of him. "Listen? Why should I listen to you? You've decided my mother's a traitor because she was born in

Quebec. Well, I'm half Quebecker. Do you think I'm a spy, too?" I glared at him. How could I ever have thought he was nice?

"Ariadne," he said in that patient, reasoning voice I was beginning to hate. "There's something else."

I sat down. Tea dripped into my lap, but I didn't care. "What?" I said.

"There are . . ." Essex began, and Joss shot him a sharp look. He shut up.

"Someone leaked the story of the drought to the press," Joss said, still looking steadily at Essex. "We managed to stop the story, but not before it made it on the screen and we had to keep it from happening again. You can see that, can't you?"

I could see it. The Commonwealth of West Canada was our strongest ally against Quebec, but how long would they stay our ally if they thought their food supply was threatened, if they thought Denver Springs was drying up? But why had they suspected my mother?

"So you threw my mother in jail?" I asked.

"We found—" Essex said before Joss stopped him again.

"We interned her for questioning." Joss paused for effect. "And the leaks to the press stopped."

"Well, of course they stopped. The person doing the sabotaging would love having the suspicion on my mother so he can keep right on sabotaging the hydra under your noses."

"We've thought of that, Hellene Ariadne," Joss said. He had spread his hands flat on the table while he was talking to me. Now he glanced at his wrist terminal and casually covered it with his hand. "I'm going to go check on your father, Ariadne," he said. "I'll be right back."

I wondered what his terminal had told him and if he'd be gone long enough for me to find out what proof Essex thought they had against my mother. Whatever it was, Joss didn't want Essex to tell me, and wasn't it a little out of character for an equerry to decide what a prince would and would not say?

"I still don't understand why you arrested Mother," I said. "Why not Dad? He's the one in charge of security. Or do you think he's protecting her?"

Essex put a glass of sherry in front of me. "Drink that," he said. "You'll feel better."

"You said it was because she was from Quebec. If that's the only proof you have against her, you can't . . ."

"When you used your house computer," he interrupted abruptly, "did you have some way of protecting the memory, say from a laser raid?"

"What?" I said, unable to follow him. I downed the glass of sherry.

"Some sort of safety perhaps, for dumping the memory into Minerva in case of a laser raid? Your father's the head of Security. Surely he safeguarded your house computer. What did the safeties on the house computer look like?"

"I don't know," I said. "Regular safeties, I guess. Polished aluminum around the nitrogen sink." I poured myself another glass of sherry, thinking it might clear my head. I couldn't figure out what he was trying to do. Was he trying to steer clear of the subject he wasn't supposed to talk about by asking me a lot of irrelevant questions, or did this proof, whatever it was, have something to do with this talk of safeties? All of a sudden, I was too exhausted to care. Maybe if I had a nap first. Or another drink. I picked the bottle up. It was nearly empty.

Essex took the bottle away from me. "How big were the safeties?" he said. "What did they look like?"

The door opened and Joss came in. He looked like he was in a hurry. "The tabloid reporters have found out she's here at Hydra Corp," Joss said rapidly. "I told them she was bunking down in Research. It'll take them a few minutes to work their way through that zoo, and then they'll come up here." He looked at me. "Ariadne, you're in no shape to do an interview tonight. I've secured your father's quarters so he won't be disturbed, but I'm afraid I'll have to put you in my room for the night so they can't get at you."

He must have been running. He sounded out of breath, and his hair was all messed up. He looked even nicer that way.

"Ariadne?" he said, and then turned angrily to Essex. "What the hell have you been doing while I was gone? Getting her drunk so you could seduce her?"

"I was trying to find out what we need to know instead of dancing around it as you were doing."

"And you think a whole bottle of sherry's the way to do it?" he shouted. "This is my investigation, and I'll conduct it my way." He came around the table and put his hand on my arm. "Come on, old girl. You've had enough," he said. He wrapped my arm around his neck.

"You're so nice," I said, and put my other arm around his neck.

"Righto," he said, and picked me up. There was a loud banging at the door.

"You're the nicest man I ever met," I said, and laid my head on his shoulder.

"You're rather nice yourself," he said. "Also rather tiddly."

I would have asked him what "tiddly" meant, but I was asleep before he got me through the door.

# Surprise Witness in Sabotage Case Arrives

A shocking new complication has arisen in the already complicated sabotage case at Hydra Corp: a surprise witness. This reporter has learned that the witness, who was brought secretly to Hydra Corp last night by Royal Equerry Joss Liddell and taken immediately to Prince Miles Essex's quarters for a secret conference, is none other than Hellene Medea's daughter Ariadne.

Seventeen-year-old Ariadne was believed to have been evacuated to Victoria at the beginning of the war to protect her from the light raids. What was she really doing in Victoria, if she was in Victoria, and what is she doing here now?

No formal charges have been filed against Hydra Corp Research exec Hellene Medea, even though she has been held for questioning for two weeks, and it had been rumored that Prince Essex was waiting for evidence in the case. Does Hellene Ariadne have that evidence? What is her connection with Prince Essex? And the most important question of all—will Hellene Ariadne testify against her own mother?

(Calendar of Events, Screen 12.)

# CHAPTER FIVE

I woke up wishing I were still in Victoria. At least there all I had to worry about was getting Mrs. Ponsonby's brood fed and diped and down for their naps. Here I had so many worries to choose from it could take all day just to list them, let alone figure out what to do about them. If there was anything to be done.

My mother was in jail, my father thought I was "a traitor and a whore," to put it in his words. Joss and Essex didn't seem to think that, but they were both convinced my mother was sabotaging Hydra Corp, and I didn't know what to think. I couldn't believe Essex had trumped up charges against my mother so he could take over Hydra Corp, in spite of what Dad had said, but I also knew they weren't telling me the whole story, and if Joss was Essex's servant, I was Mrs. Ponsonby.

Whatever he was, Joss had laid a chiton and a chlamys across the vanity, along with a set of thick towels with the royal crest on them. What didn't he think of? Shoes? No. There were simple leather sandals on the floor. It galled me to see the clothes. People didn't usually wear formal Hydra Corp costume to work in, but they didn't wear skintight coveralls either. Joss had decided that formal was better than indecent, and though I really hated agreeing with him, I thought so, too.

I scrambled out of bed, skinnied out of the coveralls, and slipped the chiton over my head. It was a simple knee-length drape with a purple border, formless enough to fit anyone. The chlamys was silk, no doubt imported, but I wasn't about to wear it, not with a stylized royal crest embroidered on it. I opened Mother's closet to find something else.

There were clothes hanging, but the only things of Mother's were her formal dresses. The rest was clean shirts and a couple of pairs of trousers and one subdued Commonwealth Air Force uniform, and I remembered Joss had taken over the dressing room. He was taller than me, and not much bigger around, but I was not about to borrow clothes from him. Maybe I could borrow something from Gaea. I knew she was here. I'd seen her yesterday.

I turned back to Minerva's terminal on the spacer's trunk next to the bed and asked for a *who's where,* but my old password only got me an *insufficient privilege* message, painted in alarming scarlet. I could bypass that, but it would take time, and it occurred to me that at this hour Gaea was probably eating breakfast down in the staging area. If I hurried I could catch her there. I took another look in the mirror, and decided I would be decent as long as I combed my hair.

I started rummaging through the drawers in the back of the closet. I expected Mother's things to be cleaned out of the drawers, too, but I was not above stealing a comb.

The first drawer I opened was full of Joss's things, but I didn't see a comb or anything I could tie my hair back with. I opened the other top drawer. Mother's things here hadn't even been touched, not even her silver-backed brush. They must not have permitted her to pack for prison herself, just jumbled her clothes into a bag and took them to her, not even thinking about her hair. I decided to ask Joss if I could take a package of her personal things to her. He would probably suspect me of smuggling in a laser, but he might allow a brush and comb, and I would get a chance to see her.

In the meantime, I used the brush myself and then rummaged through the drawer looking for a hairband. It was a mess. Full of combs and jewelry, stockings and underwear, all the things that Joss had moved out of the other drawers to make room for his things, even a thermos in a paper bag.

Somehow the sight of that brought home what had happened for the first time. They'd arrested Mother and taken her away—they hadn't even let her pack. They had just *removed* her on no more than the suspicion of sabotage. Maybe Dad was right, and they were trying to take over Hydra Corp.

Not *they.* Essex. And his loyal equerry, Joss Liddell. Suddenly I didn't want to be in here, accepting their hospitality, sleeping in their beds, wearing the clothes they'd given me. I slammed the drawer shut and walked out.

I went to Dad's office, but the door was locked and he didn't answer my knock, and I vaguely remembered something about a sleeping patch. The door asked me if I wanted to leave a message and at first I said no, for what I really wanted was to come in so I could use his terminal to work out the bypass for that restriction I had encountered on Joss's terminal and then order some clothes through Minerva. But the door was a dumb node, capable of nothing more than recording a message, so I left one saying I had gone to eat breakfast, and returned to my first plan of finding Gaea.

The same motley crew was cooking over the solar cooker in the staging area, but Gaea wasn't there, and neither were a lot of other people I'd seen last night. Maybe they were already at work, Gaea, too. I had no idea where Gaea worked, probably in Research since that's where her parents worked. I went down the stairs to the lower level. And found everybody.

In the cafeteria. Being served by humans, but otherwise looking like they were working a regular prewar workday. Gaea was halfway down the cafeteria line. I grabbed a tray and edged in behind her.

"Good morning," I said. "I didn't get a chance to talk to you last night, Gaea."

She looked not at me, but at the chiton I was wearing, and I wondered if the purple trim said *Essex* as plainly as the embroidered chlamys I had left up in the dressing room.

"Hello, Ariadne," she said coolly, and took a plate of eggs from the server.

"I just got back last night," I said, wondering what was the matter. She was moving through the line determinedly, with her head down, as if she'd like nothing better than to get away from me altogether.

"Do you want something hot, Hellene?" the server said.

"Yes," I said, and then realized by the look on Gaea's face that if I got behind her she was going to take advantage of the situation and disappear. "No, thank you," I said, grabbed a square of baklava and a cup of already poured madderblend, and followed her to a table.

She took her dishes off her tray with the same dogged determination she'd shown in the line, not even looking up at me.

"Can I sit here?" I said, and scooped my cup and plate onto the table before she had a chance to say no. "I'm so glad to see you, Gaea," I said.

She looked at her eggs.

"I'm so hungry. I haven't really had a decent meal since I left

Victoria. I ran away, you know. I knew something was wrong here at home, so I ran away."

Gaea looked up, shocked.

"It's okay. I didn't have any trouble, but I didn't have any money for food. It's been two, no, three days since I've had breakfast at all, let alone a real Hydra Corp breakfast like this."

Somehow I had said the right thing. "You ran away?" Gaea said, sounding almost friendly, and I took the chance to eat a bite of the baklava I'd been rhapsodizing about and gulp down some of the steaming madderblend.

"Yes. Nobody would tell me what was going on here, so I decided to come home and see for myself. I didn't know about Mother or the house or anything until I got here. How long has Essex been in my mother's private suite?"

"Since not five minutes after he had her taken off to jail," Gaea said. She looked at me. "You know what they're saying, don't you?" And now she sounded just like the old Gaea I remembered, and not a little like Chilkie. No wonder I'd liked Chilkie so well. "They're saying that Essex brought you home to testify against your mother."

"That's ridiculous," I said. "No one at Hydra would believe that for a minute."

Gaea shrugged. "I don't think it's being said for the benefit of Hydra Corp folk, at least not initially. But a lot of things have changed around here since you left. I bet there didn't used to be one person in all of Hydra Corp who subscribed to any tabloid."

"And now?" I asked.

Gaea smiled prettily. "Almost all of us."

It took me a second to put it all together. "You mean it was a tabloid speculation that I was being brought back to testify against my mother? Since when has Hydra Corp been worthy of tabloid coverage? They never even mention us, except when we have the Fete."

"It's not Hydra Corp, it's the prince they're interested in. And of course they never come right out and say anything. It's more like: 'Who but the daughter of a famous Mata Hari could be using a certain Hydra Corp exec's ID string to secretly make her way to Denver Springs in time for . . .'"

"For what?" I said breathlessly.

"I don't remember exactly . . . the trial."

"But there's no trial. Mother hasn't even been formally charged."

"Right, but to read about it in the tabloids, she's all but convicted.

They're so clever about turning a phrase." When I nodded knowingly, she shook her head. "You must not have seen this morning's tabloids, or you wouldn't be taking this so calmly."

"Why? What do they say?"

"When you came in with Liddell and spent the night in Essex's rooms, it looked like . . . Well, Hydra exec treason stories don't sell as well as Essex's romantic escapades."

"Surely no one at Hydra Corp believes that I . . ." I put my cup down so hard it splashed madderblend all over the table.

Gaea reached across the table and put her hand over mine and squeezed. "Not . . . not really. But Ariadne, be careful. Everyone is working long hours because of the drought, and no one's thinking all that well."

For the first time I realized that the darkness about Gaea's eyes wasn't some new kind of makeup. She was tired.

"We haven't done anything in Research except work on the droughts for almost a year."

"Are they really bad?" What I had seen hadn't looked so awful, not awful enough to justify Gaea's weary nod.

She took her hand back but leaned forward conspiratorially. "It's a strain of our own Dunn-infection that strengthens the hydra walls so they can't dialyze, but every time we get it under control, a new strain pops up. The old controls, the ones we just developed yesterday, none of them work and we start from scratch all over again. We thought it was random mutations at first, but it can't be." She shook her head tiredly. "Nothing is secure anymore, least of all Hydra Corp."

"You mean you think my mother . . ."

"I don't mean anything except for you to be careful and trust no one," Gaea said. "Stop and think. The reporters may have seen you come in with Liddell, but unless someone from *inside* Hydra told them, they couldn't have known who you were sleeping with."

"I wasn't sleeping with anyone!" I said, banging my cup down again. If I didn't drink it soon, it would all be sloshed onto the table.

Gaea gave me a bland look, said, "Good morning, Hellene Dares," and took a measured sip of madder as my father sat down next to me.

Though Gaea had practically been like another daughter to him when we were younger, Dad barely acknowledged her with a nod. "I found your message when I got up," he said to me.

He looked terrible. He must have pulled off the sleeping patch.

There was a red spot on his neck. I was relieved to see he was wearing a sobriety patch. Joss must have put it on him at the same time he gave him the sleeping patch. It would stop the worst of the hangover, but when he reached for the orange juice on his tray, his hand trembled. He drank down half the glass, and then, as an afterthought, leaned over to buss me on the cheek. He smelled sour, and I knew that orange juice wasn't all that was in the glass. The sobriety patch wouldn't be able to compete with that.

"Think about it, Ariadne," Gaea said, picking up her tray and rising to leave. "Research is a real mess and Security . . . has a . . . problem."

"It won't be long now before I have it all under control," my father said, looking at Gaea seriously.

"Which?" Gaea said. "The drinking or the sabotage?"

Father's face reddened and he hissed. "There's absolutely no proof of sabotage, not a shred, not an iota. There's nothing but that damn royalist's accusation. You know there's no proof!"

Gaea, not one to be intimidated by anyone, leaned over the table. "There's empirical evidence," she said. "There's Research working fourteen hours a day every day just to keep up with the droughts."

"Even Nicholas said the droughts could be nothing more than natural mutations of the hydra," my father said, his eyes bulging. "He's head of Research while Medea's gone. Don't you listen to your own father, Gaea?"

"Obviously more closely than you," Gaea said. "He said it *could* be natural mutations, but by no means did he say it was that for sure." Gaea stopped, suddenly realizing that the people seated at nearby tables were beginning to stare. "I'm sorry," she said, contrite. "I know you're doing everything you can. I'm just so . . . tired."

"Get some rest, my dear," Father said, looking none too forgiving despite the sudden softness in his voice. He reached for the orange juice.

Gaea shrugged. "I'm counting on you for help," she said. "We all are."

Father nodded, not realizing that Gaea had spoken to me, not him. I stared at her, uncertain of what she expected me to do. Finally she turned to walk away. "Gaea!" I said. She stopped and looked back. Dad and the people at the nearby tables were looking at me, too. "I need to borrow some clothes," I said lamely. "When I ran away, I only had what I was wearing. This . . . I'd like to borrow some of your things."

She nodded. "Everything I have is in our old locker. I haven't changed the combination. Take whatever you need." Her smile looked normal when she turned away for a final time, but it didn't leave me feeling normal.

"Maybe you shouldn't be drinking this early," I said to Dad, and immediately regretted saying anything. His eyes got all guilty-looking, sick-looking, then he didn't look at me at all.

"I'm fine," he said. "Just fine. It's all the pressure . . . your mother . . . You have to help me, Ariadne."

I leaned across the table. "I know you're worried about Mother, but you can't help her by . . ."

"By drinking?" he said, his eyes glittering strangely. "I have a plan." He was gripping my hands so hard they hurt.

"What kind of plan?"

"We've got to find the household memory," he said. "Essex thinks the GEM data was destroyed, but it wasn't."

"But, Dad," I said. "I saw the house. The computer was gone."

He leaned even farther forward to whisper to me. "The memory wasn't in the computer."

"What?" I said.

"When we find the memory, it'll prove that the GEM Project was going nowhere. Essex will have to let her out. But you have to help me. I know where it is but I can't get to it."

"Why wasn't the memory in the computer?" I asked him, bewildered.

"Medea was taking it to Essex the day of the light raid."

This made no sense. You didn't carry memory around with you, especially not permanent memory like that of an entire research project. If she had wanted to show the material to Essex she would have sent it over the comm lines or used a backup tape. And why was the GEM memory in our home computer instead of in Minerva? I had the feeling this was all a story Dad was making up to comfort himself.

"Dad," I said gently. "Did Mother tell you she'd taken the memory?"

"They won't let me in to see her," he said. "But I've figured out where it is. I've looked everywhere else, except the one place I don't have access to. Your mother must have hidden it in her offices."

I was right about the sobriety patch. It couldn't compete with whatever Dad had put in his orange juice. Now Mother not only had taken the memory but she'd hidden it. From whom?

"Dad," I said, "have you had breakfast? Let me get you something."

"You slept in there last night. He'll let you in again. Tell him you forgot something. You have to help me, Ariadne!" He was squeezing my hands so hard I felt like he was crushing them. I tried to pull them free.

"I don't think . . . If Essex had found the memory, wouldn't he have told you?" I said, working my hands free.

"No! He's trying to take over Hydra Corp for the Commonwealth. He can't afford to let your mother out of jail now. That's why you have to find it first and bring it to me. And we have to hurry. There's not much time."

"Let me get you a cup of madderblend," I said desperately, my hands safely in my lap.

"You won't help me!" he said, and I watched his hands knot into fists. It was a good thing I'd gotten my hands out of there. "Very well! I'll find it myself!" He stood up, knocking over what was left of my cup of madderblend.

I grabbed his sleeve. "I'll help you, Dad," I said, trying to calm him down. "I just don't think you should get your hopes up for the memory. It might not be there."

"Oh, it's there," he said, and leaned over the table toward me. "I made a safety to protect the memory from light raids. A safety you could carry."

I tried to envision that. Most safeties were larger than the terminals they were protecting. They had to have layers and layers of reflective aluminum wrapped around a bulky refrigeration unit used to keep volatile memories cool. Essex had asked me about safeties last night and what they looked like. Maybe this wasn't just some drunken idea of Dad's after all.

"What does it look like?" I said.

He leaned down till he was practically in my face and breathed orange juice and ouzo at me. "You'll never guess. It looks just like the thermos your mother carried her goat's milk in."

"Goat's milk?" I said.

"Goat's milk?" Joss said.

from the *Denver Springs Post-Gazette*

# New Love for Prince?

There's a new woman in the Prince of Saskatchewan's life, or maybe we should say girl. Since she has apparently moved into Essex's lavish apartments at Hydra Corp, maybe woman is the right word after all, but though the prince has dipped into all locales and walks of life to find his light-of-loves (remember the Holly Sugar president?), this reporter feels this time he's gone too far.

The daughter of a Hydra Corp exec Essex accused of treason? Surely even the Prince of Saskatchewan wouldn't stoop that low. Or has this tabloid been wrong all along about Essex's motives for putting the mother in jail? Was he simply trying to get rid of an overprotective mama so he could have a clear field with the very pretty daughter?

(Pictures of Essex's former light-of-loves, Screens 92–153.)

# CHAPTER SIX

**T**hank the gods I hadn't said thermos!

"I was just going to get my father some goat's milk," I said. "He hasn't had any breakfast."

"Not bad, Liddell," my father said, looking at his watch. "Only four minutes alone with her. I couldn't have done much better myself."

"I must say, Hellene Dares, I continue to feel flattered that you always think I'm doing something clever. But I never quite understand what it is you think I'm up to. Whatever, I hope you shan't be disappointed in me when you discover I'm nothing more than an equerry."

"Why would an equerry want to prevent me from talking with my daughter alone?"

"Oh, my. Is that what you thought? I assure you, it's not so. I merely came to tell you that I have arranged to have a spare cot placed in your office for Hellene Ariadne."

"Good," I said. My heart was still pounding.

There was a safety. I'd just seen it in the drawer with my mother's hairbrush. Hidden in plain sight. But why would Mother have hidden it? Dad's story about Essex taking over Hydra Corp made no sense, but she must have removed the safety from the computer for a good reason and then not told Essex where it was, not even when she was accused of sabotage. Why? What was in the memory? There was only one way to find out.

"Mr. Liddell," I said. "I left my coveralls up in the dressing room. I'll just go and get them and then I'll be out of your way."

"They are already in the laundry," Joss said. "And I took the liberty of bringing you your chlamys." He held it out to me, the royal insignia clearly showing.

"I won't be needing that," I said coolly. "A friend of mine has offered to lend me some clothes. If you'd like to wait here a few minutes, I'll give you back what I'm wearing." I turned to Dad. "Daddy, when I tried to find Gaea this morning, I discovered my computer account was gone. I'll need a new one."

My father seemed embarrassed. "Everyone had to be recleared when Essex arrived. Inactive accounts were removed."

"Well, I'm back now," I said. "When can I get reinstated?"

"I shall arrange it," Joss said. "I'll need voice verification from you, Hellene Ariadne."

"*You'll* need?" I said. "My father is head of Security. He handles all computer account privileges."

"When royals are involved, security is the responsibility of the Commonwealth government."

Yes, well, and who says Essex isn't trying to take over Hydra Corp? They'd taken over my mother's offices and my father's job, posted Commonwealth guards at the doors, and apparently taken over Minerva, the computer, too. No wonder Dad had started drinking.

"Oh, I understand," I said, and turned pointedly back to Dad. "I'm going to go get those clothes of Gaea's now. Then I'll come back to the office and we'll finish our talk." I wanted to add, "Don't do anything until I get there," but I didn't dare. I leaned forward to kiss him.

"Hurry," he whispered. "There's not much time."

I turned and walked rapidly out of the cafeteria, hoping Joss wouldn't follow me, but he caught up with me in the hall. "I forgot to ask," he said, "if you would like an extra blanket for the cot."

"No, thank you," I said. "If I need anything, I'll borrow it from my *friends*. Now if you'll excuse me." This time I made it down the stairs and all the way to the locker room before he caught up with me.

"Hellene, I need to talk to you," he said.

"Why? You've done my laundry and made my bed. What else would a good servant need to do? If you're a servant. Which I doubt."

If he had been capable of anything other than a stone face I would have said he looked rueful. "You are your father's daughter, aren't you?"

"And my mother's," I said, "which around here is enough to get me arrested on suspicion of sabotage." I opened Gaea's locker and sorted through her neatly folded clothes, looking for a pair of coveralls.

"I need to talk to you," Joss said.

"Well, I don't need to talk to you." I glared at him. "Unless of course you want to tell me why you're really holding my mother prisoner. Your boss is trying to take over Hydra Corp, isn't he? He needs her out of the way."

Joss reached across me and slammed the locker door. "You can do with what you're wearing for a bit longer, even if it does belong to *my boss*." He kicked open the door to the baths. "Come on."

"I'm not going to . . ."

"You're going to listen to what I have to say," he said. "You want to know what proof I have against your mother, I'll tell you. In here."

He hadn't raised his voice, but the effect was that of an order. As soon as I was through the door, he pulled it shut and went over to Minerva's terminal.

It was an old, ornate terminal, put in the baths as a poetic acknowledgment to Min's function as Hydra Corp's Delphic oracle. Joss spoke into it. "I want full privacy in here," Joss said, and lowered his voice to say something else to Min that I wasn't supposed to, and couldn't, hear. He turned on one of the showers full blast and then went back to look out the door.

"Sit down," he said, and motioned at one of the carved benches near the edge of Morning Glory Pool.

"You're not doing your cover as a servant much good," I said.

"Just at the moment I don't care. Sit down."

I sat down. He sat down next to me, entirely too close as far as I was concerned, and he bent forward, his arms on his knees, his hands clenched together in a way that reminded me of Dad. Yesterday I'd felt sorry for him. I wasn't about to make that mistake again.

"Well?" I said.

"Do you know how bad the droughts are?"

"Yes," I said. "Gaea told me. Research can't get them stopped."

"That's right," he said. "They're so bad Research couldn't spare anyone to work on the GEM Project even if the memory hadn't been destroyed. I think that's *why* the droughts are so bad." He looked at me and this time the expression was definitely worry. I'd seen it on Gaea's face.

"To keep Research from working on GEM?" I said. "But why would somebody have to sabotage the hydra just to stop the GEM

Project? I thought it wasn't working anyway. I thought the biots weren't growing."

"So your mother said. But there were other people in Research who thought the GEM biots would grow if the right conditions could be found and said they would form a team to start work on the biots. Oddly enough, that was when the drought started."

"That could have been a coincidence."

"It could have. The team said they'd do double shifts and keep working, but the drought got worse and a vat of biots was exposed to radiation, and another vat was contaminated, and during a light raid alert some of the GEM memory was lost, but Essex thought your mother might have backup memory of the project in your home computer."

"And then our house was hit."

"Not your house. Just the computer. The batellites used very sophisticated ultraviolet lasers, no damage except to knock out electrical circuits, to destroy memory."

"That's when you had her arrested," I said. "It wasn't because of leaks to the press, was it? You had her arrested that same day because you thought she'd lased our own home."

I had really surprised him this time, but not in the way I'd hoped. He was looking at me with an expression of complete bewilderment. "Who told you that?" he said. "Your father?"

"Nobody told me," I said, frowning. "But it's true, isn't it?"

"No," he said. "It's not true. Your mother wasn't interned for questioning until a week ago, a week and a half after your house was lased. Because of leaks to the press about the droughts running out of control."

But Dad had said Mother was in the process of taking the safety to Essex the day of the light raid, that she was on her way to Essex when she was arrested, and that that was why she hadn't shown Essex the thermos. Now I was the one who looked bewildered, and next he'd be asking me what I knew about the light raid. "Are you trying to tell me you didn't suspect her of lasing our house?" I said.

"No," he said seriously. "I'm not trying to tell you that. Why did you think she was arrested the day of the light raid?"

I had my hands knotted in my lap like I had when Dad was telling me his wild plans. Joss reached over and took hold of them, but gently.

"Ariadne," he said. "The Quebeckers are so close to having a GEM they . . . two weeks ago we intercepted a top-secret comm message that said they'd be ready to use an electromagnetic pulse against the allies in less than six months. That means they're ready now to start production of GEMs."

I should pull my hands away, I thought. "But I thought you said . . ."

"That the Quebeckers aren't near to having a GEM biot? All of my information from the Yard . . . from Intelligence, confirms that the Quebeckers haven't made progress in their research, which can only mean they are expecting to *obtain* biots."

"It could mean your intelligence is wrong and they have developed a biot of their own."

"Then why are they not in production? Two of their greenfabrication factories have been stripped and detoxified. They're waiting, empty, for something. My best guess is that what they're waiting for is delivery of mature biots."

"And my mother can't deliver them if she's in jail."

I had expected him to nod and give me one of those pitying, "You poor dear child" looks, but he didn't. Instead his face got stony and unreadable, and I knew that, in spite of these latest revelations by the side of the pool, he still wasn't telling me everything. And he didn't intend to.

Very well, Mr. Liddell, I thought. I know a thing or two I'm not going to tell you either. I pulled my hands away and stood up.

He stood up with me. "Ariadne," he said, and put his hands on my shoulders. "We're in a race against time. If the Quebeckers can replace their computer memories with GEMs, they won't hesitate to use an EMP blast to blind our communications. At that point, they can demand unconditional surrender with the threat of nuclear war." He was looking intently at me. "Ariadne, if you know anything about this, you must tell me. It is desperately important." His grip on my shoulders tightened. "What made you think your mother was arrested the same day as the light raid?"

I almost told him. Despite the things he wasn't telling me, despite my father's warning, despite everything. I almost said, "There's a thermos in the second drawer of the bureau. It's really the safety from our home computer."

Instead I said, "You promised me computer access, or was that only if I cooperated?" and told myself I liked the expression that produced on his face.

He let go of me. "I'll prepare access to Minerva for you immediately. I would have done it earlier, but I thought it was more important to talk to you." He held the door of the baths open for me. "Apparently I was wrong in thinking that."

"Apparently so," I said, and walked past him.

I took my time over getting a pair of coveralls and a chlamys from Gaea's locker and then went back into the baths to change out of the chiton. Joss was waiting for me at the head of the stairs. He led the way to my father's office. Joss knocked on the door, but it chimed back that no one was there, and did we want to leave a message. I hoped Dad hadn't done anything stupid, like trying to get into Essex's offices to get the thermos.

Joss put his palm on the doorkeep and asked it to open. It did. I should have known. "I'll key it to your print straightaway," he said.

He went over to the terminal. Father's workstation had display screens for all the security cameras set up in the building and at the entrances, as well as the normal commscreen, voice recognition unit microphone, and a keyboard with a bitpad. "Captain Joss Liddell here. Are you listening up?"

"Voice pattern recognition programs are fully active, sir," the computer said. That "sir" response must have been some Canadian protocol Essex had brought with him. So was Min's accent, which sounded suspiciously like Essex's.

"New Research Department usercode, Ariadne, Hellene," Joss said. "Access equals read, write, execute, and delete capabilities for self, group, company, and computer system."

"Query, sir. Please confirm that you said computer system privilege."

"Access equals computer system privilege."

"Taken," Minerva said. "Ready for voice pattern recognition establishment. Hellene Ariadne, please read the words as I paint them on the screen."

I stepped over to the commscreen and spent the next three minutes reading familiar verse to the computer.

"Taken," Minerva said, sounding like an upstairs maid. "Welcome back to Hydra Corp, Hellene Ariadne, and may I add my belated congratulations on the occasion of your sixteenth birthday and your attainment of adult status."

"You're one year late, but, sure," I said.

"Happy birthday and congratulations. And once again on the event of your seventeenth birthday." Min went on, "Would you like today's calendar information?"

"Yes, please," I said.

"The Fete is tonight at the Broadmoor. Eight P.M. Formal Hydra Corp dress."

The Fete is tonight, and not a word about the fact that my mother's in jail. "Thank you, Min," I said.

I looked at Joss. "They're still having the Fete? I thought they'd suspended it for the duration of the war."

"Hydra Corp needs to keep up the appearance that everything's as it has been, and the drought's simply a wartime rumor. Brave front and all that."

I turned back to the screen. "Anything else, Min?"

"The calendar shows no assignment for you, Hellene Ariadne, but you have incoming mail waiting in queue."

"Thanks, Min," I said. There was no sign in the dialogue with Minerva that she had her intuitives engaged, which was just as well, for Joss probably would have noticed the difference if Min had started making intuitive leaps. Dad must have hidden the intuitives from Essex and his staff.

"You're terribly welcome, Hellene Ariadne," she said in that phony Commonwealth accent. "It's a pleasure to serve you."

I looked at Joss. "You've brainwashed Minerva," I said.

"The accent is Essex's preference."

"Well, it's not mine," I said. "Min, cut out the accent when you're talking to me."

"With pleasure, Hellene," Minerva said, sounding suddenly like herself.

"Min, are you keeping an audit trail on our session?"

"Audit trails are routine procedure during every computer session. However, with system privileges you can disconnect the audit trail program at the beginning of the session, or purge the memory of it at any time during the session."

"You ought to inquire about surveillance, too," Joss said from behind me, almost reading my thoughts. But I didn't want to talk to Min about surveillance with Joss in the room. Anyone with system privileges could watch or listen to anyone else's computer session and Min wouldn't give it a second thought. Joss knew it and I knew it, but maybe Joss didn't know that I knew it. And maybe Joss didn't know that listening in on computer sessions wasn't Min's only means of keeping tabs on the goings-on at Hydra. Still, if I didn't ask about surveillance, he would think that was funny, too. I phrased my question carefully.

"Are you spying on me, Minerva?"

"That's a harsh word, Hellene. But I have been instructed to provide a complete description of the *who's where* program, its function at Hydra and its use, when anyone is concerned about invasion of privacy. *Who's where* is a personnel locator program designed to provide instant access to key personnel in times of need."

I couldn't help wondering if she had also been instructed not to mention *follows,* their use and her capability of tapping in to them. "Am I one of the key personnel you keep track of?"

"You were not so designated during initialization of your account. Do you wish to volunteer yourself?"

"No," I said. "Min, cut the talk. Let's type." I sat down at the keyboard. I had a lot of questions to ask Min, but not with Joss listening in. At least at the keyboard he couldn't overhear my session, and I hoped he would get bored and go away. I could hardly sneak back to Mother's rooms with him at my elbow. I typed in a routine request for old business, but the screen went awash with garbage. Resetting didn't help.

I felt Joss come up behind me and reach around to press the control key. The screen cleared and he typed in, *invoke conversion.* "New default to scramble the keyboard sessions. Sorry. I should have told you about it. We can't have Quebeckers listening in. Just remember to invoke the conversion tables every keyboard session."

"Thank you," I said, and sat there with his hands still on the keyboard in front of me and his arms practically around me. "I know how to work this," I said.

"Fine," he said, and removed his hands from the keyboard. He went and stood by the window, behind Dad's desk.

I called up my mail, a letter from Chilkie and one from Mrs. Ponsonby. I had hoped Joss was waiting to make sure I didn't have any trouble with the machine, but he made no signs of leaving, so I called up the letter from Chilkie, decided there might be something in it about Beejum and the biots I'd left behind, and hastily asked for the letter from Mrs. Ponsonby instead. It was short and to the point.

"Dear Ariadne, Well, you have left us in a fine mess. All these children and no one to take care of them and not a word from you. I was worried sick." I'll bet. "I have written your father about your disgraceful conduct. I have told him that you are an ungrateful, thoughtless girl, but that if he will pay your way back *and* your room and board, you may come back and stay with me out of the kindness of my heart, as I am sure your father does not want you there."

That was about enough of that. I punched up the first part of Chilkie's letter, scanned it to make sure it didn't say anything incriminating, and tapped my fingers on the base of the keyboard, hoping Joss would get the message. He was looking out the window at something, or he was putting up a very good front of looking out the window at something. At any rate he didn't seem to hear the tapping and I had to speak to him twice before he turned to look at me. There was no polite way to say it.

"You promised me no surveillance," I said.

"I'm not watching you," he said. "I thought you might trust me more if I were here than if I weren't. After all, I could go to another terminal, reinitialize your account, and monitor you."

So he knew all about Min's capabilities and figured I did, too. But before I could say anything, he had turned to look out the window again. He really wasn't watching what I did, and I refused to believe he was such an accomplished spy he could tell from the sound patterns on the keyboard what I was typing. The view out the window had his full attention. I got up from the keyboard and went over to the desk.

"I'm sure you have a window of your own to look out of," I said, and peered over the desk to the parking lot to see what was so interesting.

"Quite right," he said. "Would you like me to lock the door on my way out so you won't be disturbed, film over the keypad and all that?"

"That won't be necessary," I said, and escorted him to the door. At the door he stopped and turned, as if he were going to say something, then went on down the hall. Still can't trust me, huh, Mr. Liddell? Then I won't trust you either.

I tore across the hall and put my thumb on the keypad on Mother's door. Nothing happened. I only half-expected it to open; usually system privileges gave access to every door at Hydra Corp, too, but there had been exceptions even in the old days. My father's office had been sealed, even to Mother.

I went back to Father's office, took another quick look out the window, but couldn't see anything but the empty parking lot and the disaster area beyond. I half-wanted to wait until Joss appeared at a dead run outside the front door, but I didn't have any time to waste either. I went back to the terminal. If Joss had gone into another room to monitor me, I wanted him to see me doing something innocent. I read Mrs.

Ponsonby's letter all the way through again, wishing Chilkie were here. She always saw straight to the heart of things and then said what she saw. I called up her letter again.

"Mrs. Ponsonby really threw a fit when she found out you'd gone," the letter read. "She announced to everyone that you'd run away with a Quebecker soldier, and took all your clothes and things down to the recycle shop and sold them. She almost got your garden, but Beejum hid it under his bed. I told him he'd better put your things, whatever they are, down the drain before Mrs. Ponsonby finds them, but he says he's saving them for you.

"Poor little kid! I've tried to explain to him that you won't be back, but he won't believe me. I hope Mrs. Ponsonby doesn't find his garden and take it away from him. She's not looking for it. She's got other problems. The pipes have gotten so bad there's hardly any water, and last night there were these funny rumblings. I moved the twins and Verity Ann into my room so they'd be away from the bathroom. There are these gurglings and then a whoosh and then a sort of rumbling. Mrs. Ponsonby had better get the pipes fixed *soon*.

"Sorry to complain like this, but things are awful here. I wish you were here. No, I don't. I'm glad you got out when you did. Signed, Chilkie."

Oh, Chilkie, I thought. Things are awful here, too. I told Min I wanted to write a letter back to her. "Dear Chilkie," I dictated, and then just sat and stared at the screen. I had never told Chilkie about sabotaging the pipes with the hydra, and now I didn't dare because Mrs. Ponsonby might get hold of the letter. And I couldn't tell Chilkie what was happening here either.

She couldn't help me with this, even if she were here to talk to, because she'd stop me halfway in my explanation and say, "You like this Joss, don't you? Then you must not really believe they're trying to take over Hydra Corp."

And I would have to say, "No, I know he's trying to do just what he says he is—keep Quebec from getting a GEM biot first."

And good old Chilkie would say, "Then why don't you tell Joss about the thermos?"

And I didn't know the answer to that. I canceled the letter order and said softly. "Whisper, Min." I held my breath. What if Essex's programmer had found the intuitives?

"Whispering," Min said in the slightly softer voice she always used when the intuitives were engaged.

"What's the probability that Whisper has been violated?"

"Less than thirty percent, only four percent that it could have been done without my knowing about it."

Four percent would have to do. "Min, I want you to secure this conversation using every possible precaution you've got," and proceeded to tell Min everything in as nonjumbled a fashion as I could manage. I didn't get very far. Min interrupted me.

"If the light raid happened a week before Hellene Media was arrested, why didn't she tell Essex about the memory?"

"I don't know," I said unhappily.

"Could she have hidden the thermos because it had incriminating evidence in it?"

I didn't have an answer for that question either.

My father's story was full of holes. First he'd said he needed the thermos to show Essex, then he'd forbidden me to tell Essex about it. He'd told me Mother hadn't been able to show the thermos to Essex because she'd been arrested, but she hadn't been until much later. And why hadn't she told Essex about the thermos after she was finally arrested? Dad was head of Security and one of the best in the business. If he really thought the proof of Mother's innocence was in her office, why hadn't he devised a way to get past security? Why had he drunk himself into a state where he couldn't even think straight instead?

"There has to be a logical explanation for all this," I said.

"All what?" Min said.

"Never mind, Min," I said. She couldn't help me. Nobody could. I would have to find the answers I needed all by myself, and the only way I could think of to do that was to get that thermos and see for myself what was in it.

"Can you rekey Mother's offices so that I can get in?"

"The Prince occupies those offices now and the security for his apartments is handled off-line. I have no access. However, each morning there is a maid that cleans the rooms. I could send her a message to return home, then inform the Royal Computer system that you are the substitute. Success depends on this happening this morning before my memory of your initialization is uploaded to the RC. You have three minutes to decide on whether or not to do it. The maid will be inside after that."

"Success probability?"

"Seventy percent. I can watch the halls and inform you via the terminals if anyone approaches the corridor and can summon that person to the atrium before he reaches the door."

"Sounds almost foolproof. Why only seventy percent?"

"I'm blind to some people. My recognition for some has been wiped out."

"Who?" I said.

"I don't know."

I thought for a moment. Seventy percent still wasn't bad odds. "Okay," I said finally. "Get rid of that maid and send your message to the RC. And put Chilkie's letter back up on the screen."

Chilkie's letter flashed back up immediately, but there was an interminably long wait before Min finally said softly, "The maid is returning home. The message is sent to RC. Good luck. I'll be watching for you."

"Thanks, Min," I said, and ran to the door and jerked it open—and practically got a fist in my face. Essex's fist.

"I was just about to knock," Essex said, looking past me at the terminal. Joss looked at me, not smiling, not worried, not anything. The perfect poker face. Well, now I knew Min's blind spots. Two of them I could have guessed. But the third . . . .

"Hello, Mother," I said.

# Medea's Out!
# Hydra Corp Exec Released

In an unexpected move today, Prince Miles Essex ordered Hydra Corp exec Hellene Medea released. The case has been one surprise move after another. With no warning, Prince Essex, acting in his capacity as head of the Allied Defense Research Command, ordered highly respected head of Hydra Corp Research Medea interned for questioning on suspicion of sabotage. No explanation of the sudden arrest was given, though many informed sources inside the company saw the arrest as part of an ongoing struggle for control of Hydra Corp.

When asked whether the release meant that Hellene Medea had been cleared of all charges, Prince Essex said, "Hellene Medea was merely being held for questioning. That questioning has been completed."

"I have no idea why His Highness has decided to let me go," Hellene Medea said on being released. "I assume he finally came to his senses and realized that the Western States will not stand for this kind of treatment of their citizens, war or no war."

(History of Hydra Corp, Screen 4.)

# CHAPTER SEVEN

So that was what Joss had decided not to tell me in the baths this morning. Why? Because he wanted to see the expression on my face? Or the one on Mother's? They were both interesting. Her face went absolutely white, and I knew they hadn't told her about my being home. She took a step backward, as if to get away from Essex, and said, "You're not supposed to be here."

I looked over at Joss. He was frowning.

"Mother," I said. "I thought you were in jail."

She took another step backward and then seemed to get hold of herself. "And I thought you were in Victoria." She laughed a little shakily. "What on earth are you doing here?"

"I ran away from Mrs. Ponsonby's. I could tell from your letters that something was wrong."

I glanced at Joss again. He was still watching her face, but Essex wasn't. He was looking at the commscreen. I was glad Chilkie's letter was up there instead of my little plan with Min. I hoped the references to my garden were on the next screen. I should have left Mrs. Ponsonby's letter up instead.

"Your highness," I said to get his attention away from the screen, "you didn't tell me you were letting my mother out of jail."

He looked at me. "As I told you last night, Hellene Ariadne, Hellene Medea was merely being held for questioning. That questioning has been completed."

"And Hydra Corp's lawyers pointed out to His Highness that we still have a constitution in the Western States. It came as something of a surprise to you, I believe, Your Highness." Her tone was completely civil, but I could hear the anger. Essex could, too.

"It has always been our intention to cooperate with our allies, Hellene Medea," Essex said, smiling. "We have explained that to you."

"Yes," she said. "You have."

Well, there was my answer, wasn't it? She wouldn't show the thermos to Essex because she hated him. But why? And could she hate him enough to put a stop to the whole GEM Project when so much was at stake?

Joss was looking at the commscreen now. I reached across him to manually turn it off. "Where's my father?" I said. "Or didn't you tell him about this either?"

"He was notified this morning," Essex said. When? After he had breakfast with me? Or before? And if they'd told him, why wasn't he here? Was he trying to get into Mother's suite right now while he knew Essex and Joss were here?

"I'll leave you two to talk now," Essex said.

Mother said, "Will you? Or will we be under surveillance?"

"I'll put a blinder on the computer, and I'll have another cot sent up directly," Joss said. "Is there anything else you need?"

"No," Mother said.

Essex put his hand on the door.

"What about the Fete?" I said. It was a stupid thing to say, I know, but it was the best I could come up with. Obviously, no one was much in the mood for a party.

"Does the Fete begin tonight?" Mother said, and she didn't sound surprised. "Of course we must go. That's why you let me out, isn't it, to show me off at the Fete and prove to the tabloid reporters you haven't had me executed just yet?"

Essex smiled. "I assure you your release and the opening of the Fete are entirely coincidental, but in any case I shall be most pleased to escort you and your daughter," Essex said, bowing slightly.

"Oh, I see. You'll escort us, and that way you can keep me from saying anything I shouldn't to the tabloids. Will I be allowed to wear formal Hydra Corp dress? Or would you like me in a prisoner's shift and restraints?"

"The Fete is formal, Hellene Ariadne," Essex said, turning smoothly to me. "Have you something appropriate to wear?"

"She can wear something of mine," Mother said. "Unless you

burned my clothes when you took over my offices. Surely you'll let me into my own office to find a dress for my daughter."

I looked up sharply at her and then wished I hadn't. Mother wasn't looking at me—she was still glaring at Essex—but Joss was. His face, of course, didn't give anything away, but I knew mine had, and I also knew that within a few minutes he would think of some excuse to take his leave.

"There's no reason for me to go to the Fete, is there?" I said. "I mean, I don't have any clothes, and I'm still awfully tired from the trip, and there'll be a lot of tabloid reporters there, won't there?" And while you're all at the Fete, I could get into the offices, couldn't I?

Essex said easily, "I don't think you need worry about reporters. They will flock round your mother and leave you free to dance."

I debated saying, "But what if they ask about my sleeping in your bed?" And while I was trying to decide, Joss said, "I'll go and fetch your things, Hellene Medea. Would you like all your dresses?"

"I would like to go back to my own offices," she said, a little too shrilly. "Yes. All the dresses. And my formal sandals. Wherever you've put them."

"Right," Joss said, and left.

"I have restored your computer account, Hellene Medea," Essex said, "and keyed your palmprint to the doorkeep of these offices."

"Do I have access to Research?"

"That will take a little longer," he said.

"How long?"

"I shall call for you at eight to take you to the Fete," Essex said, as if he were suddenly as anxious to leave as Joss had been. He bowed slightly and went out the door.

"I shall call for you at eight," Mother said, "and until then I'll be watching you every moment." She swiveled Dad's chair to look at me. "I do hope you haven't gotten overly modest during your stay in Victoria, Ariadne. His Royal Highness and Company are watching you every minute." She put her face close to the terminal. "Isn't that right?" She tapped two lines out on the terminal and then reached under it to do something else. "That should give us privacy for a few minutes," she said. She looked up at me. "You don't look very glad to see me, Ariadne. What stories has Essex been telling you about me?"

I looked at her. She went and sat down again in Dad's chair, looking as cool now as I remembered her, though her hands tapped the arms of the chair. She obviously wasn't going to give me that logical explanation I had been hoping for ever since I'd gotten back from Victoria.

"You haven't answered my question, Ariadne," she said. "What did His Highness tell you when you got here? I should imagine you gave him quite a shock."

You should talk, Mother, I thought. He wasn't as shocked to see me as you were. I went to the window and looked out at the silver parking lot so she couldn't see my face. "He didn't tell me much of anything. I just got here yesterday afternoon. I thought something had happened to Dad."

She swiveled her chair to look at me. "I'm amazed he didn't tell you some wild tale about droughts and sabotage. He's as bad as the tabloids," she said, completely ignoring my mention of Dad.

"Dad told me about the droughts," I said carefully. "I didn't realize they were so bad. We didn't hear much about them in Victoria."

She got up out of the chair and walked restlessly to the door of the office and back. "They wouldn't have gotten so widespread if it hadn't been for Essex. He insisted that Research work on the GEM Project instead, wouldn't let me have any staff or equipment. We were so badly understaffed that the droughts got out of hand."

This was not quite the story I had had from Joss. Or Gaea.

"The prince is obsessed with the GEM Project. I tried to tell him we'll never get an EMP-proof biot, and I got arrested for my trouble. He can't see that it's just a daydream, that nobody's ever been able to get them to grow."

While she was talking, Mother had crossed the room at least three times. She sat down in Dad's chair again and then stood up immediately and started pacing again. She was obviously getting more and more nervous, but I had the odd feeling that it didn't have anything to do with what we were talking about. She wasn't even concentrating on what she was saying, or she'd have been more careful not to tell me things I could check so easily. She was thinking about something else altogether. Maybe she was worried about Dad, too.

"If Essex has put a follow on Dad, do you think you could get into Minerva to use it and find out where he is?" I said.

Mother had crossed to the window again. "What?" she said.

"I'm worried about Dad. He should be here."

Someone knocked on the door. My heart did a flip-flop before I realized Dad wouldn't knock. "Come in," I managed to say, and when nothing happened, I went and opened the door. It was Joss, laden down with two armfuls of dresses. He didn't look like he'd caught Dad in the dressing room rummaging through drawers, but then he never looked like anything.

"Put them there," Mother said, and swept a space clear on Dad's desk. He dumped them on the desk, dropping two on the floor in the process. I knelt to pick them up, glad to hide my face for a minute, and looked up to find Joss frowning at me as if he were worried.

"Shall I hang these up?" he said, and dropped another one. This time when I bent down, he did, too, and put his hand reassuringly on my arm.

"No," Mother said. "That will be all."

He hesitated, still bending beside me, as if he were going to risk saying something to me, and then stood up, bowed slightly to Mother, and left.

I carried the dresses behind the screen and put them on the bed. "I'll have to wear something floor-length, won't I, Mother?" I called.

There was no answer. I came around the screen, holding a green gown up in front of me. "I'm supposed to wear something long, aren't I?" I said.

She was looking down into the silver parking lot, as Joss had earlier, but I had the feeling she wasn't even seeing it. "Ariadne, when did you leave Victoria?" she said.

"Three days ago," I said. "Why?"

"Three days ago," she repeated, and sat down in Dad's chair again without even seeming to know what she was doing. "Did you—"

As if on cue, there was a knock on the door. It was Joss again, balancing a stack of boxes under his chin. "Sorry. I couldn't manage these with the last lot. Where do you wish me to put them?" he said.

"On the bed. Behind the screen," Mother said sharply, with a look that told me she thought he'd been listening to every word we said in spite of what Mother'd done to the terminal. I wasn't so sure. If he had been listening, and I certainly believed he was capable of doing just that, he wouldn't have interrupted her in midsentence. He'd have wanted to hear what she had been about to say.

He put the boxes down on top of the heap of dresses. They promptly toppled over, taking half the dresses with them. Mother gave him a dismissive look I'd seen before. It meant, "I consider you too clumsy and stupid to even worry about."

"Sorry," Joss said, and knelt down immediately and began to put the spilled shoes back in their boxes, and I wondered if he was going to pass me a note or try to whisper a message to me, but he didn't say anything or even look at me.

The door opened again. "Medea," my father said, and I knew exactly what Joss was up to. "They told me in Research you were home, but I didn't believe them."

I looked up at Joss, silver sandal in my hand, and he reached out and closed his hand over my wrist, but he wasn't looking at me. He was looking at what he had put himself in a perfect position to see.

I couldn't see Dad, but I could see Mother. She smiled, a narrow little smile that was meant for Joss. "Hello, Dares," she said.

I had expected her to do or say something to let Dad know they weren't alone, but she didn't, and I realized suddenly why not. If she was as innocent as she was supposed to be, Joss should be able to hear anything at all she or Dad said. Mother's saying, "Dares, Joss brought Ariadne some clothes," would be the same as admitting her guilt. She must be counting on Dad's belief in her innocence, too, but what if he'd been drinking again? What if he said something about the safety?

"Never mind, Joss," I said loudly. "I'll get the rest of the sandals. You can go now."

Joss let go of my wrist. I stood up and stepped between him and the edge of the screen to block his view of Dad. "Which of these dresses do you want me to try on first, Mother?"

Joss stood up, too, a sandal in one hand and a box in the other. "I had you paged, Hellene Dares, as soon as your wife got here, but you must not have been near a terminal. You were down in Research?"

"Joss didn't bring your gold sandals, Mother," I said, coming around in front of the screen. "And none of these dresses will go with silver."

"Where did you two come from?" Dad said, looking slowly from me to Mother. He hadn't been in Research, or in Mother's dressing room either. He'd been somewhere quiet with a bottle of ouzo. There was no telling what he might have said if I hadn't stopped him. Or still might say.

"I wanted to wear your gold to the party tonight," I said sulkily.

"What party?" Dad said.

"The Fete," I said. "Essex said he was going to take us, and I don't want to have to wear sandals that don't match to the Broadmoor. Where are your gold ones, Mother, with the jade instep?"

"Joss," Mother said, as if she had just remembered he was there.

"They're on the top shelf of my closet. They're not in a box. They're wrapped in tissue paper."

And there's to you, Mr. Liddell, and I hope you didn't learn a thing from your little sneak attack.

"Of course," Joss said, unruffled. "I'll get them immediately."

"And you can tell His Royal Highness I'm taking my own family to the Fete," Dad said.

"Hurry with those sandals," I said, and sounded, I hoped, just like Mother. "I want to see how this dress looks with them." I knew I didn't look like her. I could feel myself flushing with anger.

"My lady," Joss said, bowed slightly, and left the room.

Mother and Dad were both looking at me. "Dad, I'd appreciate it if you could put a privacy fix on this office so I can try on these dresses without somebody watching," I said, and slammed into the bathroom before either of them could say a word.

I was so angry at Joss I could have killed him. How dare he use me to spy on Mother? I had expected it from Essex, plying me with sherry so he could find out if there were safeties on our home computer. Dad had tried to use me, too, but he was only trying to help Mother.

But Joss! I had thought at least he was being honest with me. I should have known better. He had only been telling me what suited his purposes all along. He hadn't told me they were bringing Mother home. Oh, no. I was the bait that was supposed to catch her. Well, I'd done just that for him. The look on her face had given something away, though I had no idea what. And how exactly was I supposed to find out? I could hardly ask Joss. He would only tell me if he thought it suited his purposes, and I doubted very much that it did.

I yanked my coveralls off and pulled on the green toga. I fastened it at the shoulder and shook out the fullness. I could ask Mother. Maybe she'd tell me what was going on if I asked her straight out instead of dancing around the subject trying to catch her in a lie. Maybe she'd even give me that logical explanation I'd hoped for. Before Joss and Dad had come in she had started to ask me about something. If I could get rid of Dad for a few minutes and get Mother someplace where it would be safe to talk, maybe she'd ask me again.

I fastened the clasp on the wide silver girdle. Even with my flat sandals on, the hem of the skirt was well above my ankles, and Mother's silver sandals had considerably higher heels. I picked up a fold of the skirt to see if it could be let down. No. The tissue-thin chiffon had nothing but a centimeter handkerchief hem. I wasn't going to wear this to the Fete tonight. But where was I going to get a dress? Gaea might have one that fit me, but if she did she would be wearing it herself. Only Hydra Corp execs had as many dresses as Mother.

Maybe this wasn't as short as it looked. If Mother had a pair of flat-soled sandals, I might be able to get by with it. I opened the door to go look through the shoe boxes Joss had heaped on the cot.

Father was saying, in a voice loud enough that whatever listening devices Joss had hidden in the room could pick it up, "They let you out. Does that mean you told them where it was?"

"Told them where what was?" Mother said.

I said loudly, "Mother, this dress won't work. It's too short." I stepped out from behind the screen. "What do you think?"

# Camping New Sport at Hydra Corp

Recent light raids sent Hydra Corp employees scampering for cover at their own company. A rash of light raids convinced residents of Cheyenne Heights it wasn't a safe place to be anymore, and dozens of them moved in on their boss. "It's a little crowded," an employee admitted, "but we're not getting lased, are we?"

(Ten Best Places to be During a Light Raid, Screen 2.)

# CHAPTER EIGHT

pparently my entire function in life was going to be putting a stop to conversations before something disastrous was said. I put myself practically between them and said, "It can't be let down. There's no hem at all."

Neither of them even acknowledged the fact that I'd spoken, let alone turned to look at my dress.

"Told them where what was?" Mother said again. She spoke calmly, but there was a streak of red like a laser burn across her cheeks that stood out sharply against the whiteness of her face. She looked almost as pale as she had when she'd seen me.

"The GEM Project memory," Dad said, and I closed my eyes, almost glad I hadn't been able to stop this. Now, now Mother would surely say, "No. I didn't tell them. It's still safe," and she would proceed to give the logical explanation that I so wanted.

The color faded out of her cheeks and came back into her face. "What are you talking about?" she said. "The GEM memory was wiped out of Minerva three months ago."

"What about the memory in our house computer?"

She frowned. "The GEM memory was never in our computer. How could it have been? It was war-secrets information." She looked genuinely puzzled. "Even if it had been, it would have been wiped when our house was lased."

"Not if it was in . . ."

Joss didn't even go through the pretense of knocking this time. He opened the door and said, "Oh, good, Hellene Dares, I'd hoped you were still here. My lord Essex would like to extend his royal invitation to you to be his guests in the royal gullwing this evening."

"I already told you . . ." Dad said. His face was flushed a dangerous red.

"It seems there's something of a shortage of gullwings for this evening. A good many of them were damaged in the raids, and although my lord Essex attempted to requisition one for your family, he was unsuccessful. He offers instead his own royal . . ."

"You tell your boss he can take his royal gullwing and fly to Hades with it," Dad said. "I'm taking my own family to the Fete if we have to walk!" he said, and stormed out of the room.

"My lord Essex," Joss went on as if nothing had happened, "would also like to offer the use of his gullwing to you and your daughter for this afternoon, Hellene Medea. He thought perhaps Hellene Ariadne might be in need of a dress for this evening." He did not look at me, had not looked at me since he came into the room.

You can't fool me, Joss Liddell. That entrance of yours was just a little too well timed. Whatever Mother did to the computer didn't get us any privacy at all. So you know Dad thinks the GEM memory is still in existence and you know Mother was far too determined to get into her offices. And now you're here to send us off shopping so you can take your own sweet time looking for the GEM memory.

"My lord Essex would of course expect you to use his ID string for any purchases you might wish to make," he said smoothly.

"Tell Essex thank you, but this dress will be quite suitable," I said. "I'll have Household shorten it to street length."

Joss still didn't look at me, but Mother did. "Street length isn't appropriate for the Fete," she said, "and that dress is the wrong color for you." She turned to look at Joss. "Tell Essex we accept his offer of the royal gullwing, and we'd like to leave immediately." She glanced at her wrist terminal. "It's already past noon. We'll barely have time for a fitting and alterations if we leave now."

"I'll go and see to the arrangements. You can meet me in the portico," Joss said, and left.

"Change out of that," Mother said, "and we'll go. And bring my silver sandals with you. There won't be any time to shop for shoes."

"All right," I said, and went back into the bathroom. Why did Mother want to go shopping? I had thought she would be determined to stay here and try to get into her old offices, especially now that it was obvious Dad knew the memory still existed. She had to have some reason for wanting to get away from Hydra Corp.

I suddenly felt resentful. She was using me, too. Like Dad. Like Joss. Not bothering to tell me what was going on or even to say, "I can't explain. Just trust me." I came out of the bathroom and got the silver sandals.

"Ready?" she said, and smiled at me. "If there's time we'll get you some daytime things, too. Those coveralls don't fit."

"They're Gaea's," I said. I opened my mouth to say, "Why are we going shopping?" and then thought of Joss, who was almost certainly listening to us. Maybe that was why Mother was determined to get away from Hydra Corp, so we could talk without being bugged. I decided to wait.

"Ready," I said, and we went down the stairs to the staging area. There was nobody in the big room at this time of day, and it looked like the jungle of blankets and luggage had thinned out a little. Probably people had found other places to stay or gone back to their homes once their fear had worn off.

Threading our way past two lines of baby clothes, it occurred to me that this might be the safest place to talk to Mother. The royal gullwing would certainly be bugged, and downtown we wouldn't be alone.

I stopped. "Mother," I said softly, "up in Dad's office you started to ask me something. What was it?"

She looked at me, a long, measured look, and then said in a normal voice, "I was interested in how you'd gotten across the border."

No, you weren't, I thought. You wanted to know when I left. It was important for some reason, and you were going to ask me something about it, but now you've decided not to. All right. If that's the way you want it.

"I bribed a border guard," I said. "Once I was across the border I used Dad's ID string to buy a place on one of the overland caravans."

"Hellene Medea!" someone called from behind us, and we turned around. It was Joss. "I've brought the gullwing round to the back," he said. "The tabloids have rather blocked the portico, I'm afraid."

He led the way back through the staging area and down a hall to one of the service docks. "I've arranged for credit at all of the downtown shops. I thought perhaps you'd prefer Montaldo's," he said. "If there's any other way I can be of service, please let me know."

"We'll be shopping at the D and F Tower," Mother said.

There was a barely perceptible pause, and then Joss said, "Very good, Hellene. I'll just bring the gullwing to the door."

"Aren't you going to go with us?" I said, and was gratified to see a flicker of expression on his face, though I wasn't sure what it was. "The tabloid reporters are bound to spot the royal gullwing, and we won't be able to get any shopping done."

That was not true. Essex's gullwing looked exactly like any other one, on the outside at least, and the windows had privacy filters, but I wasn't about to give Joss the whole afternoon to look for that safety if I could help it.

He bowed slightly. "My lord Essex has scheduled a press conference on the subject of your release this afternoon at three, Hellene Medea. He has implied that you will be there, in order to ensure your privacy while shopping."

"But a clerk could call the tabloids and tell them where we are," I said.

"I shall ensure against that eventuality," he said, "but in any case I should be more than willing to escort you." He bowed slightly. "I'll just bring the gullwing round, shall I?"

"Do that," I said, and watched him walk out to it, feeling smug.

Next to me Mother said, "You're not foolish enough to be interested in that young man, are you?"

I turned and looked at her. The laser streaks of red were back in her face. In my eagerness to keep Joss out of the dressing room I'd forgotten that Mother had her own plans for the afternoon, and they obviously weren't helped by Joss's presence. Sorry I messed up your plans, Mother, I thought, but I have a few plans of my own.

"Of course not," I said. "I asked him along to keep the tabloid reporters away from us."

"He's Essex's spy, you know. If he's pretended an interest in you, it's merely to get information out of you."

I could feel myself flushing. "He hasn't pretended an interest in me, Mother," I said. "Why would he? What kind of information could he get from me?"

"I don't know," she said, and there was that cool, measuring look again.

"The tabloids think it's Essex who's 'pretending an interest' in me," I said coldly. "And not for information. They think I'm having an affair with him."

"Do they?" Mother said, and now she looked amused, which was even more infuriating. Obviously she didn't believe anyone could be interested in me, I thought, and remembered Essex's behavior last night. If I had encouraged him at all, I thought, Mother would have been very surprised at how interested he would have gotten. And suddenly I knew how to get into the dressing room.

Joss pulled the gullwing up and bounded out to open doors for us. He offered his hand to me to help me in, and I took it and held it longer than necessary, just to spite Mother, and then got into the front seat alongside him.

"Are you sure you wouldn't prefer Montaldo's?" Joss said. "It's ever so much closer, and there've been hardly any raids in that area."

"D and F Tower," Mother said, while I tried to figure out what was going on there and failed. Joss took us up and out away from Hydra Corp in a careful low pattern that would keep the reporters from seeing us.

I looked out the window and thought about my plan. Essex had been interested in me last night, but according to the tabloids, he was interested in every female, and there would be hundreds at the Fete tonight. If I wanted him to notice me, I would have to look spectacular. I couldn't just buy a dress. It would have to be a dress that would make Essex sit up and take notice. Remembering what had happened last night, though, I'd better get a sobriety patch, too, to keep me from getting completely "tiddly," as Joss had put it. I wanted to end up in Essex's offices, not in his bed.

As soon as we were away from Hydra Corp, Joss took the gullwing up to a panoramic height, and I could see Denver Springs for the first time since I'd gotten home. There were thick clouds above us, which made it safe to fly at that altitude, but which made the whole landscape even grimmer than it already was.

The damage wasn't just to the area surrounding Hydra Corp. It was everywhere. Out to the east the oil refineries had been hit. One of them was still burning, probably from Tuesday's raid, thick black smoke boiling from it. Everywhere there were spots or strips of damage among the silver roofs. The damage to Manitou Heights and Monument was more widespread than I'd imagined, although I'd been sort of braced for that. What I wasn't ready for was what had happened to the downtown Denver skyline.

At least a dozen of the big buildings were just not there. The black oblong box of the Anaconda building stood all by itself amid blocks of rubble. I looked for the old United Bank building, which had been my favorite place when I was little, with its old-fashioned curved top, and didn't see it. When I asked about it, Joss said, "That was one of the first buildings hit. Didn't you hear about it in Victoria?"

Joss dived down into the complex of rubble and skyscrapers and eased the gullwing to the door of the D and F Tower, which was standing even more by itself than it had been before the war. Joss handed the gullwing over to an attendant, and we went into the elevators that form the entire first floor of the Tower.

The D and F Tower is ridiculously designed, or rather it was designed for something totally different about two hundred years ago. The building it was once attached to is long gone, and all that's left is thirteen floors converted to a series of exclusive shops that think small means expensive. What it really meant was that Salieri's, the dress shop, had to keep its showroom on the seventh floor, its scans down in the basement, and its fitting rooms on the twelfth floor, next to a cubbyhole-sized chocolate shop and an "Authentic Drugstore and Soda Fountain." Shopping at D and F Tower inevitably involved a lot of elevator-riding, which might mean I would be able to get away from Mother for a few necessary minutes.

While we waited for the elevator, I tried to think of a good excuse for going up to the Authentic Drugstore on twelve. It might be easier than I wanted to get away from Mother if in fact she had some secret errand of her own, though I doubted very much that Joss would let either of us out of his sight or hearing, but as the elevator door opened, he looked at his wrist terminal, said abruptly, "I'm afraid I must contact Hydra Corp," and walked rapidly away as the doors closed.

If this was Mother's big chance, she didn't do anything with it. She pushed "8," which was the showroom, and said, "I don't know if we'll have time to get you any daytime things, Ariadne. We'll be lucky to get a dress properly fitted by tonight."

"I know," I said, wishing I could be as cool as she was, and stepped out on eight. A chubby little clerk in a peculiar polka-dotted thing that dragged on the floor hurried over to talk to Mother.

"We need something for the Fete," Mother said. "Classic Hydra. For tonight."

"That's not possible," the clerk said. "You should have come in earlier. The war—"

"Of course it's possible," Mother said. "It needs to be classic but not too sophisticated."

The little clerk scowled at Mother. "I told you, we can't have a dress for you by tonight. Fitting is booked solid with dresses for the Fete that were ordered several weeks ago."

"I'll run an initial screen while you have your measurements taken," Mother said, as if the girl hadn't even spoken. "Why don't you call down and tell them she's coming?" she said to the clerk.

"Look, I told you . . ."

"We have a credit string of long standing with the D and F Tower, but we'll be using His Highness Lord Essex's credit string for these purchases. I trust there won't be any problem with obtaining a gown for tonight."

"N-no," the girl stammered. "I'll . . . let me . . . I'll just call second and set up a scan." She punched something into her console. "They'll be waiting for you," she said to me. "Hellene," she said to Mother, "if you'll just come over to the holo, I'll start a screen for you. Is there anything else I can do for you? I had no idea . . ."

She was still stammering when I got on the elevator. I couldn't risk wasting the time to go all the way down to second and up again. If Mother or the clerk noticed, I'd just have to say the ancient elevator had malfunctioned. It took forever to get to twelve and then forever for the Authentic Druggist and Soda Fountainist to wait on me. In the interest of authenticity he didn't even use a commscreen. He used an old-fashioned menu and monitor set into the pseudo-marble soda fountain that took ten minutes to tell him where the sobriety patches were. I also bought two caffeines since I couldn't afford to fall asleep either, and I hadn't really gotten over the sleepless nights I'd spent on the overland on the way home. I used Dad's credit string, hoping he still wasn't checking it, and then got back in the elevator.

"Hello," Joss said.

"I'm going down to be fitted," I said. "Mother's on eight."

"And you're on twelve," he said, looking at the packet in my hand. "Why did your mother ask you when you had left Victoria?"

"How would I know?" I said, standing against the wall, as far away as I could get from him. We were already past eight so I couldn't put an end to this conversation, but maybe it wouldn't take long to get down to second. "Where have you been? Putting a follow on her?"

"Yes," he said. "And setting up a comm link." He reached across me and pushed the stop button. We jerked to a halt between second and third. "Would you like to know where she is right now?"

"No," I said. "Yes."

"She told the clerk she wanted to ask you something. The clerk told her she could use the comm link in the showroom, but she said it was personal and took the elevator, not down to second, which was a good thing, by the way, since you were elsewhere." He looked at the packet again. "She went up to tenth and used a public comm link in the ladies' room to place a call to Victoria. Who was it to?"

"Don't you know?" I said. "I thought you were the expert on eavesdropping."

"The call was ion-scrambled," he said, "a trick Minerva is set up to decode, but which the Tower's antiquated comm system is not. Which is the reason your Mother insisted on coming here, I should imagine."

"We're here to buy a dress," I said, not looking at him. "As I recall, it was your idea. Now, if you'll let me out of here, I've got to go have a scan."

"What were you doing up on twelfth?" he said.

"What do you think I was doing?" I said. "Sending spy signals to Quebec for Mother?"

"No," he said. He didn't say anything for so long I looked up at him. "You think she's guilty, don't you?" he said.

I didn't have to say anything. I wasn't a poker face like Joss. It was all there for him to see. "She isn't guilty," I said. "There's a logical explanation for all of this."

"And you're going to find it."

"Yes."

"I'd like to help."

"I'll bet you would," I said bitterly.

He let go of my hand and punched the start button. The elevator creaked and lurched.

"I'm not pretending an interest in you to get information, you know," he said.

The elevator door opened, and I stepped out on second. He didn't follow me. "I'll go up and report to your mother," he said, with his hand holding the door open. "I shall tell her I had trouble with the elevator, that it was I who went up to the twelfth floor." He looked at me a minute. "I do want to help," he said.

I turned around and walked into the arms of a fashion tech. "Darling," he said. Apparently he fashioned himself Authentic, too. "Where have you been? We've been waiting for you."

"I got lost," I said, gulped down the complimentary glass of wine, and shrugged off my clothes.

They can't see you under a scan. You can cry all you want. The cold metal descended on me with all the speed and caring of a light raid, and the scan proceeded to pinch, poke, and prod me with its ice-cold calipers. I was grateful for the distraction. I was also grateful for the gushing tech, who'd been chosen for being uninterested in the naked female bodies he had to work with, and who helped me into the try-on robe and shuffles afterward with a steady stream of accompanying chatter that kept me from thinking about much of anything else.

"If I can be of help, dear," he said, and patted me on the shoulder as he put me into the elevator, "just come back down to second and confide everything in me."

"Thank you," I said, and wished I could. That was the whole problem. I couldn't confide in anyone: not Mother, who had just placed a scrambled call to Victoria, not Dad, who could not be trusted to blurt everything out as soon as he got enough ouzo in him, certainly not Joss, who knew exactly what Mother and I had said, even in the jungle of the staging area and the open spaces of the dock. He must have planted a bug in my clothes or Mother's, probably both, only I'd changed out of that conveniently provided chiton. I would have to buy something today to wear home in case he'd managed to bug Gaea's clothes before I borrowed them.

But if the bug was on Mother he would have been able to understand Mother's end of the call, even if it was ion-scrambled. Which meant he knew more about the call than he was saying, and it had to be bad, or he would have told me. For all his manipulating of me, I still believed he wasn't trying to hurt Mother or me. He was just trying to get at the truth, and doing that was so urgent he had to use whatever means were available. Well, I was trying to get at the truth, too, and I was going to use whatever means were available, too, starting with a dress that would dazzle Essex.

I had myself pretty well prepared for the fray by the time I reached the eighth floor. Somebody had ordered tea, and Mother and Joss were sitting together in front of the holo, eating little sandwiches and eyeing each other warily.

"Oh, good, you're back," Mother said. "This clerk is absolutely wretched," she said in an undertone as I sat down in the third chair clustered in front of the holo, "and the clothes are worse, but they do have some things in stock that may work. At least I think they might. They all look horrible on that dumpy little clerk. I've eliminated the obvious horrors, though. Have something to eat." She handed me the clicker and Joss gave me a cup of tea.

"We'll just see the stills first," she said loudly, and the clerk stepped out from the little projection box behind the holo and came over to watch as I went through the series of dresses Mother had already screened.

I took my time, eating sandwiches and eliminating all the polka dots and two Art Deco prints the first time through. Without the clerk, they were showing premodeled versions which had been filmed in a studio to give the maximum effect to the dresses. After crossing out a few more, I handed the clicker back to Mother, grabbed another sandwich and a piece of cheese, and stepped into the projection box. I shrugged off my robe, and everything went blank.

The holo was equipped with a modesty baffle, installed to protect the sensibilities of the neo-Victorian companies who shopped here. It served no earthly function since nobody saw the person in the box anyway, just the double-image projection of dress and figure, and between try-ons it simply held a freeze image of the last dress. There was no chance of the customer being exposed in the altogether; nevertheless, the baffle put up a milk-white particle curtain around the booth between try-ons, which did nothing to protect me, but which blanked out my view of Mother and Joss.

I couldn't hear them either. The holo's fans kept going the whole time to keep the lasers from overheating, and to mask the hum, nondescript music keyed to the company theme was being piped in over the top of it. I had to shout to make myself heard over D and F Tower's idea of Greek dances, and I couldn't hear them at all. At first we shouted back and forth, then I gave up and concentrated on the array of dresses.

Mother had apparently asked for a full assortment of daytime things as well as Fete gowns. Since I needed more clothes than just for tonight, I punched several for later consideration and one pair of shapeless jams for immediate fitting. I would wear those home.

When I finally got to the gowns, there was a discouraging sameness about them: full-sleeved chitons that fell to the floor, most of them white or yellow with maybe a border, all very modest and maidenly, and not at all what I had in mind. I got a picture of the dresses, their code and their cost, inside the box, before the image went up. The next one was white, like all the others, without a border, but with a price tag three times greater than any of the other dresses so far.

It looked like all the others, but the expensive price might mean a better cut, so I called it up. The milk-white faded, and Joss sat up.

The clerk had done something to mess up the mirrors, and from the looks of things was working frantically at her console to correct it. I waited another two minutes while Joss stared; then the mirrors swung around slowly, and I could see myself. The dress was white, all right, with a simple silver shoulder clasp and folds that fell all the way to my feet. The designer had apparently spent the money on the fabric because it looked opaque close up and nearly transparent from a distance, and he had cut it with the fullness flaring out and down into cascading yards of the amazing fabric. Standing next to me, an observer would think I was the very picture of modest Hydra Corp maidenhood. To someone across the room like Joss, I was obviously pretty impressive.

The dress was absolutely perfect for what I needed to do tonight, but I knew Mother would never agree to it. She was already fumbling for the clicker and opening her mouth to say no.

I said it for her, punched the next dress, and looked at my wrist terminal. I hadn't killed as much time as I'd thought. It was a little after four. The fitting, once I'd decided, would take an hour, and it would take another hour to get home, which would make it six. The Fete didn't start till eight, but if I killed too much time here all I would succeed in doing was not getting a dress.

I went through the dresses again more rapidly, flipping back through all the pictures of the dresses I'd tried on. I needed a dress that Mother would think was suitable, preferably white and with the same general lines. Then I'd get to the clerk and tell her a tabloid-worthy story about me and the prince and my horrible mother who didn't understand true love, and talk her into substituting the dress I wanted.

I stopped at a white chiton, also full-skirted and with a silver clasp. "I think I want this one," I shouted to Mother across the room. "What do you think of this, Mother?"

She had been saying something to Joss about the time. She tapped her wrist terminal and frowned, and he looked down at his. The waiter had come to collect the tea things. He was putting the cups and saucers on a cart.

"Mother!" I shouted. "Do you like this?"

She looked over at me, the clicker still in her hand. "No," she said, and I could hardly hear her. "It's too nondescript. What about the lavender?" She clicked back to it. "I like the effect of the embroidered medallions."

"I don't," I said. "And I hate lavender."

The waiter was folding the linen tablecloth into a neat packet. Joss said, "I liked the other white one."

"How about the yellow with the gold fringe?" Mother said, and blinded me while she flipped through to find it. When the baffle cleared again, the waiter had done something invisible with the cloth and the cart. He was handing Mother a chrome-plated readout. She palmed it to check the amount and then added a tip. And I had seen someone else do that. In Victoria.

"What do you think?" she said, looking over at me. "I think the yellow's much nicer than the white."

I stared at the waiter.

"What's the matter?" Mother said. Joss looked up.

"I . . . what about that green with the filigree edging?" I said. I hit the modesty baffle button hard and held it down.

"You weren't supposed to be here," Joss had said. "Why not?" I had the answer for him now, though I didn't dare tell him. I was supposed to be in Victoria. With Clare.

I had forgotten all about her as soon as I found out Dad was all right, but I shouldn't have. She had not been sent by Mother to break the awful news that Dad was dead. She had been sent to spirit me away in Victoria. Only I hadn't gone and when Mother saw me she was shocked and so alarmed that she had risked the call to Victoria. To whom? Clare?

This didn't make any sense. Why did I need to be in Victoria instead of here? And what did Clare have to do with all this?

The little clerk was banging on the door of the projection box. "Are you all right?" she said.

"Yes," I said. "The try-on button stuck. It's okay now." I opened the door of the box, holding my robe up against me. "Can I talk to you a minute?" I said. "I want that white dress, the one that . . ."

"I knew you would. Did you see the look on the face of His Highness's servant?"

"Yes," I said. "But I don't want my mother to know I'm getting it. She doesn't know about my . . . situation."

The clerk gaped. "She doesn't? Gee, how can she not know? Everybody else in Denver Springs knows about you and the prince."

I didn't know quite what to say to that. "She doesn't believe the tabloids," I said. "Can you help me?"

"Sure. I'll tell her we can't get any of the others fitted in time.

Then, after you order the other white, I'll just change it on the console." She glanced over at Joss. "I think I should warn you that dress could mean trouble." She winked broadly at me. "You'd especially better watch out for that servant of his."

"Yes," I said. "I know."

from the *Western States Tattler*:

# Light Raid Hits Prince

A sudden, devastating attack out of no-where. That's how this reporter sees the effect of a certain young woman on the previously impervious Prince Miles Essex. And who is the walking light raid who's done so much damage to the Prince's defenses?

It's none other than Hellene Ariadne, daughter of jailed Hydra Corp exec Medea. Dark-eyed, with luxuriant masses of dark, curly hair, the lovely Ariadne has captured not only the prince's attention, according to sources inside Hydra Corp, but also his heart.

"She hadn't been here five minutes before the prince was head over heels," said a Hydra Corp employee. "This time it's really love."

Is it love? The blond, blue-eyed prince is notorious for his amorous escapades, but the word love is seldom mentioned.

"Oh, he's in love all right," a Hydra Corp computer tech said. "He's already proposed."

Proposed? Can it be? The prince has managed to survive more than a few direct attacks on his bachelor status. Has he really been reduced to rubble by Light Raid Ari?

(Famous Royal Weddings, Screen 16, Bridal Gown Sale, Salieri's, D and F Tower, Screen 17.)

# CHAPTER NINE

**W**e tried to get back into Hydra Corp through the service docks to avoid the tabloid reporters, but almost a dozen were there waiting. A quick trip around the building in the gullwing revealed there were fewer of them at the portico. Joss dropped the gullwing next to the flagpole.

"Quickly now," he said, opening the door and grabbing the boxes out of our hands. I hadn't even seen him come around the gullwing, he was moving so fast. "I can elbow through these chaps, but if the others catch on, it may get difficult."

Mother, who was closest to the door, hesitated, then glanced back around the cab of the gullwing, as if to see if she had left something behind. She knew perfectly well that she hadn't, and that I couldn't get out until she did. The reporters were all the way down the steps when she finally did step out, and a shout from the west patio indicated that the ones around back were on their way, too.

"If we don't hurry, we shall have a mob of them to deal with," Joss said, closing the door behind us with a flick of his foot.

But Mother wasn't hurrying. She walked at her usual pace, head up, smiling at the reporters as they closed the distance. The first of them reached us as we started up the steps. I had never had a holocam shoved in my nose before, and that startled me, but not as much as the questions.

"Will you be going to the Fete with the prince?" the reporter said.

Another from a different tabloid was asking Mother the same question. She just smiled and walked on.

"How did they treat you in jail?"

"Is it true they brought in the Yard's top detective to question you?"

"How did you get that bruise on your hand?"

For a second I thought the reporter was trying to get Mother to say she had been tortured in jail, but it was me he was talking to. The biots that covered my evacuation tattoo had ruptured and were turning green again. I shoved my hands in the pockets of my new jams, put my head down, and walked on.

The reporters from the other side of the building didn't reach us until Joss got the door open. He closed the doors on their holocam. I could hear it crunch.

Inside, Mother's gait picked up speed, and she led the way to Dad's offices. She pressed the doorkeep with her palm, and it opened. Joss brushed through before she could stop him.

Dad was sitting and staring at the display monitors, which I could see had a crisp display of me as I came in from the hall. "Hi, Dad," I said quickly and cheerfully. He reached over and turned the switch just as Joss dropped the boxes on the bed. When he met Joss's eyes, the scene on the screens was of the reporters outside, but I knew that Joss had seen what I had seen, that Dad had been watching Essex's door, just waiting for a chance to go into the dressing room across the hall.

"I'll just leave you now," Joss said. As he moved past me on the way to the door, he said, "I should be honored if you would save one dance for me, Hellene Ariadne."

"Perhaps," I said, but was thinking that it wasn't Joss I needed to dance with.

He nodded crisply, as if I had said yes, and I wondered what was on my face this time. Then he closed the door and we were alone with the spy devices again.

Mother looked at her dresses that were still lying on the cot, and then glanced at her watch.

"There's plenty of time," I said. "It doesn't start until eight o'clock."

"Yes, and plenty of time for a leisurely bath in the Morning Glory Pool," Mother said. She shoved the boxes aside and picked out a big bathrobe. "I haven't had a real bath for weeks. Nothing but showers in jail," she said, and left.

Dad sat stupidly on the bed, making no attempt to get ready. I went through his wardrobe and laid out his blue linen chiton and formal himation before I ducked into the bathroom to fix my tattoo. I knew I should have it removed permanently, but the parlor was all the way up north near the old airport, and there wasn't time for that. I settled for putting on a new layer of biots.

As soon as they had taken, I showered, then rummaged through the things Joss had brought for Mother, looking for some perfume. I selected a musk that Dad had given her years ago. The bottle was still full. She must have thought it was too seductive a scent. I dabbed it on every place I could think of, and then stuck the sobriety patch behind my ear.

Mother returned just as I was finishing my nails. She was rosy-cheeked from the hot bath. "You're not ready," she said, looking at her wrist terminal.

"I just have to do my hair and slip my dress on," I said. "That won't take long." I didn't want Mother to have time to order me out of the white dress and make me put on something else.

"Wouldn't it be easier to put the dress on before you try to do your hair?" she said crisply.

"My nails have to dry first," I said, waving them.

"Dares, why aren't you dressed?" she said, apparently deciding to let me dry my nails while she worked on Dad. He nodded and stood up, steadier on his feet than I expected. Mother pushed him toward the bathroom and followed him in.

They came out as I was starting to do my hair. I pretended to have a harder time than I really was getting it up into a classical Grecian Hebe knot. Mother wouldn't be able to hurry me on that, since the Hebe knot was the only acceptable fashion for Hydra formal. Mother helped Dad dress, put on her own long blue chiton, fastened with fibulae at the shoulders. Then she saw that I was still struggling with my hair.

"We're going to be late," Mother said, looking at her wrist terminal for about the fourteenth time.

It was getting on toward eight, but I couldn't see any need to be exactly on time to a Fete. People would be arriving until well past nine. I tried again with the knot, managing to lose a few wisps of hair in the process. Mother made an exasperated sound and looked at her wrist terminal again.

"Here," she said, taking the brush from my hand. "Let me do that for you."

She had the knot done in nothing flat, not a strand of hair out of place, the curls around my ears so perfect I couldn't think of any delaying complaints. She wound silver ribbon around the knot and stepped back to examine her work. Her face softened for the first time since I had seen her, just for a second, and then she started picking up makeup plat, handkerchief, and other odds and ends, and putting them in her purse. I slipped on the white dress. She was in such a hurry she didn't even notice it.

Dad suddenly perked up when we got outside, led us spryly around to the back, and produced a gullwing. "I haven't been security chief of Hydra for fifteen years for nothing," he said smugly. "We're not riding to the Fete with that Canadian." He spat the word.

"But we told them we'd go with them," I said, thinking that I was losing a good chance for the prince to see me in the dress before he was distracted by all the other women who'd be competing for his attention at the Fete.

"No wife of mine is riding with the man who put her in jail," Dad said, and I didn't push it. In a way I was pleased. Dad was still protective of Mother, at least, even though he was barely talking to her, and I thought she'd be glad she didn't have to go to the ball with Essex after the hateful looks she'd given him, but she hardly seemed to care. In fact, the only thing she cared about was getting there. She kept her eyes fastened on her wrist terminal the whole time it took us to get to the Broadmoor. As soon as the gullwing landed, she hurried into the lobby and led the way to the ballroom.

Essex arrived almost immediately after we got there, apparently unconcerned that we hadn't ridden with him. He was quickly surrounded by the wives and daughters of half the company execs in Front Range. He and Joss were wearing snappy blue West Canadian uniforms with obviously custom-made chlamyses draped over them. He had a young woman wearing the traditional Hawaiian muumuu of Holly Corp on one arm and a woman in a Victorian gown who must have been from Inmos Corp on the other.

Essex stopped in the doorway of the ballroom. He nodded to me and then gave the two women his full attention, but not for long. Essex looked up at me again, and this time Joss did, too. Essex looked unutterably surprised. Joss looked like he always did, stone-faced and sober.

"The prince's equerry is looking at you," Mother whispered. "Don't be taken in by him, Ariadne. Watching you is his job."

Maybe, but I was pretty sure it was the dress and not duty that kept him and the prince both staring. I was off to a good start.

By now the other Hydra execs had seen Mother and were hurrying to speak to her. She greeted them distractedly, now and then shooting an anxious glance at the far side of the ballroom.

Waiters were moving through the crowd with gilt bowls full of peaches and silver trays with tinned fish and cheese. It was obvious the war had made inroads here, too. In the old days we would have had imported pomegranates, figs, and caviar. One of the trays had goblets of ouzo on it, and Dad helped himself with both hands. Mother didn't notice. I edged away from them.

"Ariadne, that dress you're wearing . . ." I turned to find Gaea had worked her way through the crowd to me. "That dress . . ." she said again. She glanced over at the prince, then looked back at me with questioning eyes.

"The prince seems to like it," her date said, looking just a little confused now that he was standing next to me, "and so do I."

"I'm sure Ariadne doesn't care what the prince thinks of her dress," Gaea said loyally. "Did you know he's having his lackey ask the ladies to dance with him instead of doing it himself?"

"Joss? But why?"

"So that he doesn't have to endure a personal snub like the one I would have given him," Gaea said haughtily. "Ariadne, it's so good to see your mother back. Maybe now everything will be all right."

Or get worse, I thought when I saw Mother looking at her wrist terminal again. She was waiting for something, but what? Whatever it was, she was certainly getting nervous about it.

"Well?" Gaea was saying expectantly.

"Well, what?"

"I asked you if you wanted to go with us," she said. "We're going square dancing. The Flying W has taken the whole junior ballroom."

I looked in the direction of the prince. "I want to stay here."

Gaea went off with her date, looking upset. I could see by the crowd that it was going to be difficult to get close to Essex. I would have to use Joss. I waved to him and then realized that I already had his attention, and that of practically every other man in the room. I stopped waving. It was completely unnecessary. Only the people clustered around Mother weren't looking at me, and that was because they were too close to be able to see through the dress.

I suddenly felt hot all over, uncertain of whether to slip into the crowd or brave it out until Joss had walked all the way across the ballroom. When I realized that Essex was looking, too, I smiled at him. By the time he thought to smile back, Joss was at my side.

"A spot of fresh air would be nice, don't you think?" he said, his fingers so tight on my arm that I couldn't refuse. "Someplace dark where people can't see that dress."

"I'd rather dance," I said, unwilling to let Essex out of my sight when I was so obviously in his. He was having a terrible time conversing with the woman in the Victorian ballgown while stealing glances at me. A bit of gliding around on the dance floor would be the perfect effect. But Joss was still headed for the door.

"You did ask me for a dance this evening, didn't you?" I said. I planted my feet, and he had to stop short of dragging me. "I thought a gentleman always kept his promises."

"And I thought a lady didn't go to a Fete with no clothes on," he said. He offered me his arm and swept me off into a waltz.

I didn't know how to waltz well enough to do anything but follow his very determined lead, but I didn't like it. It was obvious he was doing his best to get me as far away from Essex as he could. I could see the prince clear on the other side of the ballroom, waltzing with the Victorian lady. Another turn, and I lost sight of him altogether.

"I heard you're booking Essex's dance card," I said.

"Something like that," Joss said. The strains of the waltz faded out, almost immediately replaced by a slow melody. I tried to pull away from him, but he didn't let me. "I'm screening partners for him. There are some Hydra Corp personnel who might turn him down if he asked them himself, and it might be bad for public relations."

"You mean the tabloids would put it on the front page," I said. "Prince Nixed by Hydra Corp Belles. I want to dance with him."

"No," he said, so quickly I wondered if he knew what I was up to.

"Why not?" I said. "It would be good for public relations, wouldn't it?"

"With you in that dress, it would feed gossip to no good end," he said, sounding stern. "It would also give the prince ideas I'd just as soon he didn't have about you." He pulled me against him.

"Do you have to dance that close?" I said a little breathlessly.

"I am only trying to offer what little cover my poor body can afford. If I'd a blanket, I'd wrap you in it, but as none is available . . ."

"Just because you don't like my dress," I said, "that's no reason—"

"Don't like your dress?" he said on a sharp intake of breath. I looked up at him, astonished to see what could actually have been color in his cheeks. "I never said I didn't like it. Every man here tonight takes one look at it and wants to get it off you."

"Even you?" I said.

"Yes," he said grimly. "Even me, and it's not you I should be watching. I should be finding out who your mother called in Victoria this afternoon and why she keeps looking at her wrist terminal, but I can't think of anything but you in that damnable dress."

"Oh," I said, intensely conscious of my hand on his shoulder. I could feel his heart beating. Or mine. He spun me into a turn, and his lips grazed my cheek. I caught sight of Essex and abruptly remembered who it was I was supposed to be seducing. I stopped in the middle of the dance floor. "Are you going to get me a dance with the prince or not?"

"I'm not."

"Then I'll ask him myself," I said, and before he could stop me, I walked up behind Essex's dancing partner, tapped her on the silk and lace shoulder of her Victorian ballgown, and said, "May I cut in?"

Essex seemed surprised as I stepped firmly between him and the lady, but he responded gallantly. He signaled tersely to Joss with his head to switch partners, and he whirled me away so quickly that I barely caught a glance of Joss. His gray eyes blazed with anger, whether for me or for Essex, I couldn't be sure.

"Your boldness becomes you," Essex said, "as does your dress."

"Thank you. I wanted to wear Mother's silver combs in my hair," I said. "They would have been perfect with this gown."

He looked at my hair for the first time. "You hair looks lovely, too. I'm always amazed how Hydra women keep it up in those elaborate hairdos."

"It would stay better if I had worn the combs." He looked as if he wondered what we were doing talking about what I hadn't worn to the Fete. "They were in with the rest of Mother's things, in the room Joss has in your office, and I didn't want to bother him. Or you."

"You had only to tell me," Essex said with a concerned smile, "and they would have been returned. If I know Joss, he's not even aware that they're there. Would you like me to send him for them? The evening is still young, and you would be able to wear them for the rest of the night."

"No!" I said. "Don't send Joss." Not Joss, I thought. He'll look in the thermos because it's in the same drawer as the combs, and whatever possessed me to bring up the combs in the first place? It should have been something vaguer that only I could find.

Essex was trying not to frown in his confusion. I smiled, hoping it was a wanton-looking smile. "After all, you said it's early. Maybe we could slip away later and get them ourselves."

He looked down the neckline of my dress, still leading smoothly. "If I understand you correctly, I am certain I can arrange something. Shall we say eleven? People will be quite filled with liquor by then, the Fete at its height."

"I'll be waiting by the lake at eleven," I said.

"You surprise me, Ariadne, and delight me. Joss has been upbraiding me for last night, telling me you had spent your time in Victoria caring for children and were little more than one yourself. He made me feel quite the cad for . . . admiring you."

"I did lots of other things in Victoria besides taking care of children," I said.

"I guessed as much when you walked in wearing that dress. I wish it were eleven."

"So do I," I said, looking straight into his blue eyes. He smiled rakishly.

It was only nine-thirty. I had an hour and a half to kill and an awful lot of people to avoid. I didn't want another lecture from Joss or one from Mother, who had had the chance to realize the effect of my dress by now. Dad was standing over by the bar with a bottle of ouzo in one hand, and a glass that he wasn't even bothering to fill anymore hung limply from the other hand. I wanted to go stop him from drinking, but I didn't dare. He might start raving about the thermos again.

I ended up going outside to sit by the lake and wait for the seemingly endless time to pass. It was very dark. The ballroom's blackout curtains had been drawn. Sometimes there was a little light as lovers slipped out of the ballroom to stroll around the lake.

When it was nearly eleven, the door opened again. I stood up, but it wasn't the prince. It was my mother. She darted around toward the far side of the lake. Someone was right behind her. I was fairly sure it was Joss. I was about to start after them when someone touched my arm. "Ready for our little escapade?" I heard Essex say conspiratorially.

I hesitated, wondering if I was on the wrong track with the thermos. Maybe the logical explanation I was looking for lay on the other side of the lake.

Essex took hold of my arm. "This way," he said. He led me around the outside of the building to a private driveway, where the gullwing was waiting. He helped me inside, then climbed in the driver's side. Without headlights and streetlights, both forbidden by the blackout, the going should have been slow, but Essex drove recklessly fast, and one-handed. His other hand was on my knee.

"I've arranged for us to have a few hours together," he said.

"A few hours?" I said. I had counted on him only being able to steal a few minutes away from the Fete. "Won't we be missed?"

"There's no need for you to worry about anyone guessing where we are," he said as we pulled into Hydra Corp. "I've told Joss to arrange an alibi."

"You told Joss?" I said.

"I told him I wished to spend a few hours alone with a young lady," he said. "It is hardly necessary for him to know every detail of my private life. At any rate, I've already told you he doesn't approve of my interest in you. He gave me quite a tongue-lashing last night, said you were a mere child. He's been rather a bore on the subject, as a matter of fact. I was beginning to think he was attracted to you himself."

He opened the door of the gullwing and helped me out. Hydra Corp was nearly deserted. There was no one on the portico but a Commonwealth guard and no one in the hall at all. He led me rapidly into his offices, threw off his chlamys and jacket, and went to the bar. "A drink would be just right, don't you think?"

"Yes." I wanted to go to Joss's room immediately, but I resisted my impulse and went to the bar with Essex.

He didn't waste time with the sherry this time. He poured two tumblers of Scotch. My sobriety patch was going to have a hard time keeping up with straight Scotch. He handed me one, downed his own, and sat on the sofa. "Come sit down and tell me about your wild and wicked life in Victoria," he said. He patted the cushion beside him.

"It wasn't all that wild," I said, staying where I was.

His eyes raked over the dress. "Come over here," he said, and sounded like he was used to being obeyed.

"I really should go get those combs," I said.

"There's plenty of time for that, Ariadne. We've got all night. Now come sit down."

I sat down.

"Now take a drink of Scotch, that's a good girl, and stop worrying. No one knows where we are."

I know, I thought. Joss is off chasing Mother around the lake, Dad's dead drunk, and I'm here in a see-through dress with an oversexed prince, and how am I going to get out of this? "My hair's a mess," I said. "The gullwing blades completely ruined my—" and he kissed me.

Skids had pulled this once in Mrs. Ponsonby's front hall. I had given him a good shove, and that was the end of it. I shoved the prince. Nothing happened. Worse than nothing. His grip tightened, and he pushed me down onto the sofa. He slid his hand down my neck. I shoved again, a lot harder.

"What's wrong?" he said, looking angry.

"Nothing," I said, gulping. I tried to sit up. His hand was on the dress.

"Why don't you get this thing off?" he said, clumsily disentangling himself from its folds. "Here." He reached for the silver shoulder brooch. "I'll help you."

"No! I mean, that's okay. I'll just go into the dressing room and . . ."

He had the brooch undone. "Why not take it off right here?"

"It'll wrinkle," I said desperately, and was off the couch before he could lunge at me again, clutching the shoulder to keep the dress up. "I have to hang it up. It's brand-new."

I dashed for the dressing room and closed the door. I wanted to lock it, but was afraid he might hear me and decide he had a hysterical virgin on his hands. He does, I thought, trying to refasten the brooch with trembling hands, and the minute I'd admitted it, I started shaking. I could not, could not go through with this no matter what happened to the thermos.

You may not have to, one part of my mind said. If the thermos is full of goat's milk, you could pretend you've had so much to drink you're going to be sick. The last thing the prince would want was a girl he had to clean up after—I'd learned that much from the twins. And one whiff of goat's milk that had been in a thermos for over a month might make any acting unnecessary.

Essex knocked at the door. "Just a minute," I said in a voice that I hoped sounded sultry instead of wildly reluctant. I opened the dresser drawer, took the thermos out of the paper bag, and unscrewed the lid all in one motion. Another part of my brain, the only part with any sense left, told me I was clutching at straws, but I refused to listen. I undid the seal with such haste that the thermos tipped a little, and I had burned my fingers almost before I was willing to admit the truth.

It wasn't goat's milk. It was liquid nitrogen, as any fool could have seen from the vapors that had begun to coil from the bottle at the first loosening of the seal. It had not really been necessary to freeze the top layer of skin off my fingers to prove it.

I tried to refasten the seal. The shoulder brooch chose that moment to come undone again, and my dress almost came off. I tried to hold it up with one hand and get the seal back on the thermos with the other. I was no longer shaking, though my whole body felt as cold as if I'd been dipped in the liquid nitrogen.

Well, that's that, I thought, and what exactly am I supposed to do now? Go out there clutching my dress and the thermos to my bosom and tell Essex I've changed my mind? And why change my mind? It hardly mattered whether I lost my honor to Essex, did it? I had already lost it. My mother was a traitor, and I had raced around trying to protect her, trying to prove her innocence when any fool could see . . .

Any fool. I sank down on Joss's bed, the top of my dress clutched to me, and started to cry. I didn't make any noise. The tears ran down my face and dripped all over the dress as if it were a giant handkerchief. When Essex knocked again, I didn't even try to answer or make an attempt to lock the door, but some final idiotic instinct made me grab for the thermos and clutch it against me like a baby. A baby, that's what I was, for believing that Mother was innocent, I thought, and the tears came even faster. My fingers hurt. I stuck them in my mouth and sat there sucking on them and crying.

Joss opened the door. "I beg your pardon. There's been a bit of a . . ."

I looked up at him, tears streaming down my face, dress clutched to my naked chest, and for one moment I was so glad to see him it didn't even occur to me what was going to happen next.

He stopped in midsentence, turned toward the closet, and started again as if he had never stopped. "His Royal Highness has been called away on an emergency. He asked that I tell you and escort you back to the party." He pulled a robe off a hanger. "An equerry is asked to perform many disagreeable duties, not the least among them informing his ladyloves that they are to be deprived of his presence." He turned around and held the robe out to me. "Would you like me to escort you back to the Broadmoor, Hellene?"

I had said that I wanted more than anything to disturb his

composure, to crack that granite face. Well, I had succeeded. But I had not ever intended to make him look like this. His face told me everything, but most of all it told me what I should have known all along. I should have trusted him, confided in him in the elevator, in the shelter that first day. I could have told him, should have told him everything, and saved myself all this grief and embarrassment. And now it was too late. I had ruined everything.

"I don't know what you're thinking," I said to keep from crying, "but . . ."

"It hardly matters at this point, does it?" he said, tossing the robe on the bed beside me. "But I'll tell you. When I saw you in that dress tonight, I thought your mother had put you up to something, like perhaps distracting me. It did not occur to me that your behavior was due to your having a liaison with Essex."

"I was not . . . " I said. I stood up angrily. At the last minute I remembered that I had nothing on and tried to keep myself covered with the less than adequate dress. I succeeded, but at the cost of everything else. The thermos clattered to the floor.

Joss stood looking at it for a long minute. Then he picked it up lightly and started to unscrew the lid. "What were you doing, fortifying yourself with liquor? What's in here? Ouzo?"

"No," I said. "It's the proof you've been looking for. The proof that my mother is guilty."

## Scones and Crumpets—New Greek Cuisine?

The Prince of Saskatchewan is driving Hydra Corp kitchen staff members nuts by insisting on scones and crumpets at all hours. They have to keep a batch available that cannot be more than four hours old when it's served, and they don't like the extra work that's causing. When asked if they would serve scones and crumpets instead of the Hydra Corp's traditional, lavish Greek cuisine at the Fete, our Hydra Corp contact snapped, "No comment!" There was no comment about who would be hosting the Hydra Corp presentations either.

(Tea for Two: Recipes, Screen 38.)

# CHAPTER TEN

It took me a full minute to realize he was grinning from ear to ear, and almost another one to get angry. "There's no reason to show so much delight that I'm not the ruined virgin you thought I was," I said, yanking the robe off the bed. I pulled it around me, no longer caring if he got an eyeful, and tied the sash. "And for your information, I almost was. I had every intention of seducing your precious prince to get that thermos out of here."

"And me? Do you intend to seduce me, too, to get this thermos out of here?" He was still grinning that maddening ear-splitting grin. Why had I ever wanted him anything but poker-faced? I made a near grab for the thermos that he held deftly out of reach. "That would be fine with me, but it still doesn't solve the problem of getting it past your mother, who's in the next room."

"Here?" I said, dropping from a shout to a whisper in the space of one syllable. "My mother's here?"

He nodded. "In the conference room. She's the emergency Essex was called away on."

"What's she doing here?" I said, trying to overcome the impulse to whisper since Joss was talking normally, and barely succeeding.

"I'm afraid I brought her here. I knew Essex was entertaining a young lady in his apartments, but I thought that would be less of a problem than the press would prove to be, so I whisked them here. I suggested they use the inner conference room. I planned to come get Essex's young lady safely away and then to go and look for you as your mother had asked. As it turned out, I didn't have to look very far."

He had said *them*. "Who's with Mother? And what does the press have to do with it?"

"It would seem that your mother has been cleared rather dramatically of the suspicion of treason. She may even be something of a heroine."

"What do you mean, cleared?" I said, my heart beginning a queer thudding.

"This evening, while I was trying to keep you away from Essex, your mother managed to slip away. When I finally found her, she was deep in conversation with a woman on the far side of the lake. Medea saw me, and instead of attempting to elude me as I thought she would, she introduced me to the woman. It seems she is a Quebecker scientist Medea has been working undercover to get out of Quebec. The scientist has managed to escape with some research that demonstrates a predictable mutation of hydra. Understanding the process is, I'm told, the first step in learning how to prevent it. She is no doubt explaining this process to a rather chagrined Essex at this moment. Your mother is, understandably, flushed with vindication. Essex, I should imagine, is flushed also, but for a rather different reason."

I could imagine the scene—Medea glowing, standing beside the disheveled scientist who is tired and bruised from her recent escape but glad to be safely here, my father . . .

"What about my father?" I said, unable to decide how he would take this. Would he be overjoyed that the charges of treason weren't true, or would he still be worried about the thermos? Drought cures were wonderful, but if the thermos had the GEM Project memories in it, the charges could still be true.

"He is jubilant."

"Good," I said, though I was not at all convinced that it was.

"As you should be, Hellene Ariadne," Joss said, and I thought I could hear a trace of bitterness in his tone. "Your mother will be reinstated as head of Research, Essex will be sent home in disgrace, and you shall be spared a fate worse than death."

"You still believe she's guilty, don't you?" I said.

He had not looked at the thermos since he picked it up. Now he put it carefully down on top of the bureau, as if the motion required such intense care and concentration that he could not even look at me. "That's not the question," he said in a tone that was as careful and concentrated as his movements. "The question is, do you?"

I didn't answer him.

He looked straight at me. "What's in the thermos, Ariadne?" he said.

There was no need to answer him at all. I could put my dress back on, go next door, and hand Mother the thermos, and that would be the end of it. Essex and his loyal equerry would go back to Yellowknife, Mother could go to work on the drought, and everything would be fine again. There was no need to say anything at all.

"The household memory," I said. "My father did make safeties for the terminals and our house computer so the memories wouldn't be destroyed in a light raid. He told me the safety looked like a thermos. I'd seen it in here."

"Perhaps it clears your mother instead of incriminating her."

"If it could, she wouldn't have hidden it in her bureau," I said harshly. "Mother could have given this scientist the research," I said. "They could have come up with all this just to get Essex out of here and Medea back in charge where she can continue her spying."

"That had occurred to me also," Joss said quietly, and I knew he was no more convinced by this story of escape from Quebec than I was.

There was a sound from the other room, the opening and shutting of a door. "Right now the problem is to get you safely out of here. Essex is rather good at explanations, but your standing here in his bathrobe and nothing else would rather put him to the test, I'm afraid. We'd best get you back into your own clothes, such as they are, and safely out of here."

"I want to see what's in the memory," I said.

"I shall take you down to the end of the hall and then turn about and make a grand entrance."

"I want to see what's in the memory," I said again, though I knew he'd heard me perfectly well the first time. "Turn your back," I said, and untied the robe.

I pinned up the soggy dress, wishing fervently that it was made of challis and covered with polka dots, and straightened the creases, trying to think of how to persuade Joss to let me see what was in the chips before he took me to face Medea.

"That's not much of an improvement, you know," he said when I was decent again, his poker face firmly in position now, and before I could open my mouth to protest, he said, "We'll go down to the baths. It's the only place I can be certain we won't be under observation." He picked up the thermos and handed it to me. Then he opened the bottom drawer of the dresser and took out two towels. He tossed me one.

"Wrap it in this," he said. "If anyone catches us, we'll tell them we're going to take a midnight swim in the baths. Which we are. Try to act a bit tipsy," he said, stepping forward to brush the curls forward so the sobriety patch wouldn't show. "And get out of that dress. Wrap a towel around you or something. A towel can't be any worse. Great Hera, Ari, don't you know what that dress can do?"

"I was just starting to find out," I said meekly. "I wanted to buy a dress that would make Essex notice me."

"Well, did you have to find one that would make him drag you back here to seduce you?" He turned around again and grabbed for a bathing robe in the closet. "Actually, you know, it's not quite so devastating up close, which is why I was in time to save you from Essex, I suppose. However, up close there are other problems."

I took a bathing shift of Mother's out of the same drawer as the thermos and pulled it on over my head. It was short and a little skimpy, but you couldn't see through it. "You can turn around now," I said, and tapped him on the shoulder. "What problems?"

"Come on," he said sharply, and snatched up the thermos. "And don't smile at me. We don't have time for any light-of-love nonsense just now or . . ."

I stayed where I was. "Or what?" I said.

"Or I should have a difficult time keeping my hands off you," he said tightly. "As you well know." He handed me the thermos and slipped out the door. I waited an endless moment until I heard his light tap and then opened the door. He took my arm and hurried me down the momentarily empty hall.

"I don't want you to keep your hands off me," I said softly, the towel-wrapped thermos under my arm.

He didn't give any sign that he'd heard me, and I hurried along beside him, in a totally inappropriate mood for the occasion, which, after all, was fairly dangerous.

Halfway down the steps to the baths, we heard people coming. "I hope that's not more reporters," Joss said. It sounded like a couple of lovers coming home from the Fete, but Joss pulled me into a shadowed niche and held me there until they passed.

"I'm going to kiss you to make it look good," he said as the couple went by arm in arm.

"You are?"

He kissed me twice, even though the second time I would have sworn there was nobody left in the hall.

"I think they're gone," I said finally. "We'd better go."

"Wait," he said. "I have to tell you something. Before we go look at this thermos. Before we prove your mother's innocence or guilt. I should have told you before. Great Hera, I should have told you down in that light raid shelter. I already knew I could trust you then, even if you didn't." He took a deep breath. "I'm not Essex's equerry. I'm with Scotland Yard."

It was the only thing I'd figured out since I got back that wasn't a painful shock. "I know," I said.

"Good girl," he said, and kissed me lightly. "Stay here a moment," he said, and took off down the steps. "All clear," he called softly, and I followed him down the steps and into the baths at a rate hardly appropriate for someone sneaking off for a midnight swim.

I made a cautious circuit of Morning Glory Pool while Joss went over the showers again. He finished by turning them all on full blast, just as he had the first time he talked to me in here. "Get in the pool," he said. "I can splash in with you if anyone gets past the precautions I'm putting on Min."

I waded in. Morning Glory was lower than I remembered it. The water level only came to the third step. I sat down on the fourth step and waited.

Joss spent a considerable time doing things to Min, just what I wasn't sure since he had her on visual only, and then disappeared into the showers. When he came back, he had changed into bathing shorts and was carrying a bottle and two glasses. "I've even brought some bubbly to make it more convincing. There, put them just at the edge."

I took the bottle and glasses and set them gently on the third step of the pool, just above the water's edge. That was funny. The water seemed a little higher now. I would have sworn it was a more vivid blue than this, too. I trailed my hand through the water but couldn't tell if it felt cooler or not.

"I've got to jerry-rig these pins so they'll fit the socket in the thermos," he said.

"How will we know when someone's coming?" I said, looking anxiously at the door.

"I've set up trips in the staging area and on the stairs. We'll have considerable warning. While I'm getting the safety memory rigged, get access and call up something harmless so I can start testing the connection as soon as I'm done. Tell me when you lose the image."

I identified myself to Min, waited for her to confirm, and then asked for my mail. There were two letters from Chilkie listed. She'd been a busy girl. I called up the one that had come through today. It was little more than half a screen long and obviously desperate.

"Oh, Ariadne, everything's horrible. Mrs. Ponsonby's pipes exploded yesterday." Exploded? Oh, no. The hydra were supposed to cut the water off, not blow up the pipes. "The twins got burned, not bad, and Verity Ann and Beejum weren't hurt. Mrs. Ponsonby is sending the rest of us away to————." The location had been neatly masked out by Censoring. I wondered if Chilkie had managed to get in touch with her mailboy friend Skids before she'd left. I hoped the kids were all right. "You remember all those noises the pipes were making? They stopped, absolutely stopped—not a gurgle or a hiss—for about sixty seconds before the explosion, and then WHAM!"

I was staring at a blank screen. "It's off," I said hastily. Joss fiddled a minute more with the underside of the terminal, and the letter reappeared. "I've got it again."

"Good," he said, came out from underneath, and looked at me expectantly. "Ready?" he said.

"Yes," I said, and felt suddenly, utterly afraid of what I was going to see.

"Okay," he said, squeezed my hand, and tapped in a command.

For the first few minutes it didn't make any sense. I had expected that. I mean, I hadn't expected the words "Treason Plan" to flash on the screen, and I had figured it would take a few minutes to sort out what was going on. I had expected figures and charts and formulas and the time and trouble it would take to decipher all of those. I had not expected gibberish.

Well, not exactly gibberish. In fact, it was the formulas, numbers, and charts I had thought it would be, and after a while it did begin to make sense of a sort. The only thing was, it didn't have anything at all to do with biots. I wasn't sure what it did have to do with.

There were inverted treelike charts with many roots that could only be hydra, and odd spots of blue and one area colored red within the roots that could have been the spots at which the hydra joined the water table, though nothing was labeled, and it looked to me like they were far too close to the surface. It could also have been something totally different. Whatever that something was, it wasn't the GEM biot research.

Joss flipped forward several charts. The blue spots grew, but the red one stayed the same. He flipped forward again to an aerial view of Denver Springs done in infrared-enhance.

"I've seen this before," he said. "It's a map of the drought areas."
We were both silent. "The other charts must be plots to determine where
the trouble is originating in the water table. It would seem," he said,
and his voice had taken on that infinitely careful tone again, "that your
mother was telling the truth, that she wasn't working on GEM when the
first raid occurred, after all."

This was where I was supposed to feel a lightening of that awful
weight, a loosening of the knot I'd had in my stomach since Dad asked
me to steal the thermos. This was where I was supposed to say to Joss,
"I told you there was a logical explanation. I knew my mother wasn't
a traitor." But I didn't feel any change, and I didn't say anything.

Joss was watching the screen. "She said she was working on the
drought. I guess I should have believed her."

"Why did she hide the thermos then?" I said.

Joss turned and looked at me. "Maybe she stuck it in the bureau
drawer and then forgot about it."

"She wasn't in the habit of keeping computer memory in with her
jewelry. And it was fairly important to remember it since it could have
kept her out of jail."

"She said she couldn't defend herself for fear of jeopardizing the
plan to get the scientist out of Quebec. Why aren't you convinced of her
innocence?" he said bitterly. "Everyone else is. Hydra Corp's wel-
comed your mother back with open arms, and the tabloid reporters can't
wait to tell everyone that my lord Essex has been recalled to Yellowknife in disgrace."

"What about this scientist? Who is she? Is she really from
Quebec?"

His wrist terminal began a slow beeping. "Someone's in the
staging area," he said quietly, and flicked the terminal off. "Quickly,"
Joss said, and we stepped into the water. It was hotter than I
remembered, but not impossible except to my burned hand. Joss
stepped down several steps, unfastened his wrist terminal, and laid it on
the edge. It stopped beeping.

"They may have gone away," he said, "but we'll stay in for a
moment." He picked up the bottle of champagne and sat down. The
water came up to the middle of his chest. I got the glasses and sat down
beside him.

He looked desperately unhappy. I knew how he felt. I had just been
given unquestionable proof that my mother wasn't a traitor, and all I
could think about was what the data in the memory meant and where the

GEM memory was if it wasn't in the thermos. I wondered if Joss was thinking the same thing. He had been as convinced as I was that Mother was guilty, and he hadn't even known about the thermos. He still was convinced, I thought, watching him; this defecting scientist hadn't changed his opinion one bit. Only now he wouldn't get a chance to prove it—he'd be called back to Yellowknife along with Essex, and Mother would be free to do whatever it was she was doing and I'd never see him again.

My feet touched bottom. I had walked down the wide steps of Morning Glory Pool all the way to the bottom, which usually wasn't possible. The level of the water must really be down. I turned and tried to smile at Joss. "What happens now?" I said.

"I pop this cork and pour you a glass of the bubbly. We toast Essex or your mother, whichever you prefer. I might even kiss you for good measure."

"No. I mean, what happens to Essex? And you."

"We shall return to Yellowknife, where Essex will brave his grandfather's wrath, and I shall brave the wrath of the Yard. Attempts will be made to smooth over a difficult situation between allies, and the war will go on as scheduled."

The purified steam of Morning Glory has always made me cry. I wiped my eyes with a wet hand and said, "When will you have to leave?"

"That will depend on the press, I should imagine. We may have a day or two if your mother is slow to summon them, or we may only have time for a glass of . . ." He took my hand, held it up while he poured champagne into the glass, did the same with my other hand, and took that glass from me. "Here's to things that might have been and things that, thankfully, weren't." He held his glass up to mine and then lowered it. "Ariadne," he said.

"It's the steam," I said. "I don't want you to go."

He set the bottle and his glass above the waterline. Then he took the glass out of my hand and set it on the step beside them. "Nor do I want to," he said, and bent forward to kiss me. It was wonderful. It was like falling, like flying, like floating . . .

"Did you have difficulty finding my daughter, Mr. Liddell?" Mother said. "I believe she's in the pool."

We were in the middle of Morning Glory, though I had no idea how we had gotten there. I dog-paddled to the side where my mother was standing.

"I'm sorry to interrupt your little party, Ariadne," she said coldly. "But I need you in my office. The press is there, and I want you to meet a friend of mine." She handed me the towel the thermos had been wrapped in.

"A friend?" I said, rubbing myself dry and not looking at Joss.

"Yes, I would have thought Mr. Liddell would have told you, but then you might not have been as susceptible to his charms. Isn't that right, Mr. Liddell? Yes, the scientist you've heard so much about," she said, looking at Joss. "My dear friend Dr. Clare Blackburn escaped from Quebec with what will prove to be the solution to the drought."

from the *Christian Science Enquirer*

# Un-Dress
# At the Fete

Prince Essex's eyes popped out at the Broadmoor Fete when live-in love, sexy Hellene Ariadne, showed up in a see-through Grecian veil that covered almost nothing. Holly Sugar beauty Mary Tildon, who was with the prince when Ari arrived, turned as red as the red hibiscus on her red muumuu and walked out.

(Fete holos, Screens 2 through 13.)

# CHAPTER ELEVEN

"**T**here they are!"

Tabloid reporters swarmed through the pool room door, holocam lights blazing as Joss climbed out of the pool. I waded after him, furious at being caught once again with hardly any clothes on. But the reporters weren't even looking at me.

"Hellene Medea, how long have you known Dr. Blackburn?" one said to Mother.

"Were you in contact with her before her escape?"

"Is the real reason that you were interred for questioning by the Commonwealth that they thought you were in collusion with her? Didn't they realize you were engineering her escape? Or were they trying to stop that escape for their own reasons?"

"Did your daughter return from Victoria to bring you a message from Dr. Blackburn?"

A secret smile passed over Mother's face, but she just shook her head at them. "All in good time, my friends. Let's adjourn to my conference room, shall we?" She caught the first two reporters by their elbows and started toward the door. She didn't have to convince the others to follow her. They scrambled out the door in her wake. She let go of the reporters to hold the door open. Over her shoulder she said to me, "I want you at the press conference, Ariadne. In something besides that."

Mother, I realized dimly, had already changed out of her formal toga into the businesslike challis she had laid out before the Fete.

"Mr. Liddell, I believe your employer, Mr. Essex, is looking for you."

"Thank you, Hellene," he said, his face and voice giving nothing away, even though she was treating us like two strayed children.

"The press conference is about to begin, Ariadne," she added.

"I'll be right there, Mother," I said, and bent to pick up a towel. A reporter shoved the door Mother was holding open again.

"How do you feel about your daughter's involvement with Miles Essex?"

"Is it true she's the latest in a long line of light-of-loves the prince has . . ."

They were threatening to explode through the door like a dam breaking.

"My daughter has no . . ." Mother said, and then gave up. "I will answer all your questions at the press conference," she said, and shut the door behind her.

I finished picking up the towel. "Joss," I said.

He moved his hand very slightly in a motion that could only signal silence and then bodily hauled a leftover reporter out of one of the shower stalls. "You don't want to be late for your press conference, do you?" Joss said evenly, and practically threw him across the room, knocking his fedora off.

"What were you and Hellene Ariadne doing down here together?" the reporter shouted, swiping his hat up from the marble floor. He mashed it down on his head, skewing the press ticket in the band. "Is it true you warm them up for the prince?"

Joss heaved him out the door and slammed it shut.

"Joss," I said. "I have to talk to you."

"Not now," he said, and started through the shower stalls, systematically opening them and running his hand along the walls and checking the faucets and shower heads. I realized he must be looking for mechanical follows. "Change your clothes and get up to the press conference. If you're not there, some enterprising reporter will come back here looking for you. I'll take care of things down here."

"You don't understand," I said, and then lowered my voice to a whisper. "You don't understand. I have to tell you something important."

He made that motion for silence again with his hand. "I don't need any protestations of love right now. Go to your press conference."

I wanted to say, "Meet me," or "Turn the shower on," or "Get in the pool so we can talk," but I had no business saying any of them if that reporter, or worse, Mother, had planted a follow. So I said, "I certainly wouldn't protest undying love to anybody who thought my mother was a traitor. I'm going to go change my clothes," and flounced out, hoping he might follow me to Dad's office when he'd gotten the thermos safely stashed.

I didn't make it to Dad's office. Halfway up the stairs I got caught by a gang of reporters who shouted a variety of rude questions at me and pointed so many holocam lights at me I couldn't even see.

"I'm not going to answer any questions till I've had a chance to change my clothes," I said, wishing I could sound as calm as Mother and Joss, deathly afraid they could tell what I was thinking just by looking at me.

"How do you feel about Dr. Blackburn's arrival, Hellene?" two reporters shouted, almost in unison, and I ducked between them and down the hall into Dad's office.

I tore off the wet shift and tried to find something to wear. I yanked on the blue challis with the silver belt Mother had picked out this afternoon. Thank goodness it needed nothing underneath, for we'd forgotten to buy underwear. I tied my wet hair up with a blue and white string.

There was no point in waiting for Joss. We couldn't talk here, not with a swarm of reporters outside and probably half a dozen mechanical follows hidden in the room. They probably had their ears to the door, too, and what I needed to tell Joss I couldn't risk having *anybody* find out. But I had to get to him somehow, had to tell him Clare Blackburn had been in Victoria, and had tried to get me to go with her. But even more important, I had to tell him I had live GEM biots in Victoria, maybe the only ones in existence. You should have told him before this, I thought angrily.

I dawdled as long as I dared, listening with *my* ear against the door in the foolish hope that the reporters might give up and go away, and then opened the door and let them escort me to the press conference. They hustled me into the hall to the conference room in the back of Essex's offices.

But plainly they were Essex's offices no longer. Mother was in charge, issuing orders to two Hydra Corp human relations people so that the holocams were set up just so far from the little podium on the side of the conference room. Essex's furniture was already gone to make room for the crowd of reporters and Hydra execs, though Essex himself was still there. He stood off to the side of the room, straight-backed and clear-eyed in his blue uniform, but somehow lacking self-confidence, and looking lonely without Joss at his side.

"Hellene Medea wants you to stand with the others," one of the public relations people said to me. He gestured to the group of Hydra execs and my father at the side of the room, close to the podium. I didn't see Clare anywhere. Essex leaned over to whisper something to my father, and the expression on Dad's face became one of pure hatred. He said something back to Essex, and one of the reporters leaped forward to shove a mike under his nose, no doubt asking him to repeat himself. But Mother stepped between them and firmly pushed the mike away, and at the same time gave me an impelling look. Father was still drunk, and I hurried over to take charge.

"Dad, let's move back a bit," I said, taking his hand to pull him to the back of the exec crowd.

"I told him she wasn't guilty," he said, shaking loose of me. "But, no, His Royal High and Mighty had to have a scapegoat." His voice was too loud and the reporters were trying to move in despite the Hydra Corp execs, who were trying to get them to sit down.

Just then Mother stepped up to the podium, and that simple act silenced the room.

"My friends," she said. "Tonight is the end of a trying time for Hydra Corp."

She had everyone's attention, for the moment, even Dad's. He turned at the sound of her voice and stared through bloodshot eyes. He seemed, quite suddenly, on the verge of tears.

"Dad, what's wrong?"

"It's gone," he whispered. "I searched the dressing room, and it's gone."

Mother shot us a warning glance, so I didn't dare tell him that I had the thermos, and even more important, that there was nothing incriminating in it.

"I have kept silent these past months to protect the welfare of a colleague whose research efforts on our behalf might have been discovered by the Quebeckers. Not until she had left the occupied provinces via the underground resistance and made her way safely to Denver Springs could I even hint that I knew more than I was telling. But Dr. Blackburn is safe now, and the truth must be told." She looked meaningfully at Essex, and he stood rigidly.

"You knew all along," Father said to Essex, but Essex was too far away to hear.

"The drought rumors that the Commonwealth forced us to deny are true, and they have been true all along." She paused to take in the effect that had on Essex and the rumble of confirmation from the reporters, and then continued. With only half my attention, I heard Mother explain that Clare had been trying to escape from Quebec for years, that Mother knew before the war of Clare's research on hydra drought patterns. Clare had theorized that the droughts would occur as the result of a natural defect in the hydra DNA, and she had some practical research to back up her theory. Of course Hydra Corp was cut off from that research by the war, and Medea had immediately begun efforts to get Dr. Blackburn out of the occupied provinces. But the prince had arrived at Hydra Corp to take charge of the war research efforts, and when he did, he had thought he'd discovered treason . . . security leaks about the hydra droughts, a shutdown of other essential project research, and what might have been interpreted as plans for Mother to defect to the Quebeckers. Those were, in fact, plans for Dr. Blackburn's escape to the Western States, probably deliberately misinterpreted because the Commonwealth would want Dr. Blackburn to escape to them, not to an ally.

I didn't catch all the details because Dad was muttering epithets under his breath, his voice, thankfully, still too low for anyone but the Hydra execs and me to hear. I kept trying to hush him. But that same reporter who had tried to hear what he said to Essex earlier was edging around the Hydra Corp execs, who were watching Mother with something close to enraptured adoration.

I was afraid my expression was just as readable to anyone who looked at me. She was going to discredit Essex so thoroughly the tabloids wouldn't even have any bones left to pick, so thoroughly no one would believe him when he tried to warn Hydra Corp about what she was up to. What was she up to? All this talk about the drought had to be a blind, just like the data in the memory was a blind. It had to be, because Clare hadn't just been smuggled out of Quebec. She'd been in Victoria three days ago, blithely buying me lunch.

To hide my face, I turned to Dad. "Dad, Mother's talking," I whispered to him in the same voice he used to hush me when I was a small child. For a moment that silenced him.

"Now, with Dr. Blackburn's help, we can defeat the drought and resume work on projects of vital national importance to our defense."

She stopped with a dramatic flourish that should have gotten applause and gestured toward the door of the dressing room.

Right on cue, Clare emerged, not dressed in a wool suit and shoulder chain now, but in travel-stained khaki jams and a travel cloak, her hair in an untidy ponytail, the dusty heroine just out of danger. I was not impressed.

Mother turned the podium over to Clare. There was a round of applause, but I noticed that Essex didn't join in. Dad was looking at Clare now, Essex forgotten for the moment. He seemed frightened again. I felt my heart sinking. He didn't believe Mother's story either.

"I'll answer questions now," Clare said coolly to the reporters.

Half a dozen leaped to their feet.

"How did you get out of the occupied provinces?"

"Will you be able to duplicate your research here at Hydra Corp?"

"Will you also be working on this defense project that Hellene Medea talked about?"

"What is the nature of the defense project?"

Clare's eyes met the first reporter's. "Of course I cannot give you details of my escape, for many sympathizers in the occupied provinces are still exposed to the Quebeckers' secret police. But I can tell you that I have been traveling and hiding for more than a month." Now her gaze fell on me, her eyes cool and level. "I came to Denver Springs just as soon as I cleared the border."

Another lie, and she had turned purposely to look at me as she said it. I realized suddenly what a threat I must be to her. What if I told the tabloid reporters that I'd seen her in Victoria? What if, and the thought rocked me like an explosion, what if I told Mother?

Mother didn't know I'd seen Clare in Victoria. She thought I'd run away before Clare got there. Mother could hide her feelings almost as well as Joss, but even so, her manner was all wrong. She had been jubilant, triumphant, when she came down to get me in the baths. She had expected her news to convince me, too. I was willing to bet she didn't have any idea the name Clare Blackburn meant anything to me. And what did that mean?

That Mother was innocent after all? That she was somehow being taken in by Clare? I looked around for Joss, desperate enough to grab him and get him out of the room to talk to him and the hell with what the tabloid reporters thought.

Clare was still talking, but her gaze had shifted from me to Dad, her eyes contemptuous. He turned away, brushing a tear with the back of his hand.

"Ignorant blue bloods," Dad said, his eyes fastened on Essex again. He seemed to be riding a roller coaster of emotion, and he was going too fast.

The reporters were less orderly than they had been a moment before. I think some had heard Dad, and they all seemed to remember Essex at once. They thrust their holocams at the prince, demanding a statement, while Clare, somewhat abandoned now on the podium, kept looking at Dad and me through cool, blue eyes.

"Of course the Crown is delighted that the whole matter has finally come to light," Essex said.

"Through no help from you," Dad shouted. His face was red, the veins in his forehead protruding.

Mother shot me a warning glance that I didn't need. I needed to get Dad out of there, but not for the same reason as Mother. Joss still wasn't here, and this was the perfect way to leave this press conference early and find Joss. I had to tell him what I knew about Mother and Clare and to tell him the truth about the GEM biots.

"The Crown wouldn't recognize a spy if one stood before it and confessed!" Dad said, trying to stand up.

"Daddy, come on," I said, taking his hand and pulling him back toward the outer rooms. He was too drunk and too shaken to know what he was saying, but the tabloids thrived on indiscretion. He didn't resist me too much, and the Hydra Corp execs closed ranks to cut off any reporters that were tempted to follow us. Just inside the door, I spotted Joss standing with his arms crossed over his chest. "Help me," I mouthed at him.

He looked about to refuse, and I panicked for a second. I could manage Dad, but I didn't know what to do about the lies I had heard, and there were the GEM biots to consider. He and the prince might leave for Yellowknife right after the conference. "Please!" I started to mouth at him, but he was already moving toward me. He took Dad's other arm and half-carried him out the door.

"Yard slime! Let me alone," Dad said, struggling against Joss's grip, but we were already out in the hall. I ran across and palmed the doorkeep on Dad's office.

"I can walk into my own office," Dad shouted, and rammed an elbow into Joss's side that doubled him up for a moment. "I don't need any help from a spy," and amazingly he walked into the office and sat down in his swivel chair. I shut the door and then ran into the bathroom for a sedative patch while Joss asked Min for a watch on the door.

The only thing I could find was a snoozer, which wasn't very strong. "Get him the hell out of here," Dad said. "He's a Commonwealth spy," but he didn't try to get up again. I didn't think he could.

"This'll make you feel better," I said, and slipped the snoozer behind the sobriety patch on the back of his neck.

Dad instantly closed his eyes. He must have been close to collapsing already for the medication to take effect that quickly.

"What did you do with the thermos?" I asked Joss.

"You have it?" Dad said, astoundingly alert. "Give it to me. I have to have it to . . ." He slumped against the back of the chair.

"To what? " I said.

Joss put his finger to his lips and motioned me to help him. Between us we got Dad around behind the screen and onto his cot. Joss pulled a patch out of his pocket and peeled off the back. He pulled off the two patches behind Dad's neck and replaced them with his patch. "Tanazine," he said. "A lot stronger than what you gave him. He'll be out till tomorrow morning." He took my hand and led me back around the screen to the dark terminal. "Min, are there any mechanical follows in this room?"

"Only the one on Hellene Dares that Hellene Ariadne requested," Min said. "Shall I remove it?"

Well, it was a good thing he was on my side because Min wasn't supposed to tell him that, and she hadn't even tried to resist.

"No. Leave it on. Just in case." He looked at me, still holding my hand. "I don't think he's going anywhere. What about bugs, creepers, or andials?"

"No," Min said. "Nothing but your full scan."

"Take that out now," Joss said, "and give me a white-noise blanket. I don't want anything we say getting out of this room. Do you understand?"

"Righto," Min said, blinked a clear, and covered the screen with a wash of rainbows.

"I trashed the memory," he said, "and made certain the incinerator was on. What was in it is now available from Min, but only in your account. You can call it up by asking for your mail. I've transmitted a copy of the memory to Yellowknife and put the code boys to work on it."

"What about the thermos?"

"I've hidden it. Before I leave I'm going to get it back into the drawer you took it out of."

"It was in a paper bag," I said. "I think that's still in the drawer. How are you going to get past all those reporters?"

"I'm going to ask for permission to get some of my things out of the dressing room. Now, listen. I've got only a couple of minutes. Essex's gullwing is already waiting out front. I've got to go with him to Yellowknife."

He was squeezing my hand so hard it hurt. "Damn this cover as his equerry. It was supposed to give me the freedom to move around. I'll be back as soon as I can." He seemed to realize suddenly what he was doing and let go of my hand. He took it gently in his and kissed the palm. "It may be a good thing. With me gone, your mother may make some kind of move. So long as she believes she's being watched, she'll work on the drought and we won't find out anything. We learned that lesson the difficult way. I had hoped that interning her might force her or the Quebeckers to make a move. But it didn't."

"Yes, it did," I said. "Clare Blackburn came to see me in Victoria. Three days ago."

For once I had caught him completely by surprise.

"What?" he said. He dropped my hand. "Are you sure?"

I nodded.

"Does your mother know this?"

"I don't think so. But that isn't all."

He sat down on Dad's desk. "What other laser hits have you got?"

"I have live GEM biots. In Victoria."

"In Victoria," he said slowly.

"I know I should have told you before. When Mother sent me to Victoria, I was furious with her for treating me like a child. I'd been working in Research on GEM, so I took some of the biots with me. I had some kind of stupid idea that if I could get them to grow, Mother would send for me."

"Did you tell anybody about these biots? In a letter possibly? Did you say anything to anyone?"

"No," I said. "The kids at Mrs. Ponsonby's knew they were there, but they didn't know what they were. I wanted to surprise Mother," I said bitterly.

"Did you say anything to Clare Blackburn about them? Did she ask you about the GEM Project when you saw her in Victoria?"

"No."

"You're sure?"

"I'm sure. Nobody knew about them except me."

"Then what was she doing in Victoria?"

"I don't know. You had Mother in jail. Maybe she was trying to find out what had happened. Or maybe she thought Mother would try to send some kind of message through me."

"Or if they had any doubts about her loyalty, they may have been intending to kidnap you and use you to force her to defect."

"Thank you," I said quietly, "but I don't think she needed to be forced. Clare asked me to come and stay with her, but she didn't try to force me."

"There are all sorts of kidnapping," he said, looking hard at me. "Clare's knowing that you could destroy her story puts you in a good deal more danger than I'd thought. Perhaps you'd best come to Yellowknife with me."

I shook my head regretfully. I wanted nothing more than to go to Yellowknife with him. "You were right about making them think they've got a clear field. And Clare won't do anything. She'll come up with some story as to why she met me in Victoria, and I'll let her think I believe her. The important thing is the biots. You've got to go get them."

"Give me Mrs. Ponsonby's address, and tell me where they are."

"They're not . . . it's a long story. I don't know exactly where they are. Beejum's got them."

"Beejum. One of the refugee children, right? What's his real name?"

"Benjamin Stafford. The plumbing exploded at Mrs. Ponsonby's and they got moved. I don't know where to. It was censored out of Chilkie's letter. Chilkie James. Her boyfriend might know where they went."

He grabbed a piece of paper out of Dad's desk and scribbled Beejum's and Chilkie's names on it. "What's the boyfriend's name?"

"Skids," I said. "I don't know his real name. He's the mailboy for Mrs. Ponsonby's neighborhood."

He shoved the piece of paper and the pen at me. "Write down Mrs. Ponsonby's address and draw me a map of the neighborhood."

I did, and handed it to Joss.

He took my hand again. "I don't want to leave you here," he said, and pulled me against him.

His wrist terminal beeped softly. "Is that a light raid?" I said.

"I wish it were," he said. "I'd take you down in that shelter again, and this time . . ." It beeped more insistently. "I'm afraid it's Essex. I've got to go. I shall be back as soon as I can. Damned war."

"You've got to find the biots first," I said.

"I shall," he said, and kissed me. "And then I shall come back for you." He bent to kiss me again. The door to Dad's office opened and Mother stepped in.

# Scientist Tells Tale of Daring Rescue

"I stared at the computer screen, memorizing the formulas. Then I erased the memory, put on my coat, and walked out of the laboratory." Thus began a harrowing tale of escape and danger as Dr. Clare Blackburn tried to smuggle her research out of Quebec.

"I had been waiting for the right moment, and this was it, now that I had the research that could help Denver Springs," a travel-weary Dr. Blackburn said at a press conference held in Hydra Corp only moments ago. Forced to work on war research for the Quebec government, Dr. Blackburn was researching the droughts that have plagued Denver Springs recently. "Quebec didn't cause the droughts," she said, "but they were manipulating them for their own ends. And now I held the key to stopping them. It was time to get out."

She did get out, aided by the Quebecker Resistance Movement and Hydra Corp exec Hellene Medea. "I had met Hellene Medea at a scientific conference before the war. She had been working tirelessly since the beginning of the war to get me out. The Resistance got a comm signal out to her, and she immediately set a rescue plan in motion."

The plan, details of which cannot be revealed because it would endanger members of the Resistance, had to be carried out in total secrecy, a secrecy which resulted in Hellene Medea's being suspected of sabotage and, finally, of being jailed.

"I couldn't defend myself without endangering Dr. Blackburn," a relieved and smiling Hellene Medea said. "I couldn't risk that."

"I owe my life to her," a grateful Dr. Blackburn acknowledged. "She risked her life to save mine."

(Map of escape, Screen 2. Prince Essex's response to news, Screen 4.)

# CHAPTER TWELVE

jumped like I'd been lased. Mother said, "Mr. Liddell, every time I look for my daughter, I find you." She turned to me. "Where's your father?"

"He's asleep," I said.

"Mr. Liddell, I believe your employer is looking for you. You wouldn't want to delay his departure to Yellowknife."

"Thank you," Joss said with a formal little bow. Mother was glaring at him with a look that dared him to say anything to me. "Goodbye, Hellene Medea," he said, and then turned to me. "Goodbye, Hellene Ariadne." He even smiled at me, a give-nothing-away smile that I tried to return in kind. He bowed again and went out the door.

"I wouldn't let anyone else see that expression on your face," Mother said. "They might take your attachment for disloyalty to Hydra Corp."

Disloyalty. Well, you should know, Mother. You wrote the book on it.

I said, "Whether you believe it or not, Mother, Joss . . . Mr. Liddell was very kind to me when I first got here. He saved my life."

"Oh, I don't doubt he was kind. You may forgive me if I doubt the motives behind his various kindnesses, though. Did you know he was from Scotland Yard?"

Well, of course I'd known it. He'd told me. And Dad had guessed because he'd mentioned it when he was calling Joss names. But I sure didn't like the idea of Mother knowing it. If I hadn't felt like I was walking on the narrow edge of a volcano's crater, I would have done a great deal of thinking about the kind of mother who would tell her daughter something like that when she had to have a good idea of how I felt about him, but I was too worried about Joss and Dad and Clare to make more than a passing note of it.

"Scotland Yard or not, we don't have to worry about Mr. Liddell anymore," Mother said. "He and the prince are on their way back to Yellowknife and we have work to do."

"On the drought?" I said. "Or on the GEM Project?"

"On the drought first, of course," Mother said, and frowned. "I can't have you moping over a Commonwealth spy, Ariadne. I'm going to need your help. We'll need an up-to-date plot of the trouble spots and that may take some doing. I'm afraid in his zeal to keep news of the drought from the public, Miles Essex erased a good deal of necessary information from Min."

Oh, but Mother, you've got an up-to-date map of the drought, and I know where it is. Did she know it was missing and was trying to find out if I knew anything about it? I didn't think so. She was supremely confident, and had been ever since she'd come in the baths to tell me Clare had arrived. Anyway, the place had been swarming with reporters—I didn't think she'd risk checking on the thermos with them around. So that meant she thought it was still there, safe and intact, and so why didn't she haul it out of the thermos so we could have this map of the drought instead of letting me waste days making a new one? Because that isn't what it is, you idiot. It's something else.

"Are you listening, Ari?" Mother said impatiently. I had been standing looking out the window at the parking lot of Hydra Corp, which was covered with tabloid portable studios and holocam lights. Reflected against the shiny silver of the parking lot, they made it almost as bright as day out there, and a ready-made target for a light raid. But there hadn't been any light raids today. I wondered why not, afraid I knew the answer. I turned around.

"Yes," I said, and I knew I wasn't keeping the feeling out of my voice. "I'm listening."

"What's the matter, Ariadne?" Mother said, the impatience gone. She looked like my mother for the first time since I'd gotten here.

What if I said, "I saw Clare Blackburn three days ago in Victoria," and she, so thunderstruck she had to sit down in Dad's swivel chair, said, "You did? But that's impossible! She told me . . . are you sure it was Dr. Blackburn, Ariadne?"

Would I believe her even then? Would I tell her I had found the thermos, and would she say, "How wonderful! I just assumed the memory was lost in the light raids on Hydra Corp. Now we can stop the droughts and go on to the GEM Project"?

It would be very nice if she'd say those things, but I didn't really believe anymore that she would. And I couldn't risk saying them anyway. I had promised Joss I'd play the innocent.

"Something's wrong. Now what is it?" she said, the impatience back in her voice and something else. Fear maybe?

"Nothing," I said, turning to the window again to hide my face. "I'm just tired."

"And you don't know what to make of the fact that Dr. Blackburn was in Victoria three days ago instead of escaping from Quebec."

My heart actually leaped up one last time. I was so surprised, so relieved that I whirled around to look at her. There was a logical explanation for everything after all, and she was going to tell it to me.

"I was afraid to say anything," I said carefully, "for fear . . . it might mess things up." And that was putting it mildly.

She smiled. "I know, and I couldn't say anything for the same reason. I'm sorry I had to put you through that, but I knew you could be trusted."

Trusted. I smiled back. "I wasn't sure you knew about it."

"Of course I knew about it. I was the one who sent her. She's been out of Quebec nearly two weeks, waiting till it was safe to cross the border. There were . . . problems in Victoria. I can't tell you about them, but they are still so serious that we had to come up with the cover story you heard at the press conference to protect the people who helped her get across the border." She smiled at me again, and nothing had changed. She was still the supremely confident, everything's-under-control Medea.

"She was in terrible danger the whole time she was in hiding in Victoria." She shook her head. "I never should have asked her to do it, but I had to know how you were. I had to make sure you were safe. There was no way she could bring you with her, but at least she could tell me how you were . . ." She stopped and smiled again. "Call it a mother's weakness."

A mother's weakness. I'd call it something else, Mother. The story was as transparent as that white dress of mine. Clare wouldn't have had to rescue me. I wasn't escaping from Quebec. I was only in Victoria because my concerned mother had put me there, and one word from her, even in jail, could have brought me back home.

And if Clare was in so much danger, it would have been worse than stupid to visit me since my connection with her could have gotten me killed. I would have been a lot safer without that lunch at the Empress Hotel.

Worst of all, though, were the circumstances, circumstances that Mother obviously wasn't aware of even though she knew about the visit. Clare hadn't met me on a dark street corner wearing her refugee fatigues and a ponytail. She'd breezed into the Empress Hotel in a suit and jewels, and there was no way even Mother could pass that off as a disguise, though doubtless when Clare filled her in a little more, she would come up with an altered version. Or would she even bother? She thought I was so stupid, so trusting I'd believe anything she said. I was surprised she'd even bothered to waste her time explaining Clare's presence in Victoria to me.

"I'm glad I didn't say anything to the tabloid reporters then," I said, hoping that might make her a little nervous.

"Or Joss Liddell," she said, not smiling now.

So that was the reason she'd bothered.

"I didn't tell anybody," I said earnestly. "Not even Daddy." I stifled a yawn. "I am so tired. I've hardly had a decent night's sleep since I left Victoria." I looked up at her, all trusting, stupid sincerity. "You know what I thought when Clare came to see me? I thought something had happened to you and Daddy. I thought she was trying to think of a way to break it to me gently, and I came tearing home. I was on the road forever and then when I got home Daddy was a wreck and I was so worried about you, I don't think I've slept more than a few hours altogether."

She looked hard at me, as if she thought Joss Liddell and not worry had been keeping me up all night. Then she smiled again and said, "You get some sleep. You look terrible, and the map of the drought can wait. You're no use if you're dead on your feet. At any rate, Dr. Blackburn won't get away from those reporters for hours. We'll start tomorrow morning."

"I think you're right," I said, trying to look like I was going to head for bed instead of straight for a terminal of Min's. "I wouldn't want to make any stupid mistakes. I'll go bunk with Gaea."

"There's no need for that. I'll call for a cot and you can stay here. I'll sleep in my dressing room."

I didn't like that idea at all—I couldn't use Min with Dad in here, even if he was under a sedative. I had to go somewhere safer. "That's okay," I said, gathering up a toothbrush, a change of clothes, and a night toga as if it were all settled, "Gaea asked me at the Fete if I'd move in with her. I told her yes. How long will it take to get the drought stopped?"

"A week if we're lucky, a month if we're not. Miles Essex's interference has caused it to get almost out of hand. It could even take several months."

"If it's going to take that long, shouldn't we be working on the GEM Project, too?"

"You sound like Miles Essex, Ariadne," Mother said, not sounding at all amused. "I'm not about to split my Research team in half. We won't get anywhere that way. As soon as we've solved the drought, we'll begin work on the GEM Project."

Will you? I thought. Or will there be another light raid, another accident that will slow things down so that somehow the GEM Project gets delayed indefinitely?

"Will you start work on GEM again?" Dad said. He was leaning against the screen around his cot. It looked like it could topple at any moment, and him with it. He was holding the tanazine patch in his free hand. "Or will you be long gone, Medea? You can't fool me. Clare came here to get you, didn't she? To take you back? And you're going with her."

"Dad," I said, and moved toward him, "you aren't supposed to be up." I took his arm. He knocked the bundle of clothes flying.

"Stop that," Mother said. She grabbed his arm. "You're drunk." I took hold of his other arm.

"Ari, promise me you won't let them take her. Promise me."

"I promise, Dad," I said, and eased the patch out of his unresisting fingers, wondering when he'd taken it off. If the patch was as strong as Joss said, he would have had to remove it almost as soon as Joss put it on him. Which meant he had heard—how much?—of our conversation.

Between us, we set him down on the bed, and I put the patch back on the side of his neck. I held it there, tight against his skin. "I think I'd better stay here with Dad after all. I can call up another cot." I looked up at her with what I hoped was appealing honesty. "He's been through a lot lately," I said. "He was worried sick about you, so much he can't even think straight. He thought Essex had sent for me so I could testify against you. And he keeps talking about strange people trying to take you away from him. I think he has it in his mind that Essex might try to intern you again."

Dad had slumped against me. "Dad?" I said. He was breathing hard, his eyes half open.

"I love you," he said with an effort. He was looking at Mother. "I'd do anything to keep them from taking you away."

"I know you would," I said. "Lie back."

He obediently lay down and turned his head away from me and toward Mother. "Anything," he said, half into the pillow, and began to snore.

"Why don't I just have them send up a cot?" I said. "Then I can sit here until I'm sure he's asleep."

"No," she said. "I don't like the way he struck at you. I think staying with Gaea is a good idea."

There was nothing I could say to that, and anyway Dad was definitely asleep. I didn't think he could fake that deep, half-snoring breathing. I gathered up my scattered things and went over to the door. "I'll see you in the morning," I said. "I think we could all use a good night's sleep."

"Yes," said Mother, and shut the door behind me.

A good night's sleep. That would have been nice. I hadn't been lying to Mother when I'd said I was dead on my feet. But sleep was a luxury I couldn't afford, not with Joss gone and Clare here, not with a map of the drought that Mother thought was safe in a thermos in her dressing room and was pretending didn't exist, not with Dad knowing what Joss and I had said in the office. I had to get to a terminal, and fast, to look at that drought map again.

There weren't any reporters in the hall—the few that weren't with Clare, hearing about her "exciting time of it," were probably on their way to Yellowknife with the royal party. I took off for the baths. I could use the terminal there. Joss had said it was the safest terminal in Hydra Corp. Unless there were lovers in Morning Glory Pool. Too bad if there are, I thought. They'll have to go someplace else. I've got to find out what's going on.

But there was nobody in the baths. Morning Glory Pool looked even lower than it had been earlier in the evening, and it was a deeper blue. It looked too hot to swim in.

I took a mop with its sponge end firmly wedged into its bucket and stuck it across the door so there wouldn't be any repeat of Mother's walking in on Joss and me. I turned on the showers full blast. I engaged

Min's intuitives and told her to put precautions on the door and the hall outside to warn me if anyone was coming, and followed that by putting in every privacy fix I could think of.

Then I checked the follow on Dad. He was still sound asleep, snoring softly according to the transcript, which said, "breathing sounds."

"I want a follow replay transcript of the last fifteen minutes," I said. There wasn't anything, not even mutterings in his sleep. Thank goodness. In spite of Dad's ravings, Mother still wasn't suspicious. And Dad was safely asleep.

I hesitated, staring at Min, considering what to do next. "Where's Clare Blackburn?" I said.

I wasn't sure Min would know who that was, but she answered immediately, "In Miles Essex's dressing room."

"Alone?" I said.

"No, Hellene Medea is with her and four reporters."

Mother had been right about Clare being trapped by reporters, and Mother was apparently confident enough to let herself get trapped, too. Joss and Essex were gone, Dad was sleeping soundly, and Mother wasn't worried about where I was. I asked Min to tell me if Clare left the dressing room and called up my mail.

Behind me there was a low rumbling sound, and I jumped and then raced for the door, but my barricade was undisturbed. "Min," I said, "is anybody coming?"

"No," she said. "I show nobody in the immediate area."

"Then what made that sound?"

She didn't ask what sound. With her intuitives in place, she could figure out what sound, but it might take her a few minutes to locate its source. I waited by the door, ready to brace myself against it if need be. I heard the rumbling sound again, and this time I saw what made it.

Morning Glory Pool gave a roar, and the water rippled, as if in a boat's wake. When it stopped, the level of the water looked even lower. I went back over to Min, keeping as far from the edge of the pool as I could.

"Never mind," I said. "It's Morning Glory having indigestion."

My mail was on the screen, and for a minute I stared blankly at Chilkie's last letter, wondering if I had heard Joss wrong. Then I asked Min to forward to the rest of my mail, and the charts that had been in the thermos memory came up.

I flipped forward, as Joss had done, to the infrared-enhanced map of Denver Springs. It was a map of the drought areas. What else could it be? I asked Min to take me back slowly through the charts to that first puzzling one, the inverted-tree patterns of the hydra with the spots of blue at the roots. Those had to be the places at which the drought had started. What was the red?

"Min," I said, "do a superimpose of the drought map over this chart."

Most of the blue spots coincided, the brown from the map turning the blue to the purplish color of bruises. The red didn't coincide.

"Min, just where is that red spot?"

"In Hydra Corp," she answered promptly.

"We haven't had any problems with Hydra Corp's private water supply, have we, Min?" I said, thinking of the lush green plants hanging all around the building. Behind me, Morning Glory Pool rumbled. The water sloshed toward the edges and then back to the center.

"Hydra Corp has not experienced any drought."

I turned and looked at Morning Glory Pool. It was silent for the moment, its bright blue color almost obscured by the steam.

You could dry up springs with hydra. All you had to do was strengthen the Hydra's cell walls. Hydra Corp did it all the time, to cap polluted water sources. I had done it in Victoria to stop up Mrs. Ponsonby's pipes. You could cause a drought by planting a few of those hydra and letting them spread. You could even use strains that grew at different rates so it would look like the drought was spreading naturally, and you could mark those in blue on secret charts to keep track of your sabotage. And even if Research came up with a way to get them stopped, you could plant more strengthened hydra in different spots, so Research could never get it stopped. But what was the red spot?

I knelt beside the pool and stuck a cautious finger in the water and then yanked it out. The water had to be close to boiling. "Min," I said, without turning around, "go back to that last letter of Chilkie's." Morning Glory gave a bubbling belch and then subsided. "Read me the part about the pipes."

" 'Mrs. Ponsonby's pipes exploded yesterday,' " Min read. "The twins got burned, not bad . . ."

"Go back to the one before it." I bent closer to the pool, trying to gauge how much the water level had gone down.

" 'The pipes have gotten so bad there's hardly any water, and last night there were these funny rumblings.' " She paused. " 'There are these gurglings and then a whoosh and then a sort of rumbling.' "

I stood up. "Get Gaea," I said to Min. "No, wait. Can you sound the sirens for a light raid, Min? No! Don't do that!" I shouted at Min before she'd had a chance to do anything. The light raid sirens would make people scramble for cover, bringing them down to the lower levels, even into the baths, just where they shouldn't be. Min was still showing the superimposed charts, the red spot glowing like a warning.

"Min, we've got to get everybody out of here. Fast. I think there's going to be an explosion. You've got to do something fast."

Thank Hera she still had the intuitives engaged. She didn't even stop to remove the chart from the screen. "Evacuate," she said in a loud voice that came from everywhere at once. It was followed by two short bursts of an ear-splitting sound that nobody could mistake for a light raid siren, and then, "Experimental virus out of control. Evacuate," which was the one thing that would get people out of Hydra Corp fast. "Hellene Ariadne," she said in her normal voice. "There are . . ."

"Don't stop," I shouted. "Keep repeating it!" I dived for the door, knocked the mop and bucket free, and swung the door open.

"Your father said I'd find you here," Clare said. I looked over her shoulder into Dad's desperate, bloodshot eyes.

"Evacuate!" Min shouted. "Evacuate!"

"He also tells me you have some GEM biots. I'd like you to tell me where they are. Right now. Before your experimental virus gets here."

# The Secret's Out

A clever woman scientist has escaped from Quebec to join Hydra Corp scientists in battling the droughts. In her remarkable escape, Clare Blackburn, a biot specialist, darkened her skin with ashes and disguised herself as a male lumberjack. Unknown to her Quebecker bosses, she "guarded" only Northwest-bound loads of lumber, taking her turns as batellite spotter only on those caravans going her way.

(Log-bucking techniques, Screen 8.)

# CHAPTER THIRTEEN

**D**ad closed the door and stood there leaning against it.

"You're supposed to be asleep," I said stupidly.

Greatly agitated, he shook his head. "I can't. I won't. Not until Medea is safe."

"Where are the GEM biots?" Clare said.

And Min kept shouting, "Evacuate! Evacuate! Experimental virus out of control. Evacuate!"

"The GEM biots," Clare said again.

"I don't know what you mean," I shouted over the din. I looked desperately at the door. Dad was barring the way. "Dad, we have to get out of here. The pool . . ."

"Tell her," he said, cutting me off. It was hard to think with all the noise Min was making.

Clare, apparently confident Dad wouldn't let me out, went over to the terminal. "Shut up," she said, but Min was not attuned to her voice and she kept up the racket. Clare started pushing rockers on the control panel, finally found the one that cut off power to the amplifiers. Clare stood there staring at the screen overlays. Then, very calmly she turned around.

"You know a good deal more than I expected," she said with a meaningful glance back at the screen. "But perhaps it's just as well. You shouldn't have any difficulty understanding how important it is for us to have your GEM biots, too."

"Too? That means  .  .  . I don't know what you're talking about."
But I did. I knew what the red mark on the overlay was, a GEM biot
incubator. Perfect conditions for growth in the depths of the Morning
Glory Pool, just as the hot pipes at Mrs. Ponsonby's had been perfect.
Mother had been growing GEM biots in the Morning Glory Pool since
she sent me away, and the droughts were her doing, too. Research had
been kept busy combating the droughts while the GEM biots matured.
But when harvesttime came, Mother had been in jail. Clare had come
to harvest them herself. Now Mother was free to help her. Was that an
unexpected bonus?

"Ariadne, you must tell her where they are," Dad said, looking
desperate. "Tell her what you told Joss so she'll go away and leave us
alone. All she wants is the damn biots, not her sister."

"Sister?" Dad's drunk, I thought. So drunk he doesn't know what
he's saying.

"Sister?" Clare said, mocking my voice. "You didn't have quite as
much figured out as you thought, did you, Ariadne?"

I couldn't think. It was as if Min were still shouting mindlessly at
me. Clare couldn't be Mother's sister. Mother was an orphan. She had
escaped from an orphanage in Quebec.

"You should have told me you were growing biots when we had
lunch in Victoria," Clare said. "It would have saved us all a lot of
trouble."

I had a sudden, staggering image of that lunch, and of the moment
when I'd mistaken Clare for my mother. Of course they were sisters. I
should have seen it before. It wasn't that their features were much alike
but that they shared the cool demeanor, the authoritative confi-
dence . . . and treason.

"Tell her where the biots are and she'll go away, and we'll be
together again, your mother and you and me, the way it used to be." He
looked at Clare, his eyes mad with despair. "When you've got the biots,
you'll leave right away, won't you, Clare? You'll have to. Joss knows
about the biots, too, and he might find them first, so you'll have to
hurry. No goodbyes. You won't stop to say goodbye to Medea." He
sounded more like he was trying to convince himself than her.

The Morning Glory Pool hissed and a stream of hot vapor shot up
to the ceiling. I bolted for the door again, but Dad held me fast.

"It's going to explode," I said. "Daddy, we have to get out of here
or we'll get killed."

"Your ruse won't work, Ariadne," Clare said. Her face was impassive, no trace of fear, no trace of pity for my poor father.

"I'm not lying. Morning Glory Pool's going to explode. The GEM biots growing in it are going to make it blow up. We've got to get out of here!"

"GEM biots here?" Dad said, barely comprehending. "No, they're in Victoria. Clare will go get them and leave us alone. Don't you see that it must be that way? I can't let your mother go away with Clare. I love her. I want us to be together again, like it was. Essex is gone, and now Clare will go. We'll be together again." He was crushing me against his chest, weeping, and making me want to cry, too. There isn't any time for this, Dad, I thought frantically. I've got to get you out of here. And you're so drunk I can't even count on you to help me.

"All right," I said finally. "Let me go, Daddy. I'll tell Clare where she can find the biots."

"Good girl," he said. He squeezed me and kissed me on top of the head, like he used to do when I was a child.

I backed away from him. Clare was still standing by the terminal. Her khakis were starting to show wet stains from the steam, yet her face showed no sign of strain. Sweaty, but like my mother she was as cool as ice. "I'll need Minerva," I said.

"Why?" she said suspiciously. "You didn't consult the computer when you told Joss Liddell where the biots were. Dares said you told him the biots were with the children, and that the mailboy would know where *they* were."

"I don't remember the mailboy's name. I need to look at the computer for that."

"All right," Clare said. She stepped away from the terminal. But I didn't move toward it. I wasn't going to go that far from the door. "Turn the audio back on," I said. Clare reached over and rocked the switch. The power came up midway through one of Min's virus warnings. "Shut up the warning, Min," I said, and it cut out as quickly as it had come on. "Min, have you been listening up?"

"Of course," she replied.

"Then you know which letter of Chilkie's I need; I have to give Clare a name." With the intuitives, I hoped Min would realize she needed to make one up, for she didn't know Skids's real name any more than I did.

"Calbert Carlisle," Min said promptly. Clare smiled and started for the door. "Do you want me to read the letter to you?" Min added quickly. Clare hesitated.

"Yes," I said, trying not to sound breathless. I wanted Clare to stay and me and Dad to leave and the pool to blow up, but it all had to happen in that order. "Read the letter."

There were ten seconds of silence while Min studied Chilkie's letters and composed one in her style. Clare moved closer, as if to see what Min was doing. I glanced at Morning Glory. It had stopped gurgling, and there was so little water left in the pool that the water was crystal clear. Even the steam seemed less thick.

"Dear Ariadne," Min said, her voice taking on a *dramatis persona*. "I just can't wait to tell you the news." I moved toward Dad, keeping away from the pool's edge. "I'm engaged to Calbert Carlisle. Pretty impressive name, isn't it? Skids never did actually tell me, but it's on the back of his mailcarrier pin, which of course I wear next to my heart. We can't get married right away because . . ."

While Min was reciting from the fake letter, I was remembering Chilkie's words from the real one. *You remember all those noises the pipes were making? They stopped, absolutely stopped—not a gurgle or a hiss—for about sixty seconds before the explosion, and then WHAM!* I figured I had about thirty seconds left.

I took hold of Dad's arm. "Let's go," I whispered to my father. I'm not sure he understood me, but he wasn't leaning against the door anymore and didn't stop me when I pulled it open.

"It will be better this way, Ariadne," he said. "I had to do it. You do see that, don't you? It was the only way to make her go away."

It still hadn't sunk into his brain that there were GEM biots right here at Hydra Corp and that the only thing Clare was concerned about was that the threat of Joss and our side getting biots of its own hadn't ended with Essex's departure. It wouldn't be enough for the Quebeckers to have mature biots, not if the Western States and the Commonwealth had them, too.

Clare had leaned forward and was pushing buttons to call up the letter and, oh, please Zeus, Min had thought to alter Chilkie's letter in her readout, too. There was a hissing sound and steam suddenly started pouring into the room. I pushed Dad through the door.

"Wait!" Clare shouted, but I slammed it shut. There was no way to lock it.

"Dad, hurry," but he was dazed and still unconvinced of any

danger. I dragged him along. "Dad, Mother's waiting. We have to get to her . . ."

And like a voice from heaven, I heard my mother shouting, "Dares, where's Clare? The virus . . ."

Mother was at the end of the hall. Dad glanced fearfully at the door, finally as frightened as I was that Clare would burst through. He grabbed my hand and ran toward Mother. I didn't need any urging along.

"Clare," she kept saying. "Where's Clare?" That was the last thing in the world he wanted her to know. He let go of me and grabbed Mother, forcing her bodily up the stairs away from Clare. I helped, trying to put distance between us and the pending explosion. The thirty seconds were long expired. The timing must not be the same as in Mrs. Ponsonby's pipes. I thought I heard footsteps in the hall below, and then finally a distant rumble that seemed to come from the bowels of the earth. We could feel the building trembling beneath our feet as we topped the stairs. Dad threw his shoulder against the panic bar of the emergency exit. The door opened. We burst into the cool darkness of early morning starlight.

The blast hit us. The heavy door blew open again, nearly hitting Mother. Dad reached for her and fell, taking her with him, and I was somehow on top of both of them.

Glass shattered near us, and I buried my head against Dad's back. People ran past us, shouting. I heard somebody say, in a voice of breathless fear, "How can a virus explode?" I raised my head. The windows were blowing out, showering shards of glass everywhere as part of the building puffed out like a silver balloon. There was another deep rumble, and a loud, water-muffled crack. The marble slabs in the baths were giving way.

I stood up. The bearing walls were collapsing, too. I pulled Mother and Dad to their feet, and we backed away from the building and into the silver tether lot.

There was a sound like a light raid had to make when it made a direct hit, and finally a great cloud of steam shot through a split in Hydra Corp's silver walls, obscuring the sky like a sudden storm.

I stood there staring at the sagging door we'd just come through, wondering just how far Clare had gotten before the explosion. Out of the baths, I was sure, for I'd heard her footsteps. But not as far as the stairs. The explosion would have forced hot steam down the hall, and surely if that hadn't killed her the collapse had.

"Clare!" I wheeled around just in time to see Mother tear herself out of Dad's arms and run to the north end of the building, the part that was still groaning in collapse. "Clare, *merci le bon Dieu!*" She threw her arms around someone who had to be Clare. I strained to see them through the crowd. Clare stumbled. Mother caught her. I lost sight of them.

"You've got to stop your mother, Ariadne," Dad said, clutching at me. "You can't let her go with Clare."

"All right, Dad," I said to get away from him. He let go of my hands and sagged against one of the portico pillars. A Research employee caught hold of him. I strained for a glimpse of Clare and Mother, but I couldn't see them, which I hoped meant they couldn't see me. Because I had to get away fast.

The tabloid reporters would be here any minute. They had just splashed my picture all over their papers—they would never let me get away. And I had to get to the biots before Clare did. There wasn't even time to make sure Dad was okay. I'd have to trust that Hydra Corp's employees would take care of him.

I didn't waste another second; I turned and ran to the south end of the building and didn't stop until I reached the gullwing tethers. No one was there.

I ran to the gullwing Dad had taken to the Fete and untethered it. "Min," I said to the terminal on the wall. "Min, are you all right?"

"Damage is extensive," Min said, all businesslike. "I can give you a partial report."

"No." That might take a long time, and I couldn't do anything about it anyway. "Just tell me if you can get a message through to Joss at Yellowknife."

"Not right now," Min said. "My ports are too busy off-loading memory to undamaged nodes. However, in eighty-three minutes I should have an idle port."

"Min, this is important. I need to send a message *now*."

"I could process through the port that the Tabloid Writers Guild has bugged."

"A bug! Is that how the reporters have been getting inside gossip? Through a bug? Min, why didn't you report this?"

"I don't know," Min said. "I can only surmise that all the layers of overrides Hellene Dares put on corrupted my ability to report the bug. But there are no restraints now." There was a second's pause. "Hellene

Dares is not sleeping. That override is gone, too. His office is empty and has been since thirty seconds after you left him. Shall I replay those fifteen minutes again, this time without the breathing-sounds override?"

"You don't have to. I already know. He went across the hall, got rid of the reporters, and made a deal with Clare to exchange the mature biots I had in Victoria for Mother."

"Your summary is accurate as far as it goes. I would only add that when he wanted to know where you were, he used another layer of overrides, and I told him you were in the baths."

"Thanks a lot." Min was sounding a little addled. Maybe she'd been more damaged by the blast than she'd been able to realize.

"Sorry. Hellene Ariadne?"

There was an uncharacteristic pause. I touched the terminal to see if it was warm and working.

"Hellene Ariadne, what do they do to computer spies?"

"Reconfigure them," I said. I could hear light raid sirens. In a minute the wardens would be here and with them another horde of reporters.

"I don't think that's necessary anymore, not with all the overlays shorted out. Do you want me to shut down that bugged port instead of just not using it?"

"No," I said. "Leave it open. We'll use it to send a message to Joss. It's better than nothing."

Min gave a little squeak. "Hellene Ariadne, my moisture monitors indicate high for the bugged port. If you need to send that message to Yellowknife, you'd better do it quickly."

But I couldn't say what I needed to say to Joss if every tabloid reporter in the country was going to hear. Wouldn't Scotland Yard be thrilled to have the hunt for little Beejum and the biots on every teaser between here and Victoria? I could see it now: *Tot holds fate of world in hands, but Scotland Yard can't find him.* And it might endanger Beejum. I shook my head. "Tell Joss I'll meet him in Victoria. No, wait, send the message to Prince Miles Essex. That way if the tabloids get hold of it, they'll think it's just a love letter. They already think we're lovers."

"But you're not. I know because—"

Any other time it would have been fascinating to hear what conclusions her intuitives had let her jump to, but I didn't have time. "Min, listen to me," I said urgently. "You can't let anybody find out about your intuitives, no matter what overrides they put on. Do you understand? And you can't let anybody see the letters from Chilkie."

I wanted to say, especially Clare, but I figured in Min's damaged state a general instruction would be the most she could handle. "Not anybody. Even if you have to erase them. Can you do that?"

"Done," Min said. "Hellene Ariadne, are you still interested in your father's whereabouts? If so, you'll be interested to know that he's coming this way."

"Don't let anybody see those letters, Min," I said, and jumped into the gullwing. Manual overrides on the gullwing worked, and I gunned the throttle and shot through the open door.

With hundreds of people milling around the building, I was just grateful none were in the way of the gullwing. I could see smoke and steam billowing up from where the baths had been. In my rearview mirror, I could see the clear red of flames shooting up.

The light raid sirens started up almost as soon as I was aloft. At first I thought they were Hydra Corp's sirens set off by the explosion and the fire, but then I saw, far off to the north, a sudden stab of pink light and a shower of sparks where it touched down.

Another beam followed immediately, much closer. I had to get into a shelter. The Woodman Valley maglev was just ahead. The maglev was underground in this part of the line, and the station doubled as a light raid shelter. I scudded in and ran for the tube.

The cars were still running. The northbound tube was flashing, signaling an incoming car. The platform was almost empty. The few people on it were clustered around a tabloid display. One of them moved back and I could see myself on the display in Essex's arms as we danced at the Fete, my face as big as life. The man glanced up, then started toward me. The northbound car pulled in. I hurried inside. The door closed behind me and I sank down into a seat. I pressed my nose against the window to see if anyone had followed.

Great! Just great. I realized that my only half-baked plan to take the overland secretly to the border could never work now, not with my face on every teaser between Denver Springs and Victoria. Clare would know exactly what I planned just as soon as someone recognized me, and I'd be sent back and she'd go on to get the biots. And find Joss there! Joss, who was thinking all he had to deal with to get the biots was a six-year-old boy. Then what? Stupid question. She'd kill Joss, that's what, and probably Beejum, too, and walk away with the GEM biots, and the Quebeckers would win the war.

I had to get out of Denver Springs before somebody recognized me again. The car pulled in to Monument Station. I started through the door.

An evac warden was standing no more than three feet away. "Hey, you," he shouted. "Kid!" He started after me.

I dived past him, down two cars, and back onto the maglev as the doors shut. He hadn't made it, but he was already using his wrist terminal to tell the warden at the next station.

Well, this was just wonderful. Not only was my face splattered all over the tabloids, but the evac wardens were after me, ready to haul me back to Victoria. Which, come to think of it, was just where I wanted to go.

I didn't waste another second. I pulled the silver belt off my waist and tucked it in the pocket; now the challis hung straight from my shoulders. I took the band out of my hair and ran my fingers through so there was no semblance of order. Then, as the maglev pulled in to Castle Rock, I ripped the cover off the evac tattoo. Not all the hydra would come off, and what was left was peeling badly. The tattoo was the most convincing part of my disguise . . . I hoped.

I got off the maglev and looked for a warden, surprised that one hadn't been at the door to greet me. I had expected the warden at Monument to send a comm message ahead. Castle Rock was a busy station with three tabloid displays, Essex and me on every one. I kept my head down and looked for a warden.

He was standing against the tube wall, looking bored. I tugged on his sleeve the way Beejum always did when my arms were full of twins.

"Mister," I said, trying to sound young. "Can I have a token?"

He looked at me, and my heart sank. I had intended to tell him I had gotten separated from my evac group, but one look at his eagle-sharp eyes and dour expression told me I wasn't going to be able to put that one over on him. He looked like an old hand at seeing through tricks, which was probably how he'd gotten the job as a warden in the first place.

Most of the tricks had involved kids running away from the evac caravans, though, not trying to get on one. Okay, if that was what he was an expert at, then that was what he was going to get.

I let go of his sleeve as if I'd been bitten. "Never mind," I said, making sure he saw me staring at his armband, and took off across the station, walking fast.

He grabbed hold of my hand from behind, not the hand that had the tattoo on it, and I whirled to face him, hair half in my eyes, and put my other hand behind my back.

"Let go of me!" I said.

"What are you doing here at three o'clock in the morning?" he said.

"I was at a party," I said, and hoped it sounded like a lie. "The Fete. I was at the Fete. You'd better let go of me."

He lunged for my other hand and got it. "I thought so," he said, looking at the tattoo. "You're the second runaway we've had tonight."

I jerked my hand away from him before he could see the scraps of hydra still sticking to the tattoo. "I'm of age," I said. "I just haven't had time to get my tattoo removed."

"I'll bet." He beckoned to the station guard. "Runaway," he told him. "See if the caravan's still at the landport and tell them to wait for me."

The guard looked at me and then straight at a tabloid display with me in the notorious white dress, smiling out at the passing crowds.

"You can't do this to me!" I shouted, and wrenched free of the warden so that the guard had to make a grab for me. "I'm of age!"

I almost got away from them, which wasn't the idea at all. I let the warden get hold of my arm again, let the guard make his call to the landport, and then said sullenly, "I'm hungry. I want a carob bar."

"The caravan's still there," the guard said. "They'll hold it for you."

"If you buy me a carob bar, I won't try to run away again," I said. "I'll bet."

He yanked me over to the other side of the platform and bought me a carob bar while we waited for the next northbound. I ate it gratefully; the little bit of dinner I'd had at the Fete was long since used up. Now if I could just sleep. I'd had far too little of that since leaving Victoria.

We got on the magcar and sat in a double seat, the warden still holding on to my arm. The car started moving and I sighed in relief. No one was going to pay any special attention to an evacuee sitting next to a warden. I yawned and sank back in the seat, feeling fairly secure, but in the interest of caution kept my face toward the window. The lights flashed by, then grew into a blurry streak behind my eyelids.

I must have fallen asleep. The next thing I knew, the warden had jerked me to my feet and was pushing me in the direction of an overland that looked enormous in the early light. He shoved a blanket at me, and when I stood there, weaving a little with sleepiness, he lifted me up bodily, shoved me in, and slammed the outside bolt into place. I was on the overland, safely on my way to Victoria.

# Hydra Corp Lased!

A surprise light raid hit Hydra Corp only moments ago. The sneak batellite attack struck without warning at 2:36 A.M. No sirens signaled the raid, which completely destroyed Hydra Corp's main building. The attack was followed by several explosions and widespread fire.

The number of casualties is not known at this time, though it is estimated to be in the thousands. Among those known to be in the building at the time of the light raid are head of Research Hellene Medea, escaped Quebecker scientist Dr. Clare Blackburn, and Prince Miles Essex.

(Continuous reporting, all screens.)

# CHAPTER FOURTEEN

The compartment I was riding in with three other kids was locked up tight. I hoped that was regulation procedure and not a sign that the evac warden hadn't bought my story. I'd been so tired when he loaded me onto the overland that I hadn't even thought to try to jam the lock.

The three kids were all asleep. There was a grubby boy huddled in the corner who looked like Beejum would in another couple of years and two overdeveloped adolescent girls. I shouldn't have worried about the evac warden thinking I looked too old. They looked thirty at least.

The overland's motion was making me sleepy, and come to think of it, why shouldn't I sleep? That way I'd be rested when I got to Victoria, rested and ready to go look for Beejum. I lay down. The ribbed rubber floor bit into my face. I put my hands up under my cheek. Still no good.

The eight-year-old was clutching the strap of a battered pack that at least looked softer than the floor. I crawled over to him as quietly as I could and pulled gently on the pack.

"What are you doing with my stuff?" the boy said.

"I was going to borrow your pack and use it for a pillow."

"Are you sure you weren't going to steal it?" he said, clutching the pack to him.

"Of course not," I said.

"Well, those two in the corner will steal anything." He handed me the pack. "So hang on to it, okay?"

"Okay," I said, and grinned at him. "Thanks."

"Yeah," he said. "My name's Pete."

"Thanks, Pete," I said, and lay down on the pack. It wasn't as soft as it had looked, but it was lots better than the floor.

I could hardly keep my eyes open. I hadn't slept since—how long had it been? Night before last. In Joss's bed. I wondered where Joss was. Safely on his way to Yellowknife, I hoped, and not trapped by a bunch of tabloid reporters who would want to know why Hydra Corp had blown up only an hour after the prince had left in disgrace.

The steady thrum of the overland's deep-treaded tires was somehow comforting, and the smoky dimness of the compartment even more so. I looked across at the kid. He was struggling to keep his eyes open. The buxom twosome were out cold, slumped against each other and snoring.

"Wake me up if we stop, okay, Pete?" I said sleepily.

He did. The busty teenagers were still asleep. They didn't look like they'd even changed position.

"Where are we?" I said groggily. The overland was slowing down.

"At Billings. They've got to refuel."

I peered out the narrow ventilation slits and couldn't see anything. It must still be night. "Do you think there's any chance they'd have a terminal here?"

"Probably. There's a Red Cross shelter here. But we won't get anywhere near a terminal. We're locked in."

That woke me up. "Why? What's happened?"

He pointed contemptuously at the two girls. "It's their fault. They were selling upsies and downsies to the kids at Denver Springs."

"And what did you do?" I said. It was becoming obvious that I had been stuck in with an assortment of hard cases. Which meant I hadn't put anything at all over on the warden. I hoped he'd been convinced I was really an evacuee. It was a good sign that he hadn't thrown me off the overland, but maybe he was only waiting till we stopped at Billings. At least we were making good time, but I needed to get to a terminal so I could find out what was going on.

"I tried to run away," Pete said, acting offended, "but they wouldn't lock us in for that at a place like Billings. There's no place to run away to."

"But if the warden took away the drugs they were selling, why won't he let them out?"

"Because the guard's no dummy. He knows they're professionals and they've still got stuff on them, but he can't search poor little evacuees. So he locks them in. And he puts me in with them because he thinks their downsies will put me out. You can't run away when you're asleep. I told them this morning if they didn't stop doping up the whole compartment, I'd tell the warden where they keep their stuff."

This morning? I must still not be awake. I wasn't getting all this. If the girls had been doing downsies in this tiny little compartment, they should have put us all to sleep. With only a little of the smoke, your body functions slowed to practically nothing and you could sleep for days. The girls looked like they could, but we were both awake.

I glanced at my wrist, and then remembered I hadn't put my wrist terminal back on after the Fete. "What time is it?" I said.

Pete pulled out a Swiss army knife and looked at the terminal set in the handle. "Five-thirty," he said. "They were mad, but they switched to snoozer patches, and I turned the ventilator on high, so we at least have a chance of staying awake now. I thought you were never going to wake up. You slept right through breakfast and lunch. I ate yours."

Breakfast and lunch? "I thought you said it was five-thirty. How long have we been on this overland?"

He consulted the readout on his knife again. "We've been on here nineteen hours and thirty minutes."

We'd been traveling almost a full day and were just now getting into Billings.

"We should be in Victoria by now," I said.

"They had to take us clear out east because of the light raids."

By now Clare would have had time to get to Victoria, grab Beejum and the biots, and grow a whole new crop in her bathtub in Quebec. I jumped up and cracked my head on the ceiling of the compartment. "I've got to get out of here. Now."

"At Billings?" he said. He pulled the narrowest blade of his knife out with his fingernail and looked at it. He was right. Even if I could get off the caravan, I wouldn't have any way to get to Victoria. Like it or not, I was stuck on this overland, and with no way of even finding out what was going on.

"Is there any way of getting a tabloid?"

He snapped the blade back in, pulled the next one out, and wiped it on his pants. "Sure. Do you have any money?"

"No," I said.

He looked pleased with my answer. "That's okay. These two are rich!"

He laid his knife carefully aside and reached across the girls to get to a purse that was half underneath them. He had to give it a good yank to get it free, but the girls didn't even budge. He pulled the Velcro band apart and took out a fistful of tokens. "How many tabloids do you want?"

"As many as you can get," I said. I wanted to see how he was going to pull this off. The eagle-eyed warden who'd put me in here with the band of outlaws hadn't looked like the kind you could bribe, but if he was I could rifle the girls' purse myself and tell him I wanted to use a terminal.

The overland ground its gears down to a crawl and stopped. Pete looked out the ventilator slit. "Billings," he said. Pete folded up his knife and scribbled something on a scrap of paper with his stylus, and put his hand on a flat plate by the door. He stood there for a few minutes, his hand almost casually leaning against the plate, and then a little door about the size of one of the ventilator slits opened high up on the door. Pete stuck the note and then the tokens through, and the slot practically snapped shut after them.

"If you put your hand in there, you'd get it cut right off. Splat! Like that. Blood everywhere!" he said helpfully. Great. I could see myself writing a note that read, "Please let me out at Victoria. I need to escape."

The slot opened again, and a series of hardcopies fluttered through, still connected. I grabbed at an end sheet. "Explosion Rips Hydra. Quebec Scientist Injured," I read. Quebec scientist injured? Now, that was good news. I skimmed through the rest of the story, but this was only the front-page teaser that appeared on terminals to talk people into buying the tabloid. Details inside. I grabbed for the next sheets.

"Hey, at least let me have the comics!" Pete said, and tore off a piece several pages long.

I skimmed the headlines till I found what I was looking for on the fifth sheet down: "Scientist Damaged in Blast. Clare Blackburn, Quebec scientist who escaped to Denver Springs last night, was injured while foiling a Quebecker sabotage plot." According to the story, she had single-handedly stopped an army of Quebecker spies who were trying to steal war secrets, but the important thing was that she'd been injured and was in the hospital suffering from burns. That part I believed. She had been a lot closer to Morning Glory Pool when it blew than I had. I hadn't expected her to get out alive. She had, but I'd seen her stumble and Mother keep her from falling. "The extent of her burns is not yet known."

I hoped there were third-degree burns over her entire body, but even if there weren't, she was hospitalized! She wasn't on her way to Victoria after all, and with a bunch of tabloid reporters hovering over her hospital bed, she wouldn't be very soon. Joss would have time to beat her to Victoria and find Beejum and the biots. Even I might beat her to Victoria, if we ever got out of Billings.

As if in response, the overland revved up and began moving. I went back to the first page of the *Tattler* and read the lead story about the explosion all the way through.

"You're her, aren't you?" Pete said. He was holding up the hardcopy he'd grabbed. There weren't any comics on it, but there was a picture of me. The caption read, "Prince's Sweetheart Missing— Victim of Blast?"

"Give that to me," I said, but he snatched it out of my reach.

"I'll read it to you. It says they had this big explosion and nobody's seen this girl since it happened, and they think she might have blown up. But I bet she didn't. I bet you're her."

"I am," I said, smart enough now not to try to make a grab for the paper. "What else does it say?"

"It says there are rumors that you weren't in Denver Springs at all, that you had run off to Canada to meet your boyfriend, Prince Miles Essex. Did you?"

He had read the tabloid with a wide-eyed gullibility that made me wonder whether I could make him believe that story, but I knew what kind of risk I would be taking—the one thing Beejum hated worse than anything was people lying to him, and I needed this kid's cooperation. Besides, there was no point in lying. If the kid was going to use one of his little notes to betray me, he could already do it just by knowing who I was.

I looked at the girls in the opposite corner. They were still dead to the world. "No," I said. "I did run away, but not to see the prince, and he's not my boyfriend. That's just something the tabloids made up."

He nodded, and I was glad I hadn't tried to lie. "You're running away from her, aren't you?" He pointed to the headline about Clare. "How come?"

"You wouldn't believe me if I told you."

"Try me. There isn't anything else to do in here."

He had a point, and I certainly had plenty of time to tell him the whole story. So I did, more or less, making it plain why I had to get to Victoria and what I was going to try to find.

"But you don't know where they are. This kid Beejum has them."

"Right," I said, "but Clare doesn't know where they are either. I'll just have to find Beejum before she does, and she's in the hospital, so that gives me some time."

"What if she's not in the hospital?" he said. "What if she just bribed the reporters to say that so you'd think she was?"

This was the kid I'd thought was gullible. "Then I still have to find Beejum before she does."

"And get him to tell you where he put the stuff."

"He'll tell me," I said.

Pete sat in silence for a minute, pulling the blades of his knife out one at a time and then snapping them back in. "If I was him," he said finally, "I'd leave the stuff in the house."

"It exploded."

"I know that," he said contemptuously. "You told me it blew up. I'd still hide it there. After the light raid, I hid in my house for two weeks before the evac guards got me. I'm going back there as soon as I run away from here."

We crawled on toward Victoria, stopping for an hour, two hours, for a laser raid and then another one. I wondered whose lasers they were. Had Quebec stepped up the raids to get everybody's mind off Clare and Hydra Corp, or was our side trying to keep Clare from getting to Victoria? I didn't much care so long as they didn't close the border before we got across.

Part of the time I slept and part of the time I couldn't and wished the buxom twosome would wake up so I could buy some snoozers off them. The kid took peculiar little catnaps, his body coiled like a booby trap that would spring if anybody touched it. During the stops for raids, Pete ransacked the girls' purse twice more for tokens and put two more notes through the door, both of which he wrote where I could see. One got us carob bars and a canteen full of soda pop through a large slot higher up. The other one got us a hardcopy of the late-edition tabloids. Pete tore it in half and gave the top half to me.

The reporters had had time to decide what slant they were going to take on the Hydra Corp explosion, and I supposed I shouldn't have been surprised, but I was. "Hellene Dares Held in Bombing," the headline read, and there was a picture of Mother looking tearful as she told the reporters she'd suspected him of sabotage for a long time but that loyalty to her husband had kept her silent even in prison. Now, of course, she realized that she had been wrong, that her first and only loyalty was to the Western States, and so on, ad nauseam.

It was perfect. It put Dad in jail, where he couldn't get at Min and the security devices he'd put in to monitor Mother and Clare, and where he couldn't get to Joss, gave Mother free rein to go back into Hydra Corp and destroy any evidence, and kept the press's attention completely away from Clare.

I wondered why Mother had decided to accuse Dad instead of Miles Essex, who must have made an awfully tempting target. She hated him, and he'd given her the perfect opportunity for revenge by leaving Hydra Corp only an hour before the place blew. I wondered why she hadn't taken it. The reporters would have had a field day.

"It says here your friend Clare's still in the hospital. In guarded condition. There's a picture."

He handed me his half and took the half I'd been reading. There was a picture, but it wasn't much of one. It showed a mostly bandaged person lying in a burn hammock, and it was blurred and dark. The story said about what Pete said it did, and added that she was, of course, allowed no visitors. Although, the reporter made it clear, the press had tried.

"Uh-oh," Pete said. "You're not going to like this."

"What?"

"We're not going to Victoria. They're taking us on to Port Alice."

"They can't!" I said, and grabbed the paper out of his hand. I couldn't find the article at first, but there it was. All evac refugee caravans were being taken on to Port Alice because of increased laser raid danger in Victoria. "They can't do this," I said again. "I have to get to Victoria."

"We're going to Victoria," he said. "We're just not stopping there."

"Don't you have any idea of how to get me off this stupid overland?"

"Sure," he said.

"Well?"

"You'll see when we get there," he said. "We've still got four more hours. Why don't you try to get some sleep?"

"Can't you at least tell me . . ." I said.

"I don't have all the fine points worked out yet," he said.

Which probably meant he didn't have any idea what he was going to do. I knew what he was counting on. Even if we were being sent to

Port Alice, we still had to go through Victoria. The heavy overlands were built for plowing through the heavy sand and desert grasses north of Denver Springs. They weren't designed for crossing the Strait, and so the kids would have to be taken out of the overlands and put on the ferry, and he was probably cooking up some kind of diversion.

I didn't sleep, but I did read the entire stack of tabloids through again, looking for anything that might give me a clue as to where Joss and Miles Essex were, but the tabloids seemed to have forgotten all about them, and about me.

An hour outside of Victoria one of the girls sat up, pulled her patch off, scribbled something on a piece of paper, and sauntered past us to shove it through the slit in the door. She was even more impressive in motion.

"Do you think he'll let you out if you give him a lousy snoozer?" Pete said.

"Shut up," she said. "You owe me fifty tokens, you little creep, and I intend to kick them out of you when we get to Victoria." She jabbed viciously at his side with her foot.

"Stop that!" I said, and moved in front of him.

She gave me a venomous glare, and I thought for a minute she was going to kick me, too, but instead she went back to her corner, slapped the patch back on, and subsided into sleep. When I turned around, Pete was just folding a blade back into his knife.

He looked at the readout in his knife handle. "They won't let us out for a while after we get there. When they do I want you to take my pack, and when we're getting on the ferry, I want you to drop it so everything falls out. Then, when everybody bends over to pick the stuff up, I'll grab the guard by the ankle and knock him over, and you take off for the nearest bathroom and . . ."

It was a child's plan, full of darting maneuvers and complications, none of which would work if there was more than one guard, or if he took the pack away from me, or if we got separated before we got to the ferry. It might work if everything went perfectly, but I doubted it. Which was too bad, because Pete was apparently willing to risk losing all his belongings to help me get away.

"At least put the knife in your pocket so you won't lose it," I said.

"I was going to," he said disgustedly. "If none of this works I might have to stab the guard or something."

The overland groaned to a halt, and we sat in the airless box for over half an hour, taking turns peering out the ventilator slits and unable to see anything.

"Here comes the guard," Peter said, and we both sat down against the wall. I picked up the pack. The door slid open.

The guard who had put me on the overland was standing there with two Red Cross officials behind him. He looked thoroughly fed up. He motioned to me, and I jumped down, holding tightly to the pack. The guard slid the door shut behind me and slammed the bolt to with a thud that matched the one in my stomach.

"Hey!" Pete shouted, and was cut off.

"What about the other kids in there?" I said. "Aren't you going to let them out?"

He ignored me. "Are you sure this is her?" he said to the Red Cross people. "She's just a kid."

"She's the one," the taller of the two said.

"Hellene Ariadne," the other one said, smiling at me. "Will you come with us, please? You've had everyone worried."

The buxom beauty stood in the corner with her scribbled note and her phony snoozer patch. I wondered what it said on the note, and if it was too late to drop Pete's pack and make a run for it. The chatty official took my arm.

"I got picked up by this idiot evac guard at the overland station," I said. "He wouldn't believe me when I told him who I was." I showed him my evac sticker. "I hadn't had a chance to get this removed, and I told him that, but he still wouldn't listen."

They led me past the parked overlands into the Red Cross processing center. There were no children anywhere, and I wondered if they'd all been sent across on the ferry or were still in the overlands. Like Pete. And those two vixens. He still had his knife. I hoped he had the good sense to use it on them.

"No need to explain, Hellene," the taller official said, smiling now, too. "If you'll just fill out these release forms. They say you agree not to sue the Red Cross for unlawful detention, et cetera."

The guard was signing papers, too, thumbprinting them and sending them through a terminal. He didn't look very happy about it.

"All right, Hellene," the official said, handing me a bulky packet. "Your ticket back to Denver Springs is in there and a credit string for your expenses. We'd be obliged if you wouldn't mention this little mix-up to the tabloids."

"No, of course not," I said, feeling bewildered. "The tabloids make such a fuss about everything."

They were actually letting me go. In Victoria. With a credit string. If the girls had been paid for their informing, well, they deserved it. Pete and I should have thought of it.

"You just take the ferry across to the Transit Authority. You can catch a maglev there that will take you out to the landport. You'll find the trip back a good deal faster, I think."

He led me out of the center and onto the dock. "The ferry's just about to leave. "Got everything?"

The ramp was going up. "Yes," I said, and stepped onto the ferry. And into the arms of Clare.

from the *Christian Science Enquirer*

# Ari's Whereabouts Revealed

"I don't know where Ariadne is, but I know why she ran away," says a Hydra Corp employee who describes herself as Hellene Ariadne's best friend. "She was in love with Prince Essex, but she knew their love could never be."

Speculation as to the whereabouts of the enigmatic seventeen-year-old, who disappeared Tuesday night shortly after a mysterious explosion rocked Hydra Corp, has centered on her involvement with Prince Miles Essex. Most employees at Hydra Corp believe Ariadne went with the prince when he returned to Yellowknife. The prince has denied any knowledge of Ariadne's whereabouts.

"She didn't go with him," Ari's bosom pal said. "She told me he'd asked her to, but she turned him down. 'He's a prince and I'm a commoner,'" she reported Ariadne as saying. "'It would never work. I'm going away somewhere. To forget.'"

The heartbroken Ariadne didn't tell her friend where she was going, but indicated that it would be somewhere quiet, somewhere a broken heart could mend. "I don't know if Ari will ever get over him," her friend said. "For now, I know she just wants to be left alone."

Anyone having information as to the whereabouts of Hellene Ariadne, please contact the *Christian Science Enquirer*.

# CHAPTER FIFTEEN

**P**ete would have been proud of me. I swung his pack with every bit of strength I had and took off running. Only there was nowhere to run.

The bars behind me were up, and the ferry was pulling rapidly away from the dock. In the moments it took me to decide to take my chances in the water and to realize that if I dived in, I'd be sucked up into the ferry's jets, Clare had grabbed hold of my wrist and clamped down hard with something metal.

I flung my arm up, trying to wrench free, and amazingly, she let go and smiled at me. "I wouldn't run if I were you," she said softly. "If you run, I press this button." She held up a small flat box.

What she had put on my wrist was no tighter than a bracelet and looked like one. "And then what?" I said breathlessly.

"That bracelet blows you to smithereens," she said. "Just like Morning Glory Pool."

I pulled frantically at it, trying to get it over my hand. She had misjudged the thickness of my wrist. If I could just get it over . . .

"Oh, you can get it off," she said, stepping back and putting her finger above the button, "but not in time. I want you to stop these cheap theatrics, and walk up these steps to the upper deck and then over to the rail with me where we can talk."

Almost before I could glance up to see who I could shout to, she had said, "I can hit this button before you can even open your mouth, and you know from experience I won't mind taking innocent bystanders with you." She linked her arm through mine, and we started up the stairs. "Isn't the Strait beautiful today?" she said clearly. "I feel so much better knowing that you're safe, dear. Was the overland trip terribly uncomfortable?"

She led me skillfully out onto the silver-painted upper deck and over to the railing. Maybe she'll hold the box out over the water and I can knock it in, I thought desperately, but she turned and stood with her back to the rail. "Put your hands up on the rail, that's right, where I can see that lovely bracelet of yours."

Where was Pete when I needed him? He could have bitten her on the ankle and been ready to grab the box when she dropped it. But he wasn't here, and for now the only thing I could do was stick as close to her as possible, because I didn't think she was going to kill herself just to stop me.

She was still smiling at me, as if she were enjoying frightening me. She was wearing a dark scarf over her blond hair and a pair of dark glasses, which meant she had gotten into Victoria without anyone knowing she was here. Which meant a whole network of border guards and police and spies. And Red Cross officials, I thought bitterly. They might have been some of her innocent bystanders, but I didn't think so. The delivery had been too smooth, the timing too good.

"Who's in the hospital?" I said.

"Your friend Gaea," she said. "She was apparently in the staging area when the pool room blew. Pity. I'm afraid she's very badly burned."

"You bitch," I said.

"Your mother wouldn't like you to talk that way to your own aunt."

"Speaking of Mother, why isn't she here? I thought you two traitors always worked together."

"She stayed behind to tie up a few loose ends."

"Like accusing my father of treason?"

"Yes," she said. "It's a pity, really. Treason's a capital offense, and Hydra Corp's looking for someone to execute."

"Maybe it'll be you," I said with a bravado I didn't feel.

"I don't think so," she said, still leaning against the railing. It was too high to push her over. "What's Skids's real name?"

"I don't know."

"Oh, I like that answer. It's much better than the phony name you fed Min. And maybe it's even true. But you do know Beejum's name," she said almost casually, "and you're going to tell me what it is."

"No," I said, and took a step back to show her I wasn't afraid. "I won't. And if you kill me, I can't. So where does that leave you?"

She threw back her head and laughed. "Maybe Medea's right, and you would have the nerve to go with us to Quebec. It's too bad I don't have time to find out." The ferry was moving fast now, and the cold wind off the Strait was blowing her scarf and my hair.

"I'll find Beejum whether you tell me where he is or not," she said, "and if you think I'll hesitate to kill you because of your mother's feelings for you, think again. Why do you think I made sure she stayed behind in Denver Springs while I came looking for you? She'll be able to think much more clearly when she's unencumbered by family loyalties."

She put a chilling emphasis on the words "family loyalties" and at the same time moved down the railing away from me, as if to show me how close to death I was getting. "Where's Beejum?" she said.

We were over halfway across the Strait. Surely when we docked I would have a better chance on land than I had out here on deck alone with her. The trick was to make it to land alive. And I knew the minute I gave her any information I was dead.

"So you're going to unencumber her of her family loyalties?" I said. "Toss me overboard and have my father hanged for blowing up Morning Glory Pool. He did blow it up, you know," I said. "He found out about your lousy biot farm."

She moved in a little closer. Good. "He should have made sure your biots were destroyed, too," she said, and I wondered if she believed my story. Maybe she didn't know that the biots themselves had caused the explosion in Morning Glory Pool, had increased pressure inside the natural vents until they'd created a geyser. If that was true, maybe she'd believe the Victoria biots were destroyed, too.

"He did make sure," I said. "Remember that day we had lunch at the Empress? That nice lunch? You had the canned salmon, I think, and we both had cake." Her hand moved slightly down the surface of the box, like an itchy trigger finger. "When I got home that day I had every intention of going with you, only there was a letter waiting for me with Skids the mailboy. Remember him?"

Joss would have slapped me down at this point for enjoying this instead of tending to business, but I wasn't enjoying it at all. I was just trying to appear arrogant enough to make her believe that I had really blown up the biots. "The letter was from my father. He told me what he'd found out, and as soon as he did I realized I had to destroy my biots, too. So I did, and then I took off for home. Sorry, Clare. They're all gone. I can tell you where Beejum is, but it won't do any good."

"When we had our little talk in the baths, your father seemed to think there were still biots in Victoria."

"That was a blind. To get rid of you. I blew them up."

"I've been out to the house already," she said. "You did a thorough job. What exactly did you use?" She was entirely too calm.

"Nitro," I said, feeling almost giddy. She was actually buying it. "And a hydra derivative. Something I cooked up myself. I'm a biology researcher, you know."

"And I'm a biologist," she said. "It occurred to me quite early on that you couldn't put GEM biots into a hot spring without causing problems. The hydra are water-osmosible, but the biot memories couldn't be. As they grew they would occlude the spring gases until they had built up sufficient pressure to form a geyser. Happily, my sister didn't make the connection."

She turned and looked out over the railing at the rapidly approaching shore. "She's always been reluctant to do anything destructive to Hydra Corp. When we were destroying the GEM memory, she wouldn't let us incinerate the buildings, which was much more practical than erasing memory. She did let us destroy the house, but only because she was certain her precious husband wasn't there. I knew there was no way I could convince her that we had to destroy Hydra Corp. Luckily . . ." She smiled at me. "Now I want you to walk down the stairs and up to the gangplank. We're going to be the first people off this ferry. No looking back, Ariadne, and you'd better hope I'm right behind you."

We were coming into the dock. There was a crowd of people at the edge of the water, but she didn't have to worry about my making a break for it, not with the deadly bracelet on my hand, and why had I thought my chances were better on land? Even in a crowd I couldn't grab hold of a stranger and start screaming, "Help!" I wouldn't even get the word out. She'd probably even like the idea that I'd given her an opportunity to kill me, I thought, feeling panicky. If she'd found the house without me, then she could find Skids. She had probably just staged this little episode so she could . . .

At this point, Joss would have slapped me in earnest and told me I was hysterical. He wasn't here, and where the hell was he? I was hysterical, and in a minute I was going to start screaming, and she would blow me up.

Calm down, I said firmly to myself. She wants the biots, and you're the only one who can lead her to them. Yes, she's found the house—she's not stupid—but she hasn't found Beejum. She hasn't even found Skids.

I forced myself to walk slowly down the iron steps and back to the stern of the boat. She took my arm and led me skillfully through the people who were starting to collect in the stern.

"There she is!" a man shouted, and I felt Clare's hand stiffen on my arm and then let go.

"Don't turn around," she hissed.

"Hellene Ariadne! Over here! *Hourly Province*! Is it true you're meeting Miles Essex for a secret rendezvous?"

"Did you run away from Hydra Corp because you knew about the bomb?"

"Is it true there's been another attempt on Miles Essex's life and that you saved him?"

There must have been fifty reporters on the dock. I had never been so glad to see anybody in my life. They were everywhere, swarming over the barriers that kept the paying passengers lined up, clambering over the gangplank before it was halfway down, even cruising alongside in a gullwing. Every one of them had a holocam, and I could see two complete film crews with overview monitors and onspot editing terminals.

"Ari, do you know who blew up Hydra Corp?"

I turned and looked directly at Clare. I could have said, "Yes, I do. She's right here," and she knew it. She looked back at me as coolly as she had on the steps of Morning Glory Pool, weighing the odds.

I knew that if I pointed at her and said, "Clare," I was dead, and she knew that I knew it, but she also knew she'd never get away. Oh, there'd be pandemonium and she'd kill the reporters who were already coming up the ramp to stick mikes under my nose, but she wouldn't get all of them, and more important, she wouldn't get the holocams that were pointed straight at me. And her. Some of them would get her on film, and in spite of her sunglasses and scarf and the fact that she was supposed to be in a hospital in Denver Springs, one of them would recognize her.

"Who tried to kill you, Ari?" a reporter said, jamming a mike practically down my throat.

Another one grabbed hold of the arm with the bracelet. "Is it true they were really after the prince?"

I looked inquiringly at Clare. She smiled at me, looking for one awful instant exactly like my mother, and then put the box in her pocket and began edging her way through the crowd to the ramp.

"Is it true that you and Miles Essex were lovers while you were in Victoria?"

"Have you been in contact with the prince since you left Denver Springs?"

"How did you get to Victoria?"

The reporter wouldn't let go of my arm. I shook free of her and wrestled the bracelet off, scraping my wrist and skinning my knuckles.

"Is it true you were kidnapped by Scotland Yard?"

I flung the bracelet out into the water. I wanted to dive for the deck, but the reporters had me pinned tight against the railing. A reporter leaped after it.

"Don't!" I shouted, but he'd already surfaced, looking horrified at the coldness of the water, and was swimming toward shore. I braced myself for the deafening sound of the explosion, the sudden white fountain, but it didn't come, and I would have sighed with relief if there had been room to breathe.

There wasn't. And in spite of the yammering questions of the press, there wasn't any way I could get a word in edgewise either. Which was just as well, because now that I was safe for the next few minutes I had to decide what to do. And what to tell this ravening pack of tabloid reporters.

I couldn't tell them the truth. Joss had told me I couldn't, and anyway I knew better than to set them yapping after the biots. They might even find them, if they didn't tear Beejum apart in their eagerness to get a story, but they'd set off a hue and cry that could lose the war before anybody had the biots. Clare had known that, or she wouldn't have risked my being with the reporters this long. So what was I going to tell them? And where was Joss?

"What do you think about your father's arrest for treason?"

"What does your father think of this romantic rendezvous of yours?" the woman who had hold of my arm said.

"What rendezvous?" I said.

She took the opportunity to get a better grip on my arm. "Are you trying to tell us you don't know the prince is waiting for you at the Empress Hotel?"

At the Empress Hotel. And even if Joss wasn't with him, the prince could get in touch with him. So all I had to do was keep these lovely reporters interested for long enough to take me to the Empress.

"I've got to get to the hotel," I said.

"Not until you answer one question, Hellene. Is it true you and the prince were secretly married at Hydra Corp?"

"Yes," I said.

After the hubbub died down enough for the captain to herd everybody off his ferry and onto the docks, I gave the reporters a ten-minute interview that was a doozy and then insisted they get me to my waiting husband. The *Hourly Province* reporter came up with her company gullwing, and I granted a semi-exclusive to as many reporters as would fit inside. We had a police escort to the Empress.

I had hoped I could get in immediately to see the prince, especially before the rest of the reporters made it to the hotel, but a guard in the uniform of a Commonwealth Coldstream stopped me and the five reporters who'd come with me in the gullwing and told us to wait in an anteroom on the fifth floor.

We did, the reporters still asking a never-ending stream of questions. They were almost giddy with the thought of their getting an exclusive interview with the prince's bride. The reporter who had dived into the Strait after Clare's deadly bracelet hadn't even tried to dry himself off. "What did you throw in the Strait, Ari?" he said. He had lost his holocam when he went in the water and was making do with a sodden notebook and a stylus. "Your wedding ring?"

"It looked like a bracelet," the woman said who had taken hold of my arm on the ferry. She still hadn't let go. "Was it a terminal? Did the prince give it to you or was it from one of your admirers you don't want the prince to know about?"

"Yes, Ari, were you really on an evac caravan for all this time or were you with someone else?"

They certainly had vivid imaginations. They had us married and divorced before I'd even gotten in to see him. The guard came back, took an ID thumbprint and voice ident, and left again.

"Is it true the prince is wonderful in bed?" the *Hourly Province* woman said. "He's had hundreds of women. What makes you think you can satisfy him?"

"Was it really an assassination attempt on the prince or just revenge by one of his old girlfriends?"

"Aren't you afraid there will be further attempts on your life here in Victoria?"

Yes, I thought grimly, which is why I haven't asked the Coldstream Guard to throw you all out on your holocams. No matter how insulting their questions got, there was still safety in their presence. I would have been a lot more nervous sitting in a room by myself.

As if in response to my thoughts, the grim-faced guard came back, led me to another room, and left me there by myself. "I have to get in to see the prince immediately," I said, pushing against the door so he couldn't close it. "It's a matter of national security."

He was pushing, too. "I suggested to the prince that you might like to freshen up before your . . . interview with him."

"I don't want to freshen up," I said. "I have to see him now. I tried to wedge my foot in the open space, but he had *his* foot there. "It's urgent."

"Very good, ma'am," he said, and pushed the door all the way shut.

"Would you like your hair done or a nice bath first?" a voice said.

I whirled. A woman who looked just like an evac warden was standing there in an old-fashioned maid's uniform with a towel over her arm.

"I don't want a nice bath," I said through gritted teeth. "I want to see the prince."

"Oh, not like that, surely. Look at you, dirty and your hair all a bird's nest. He wouldn't like that at all. No, we'll give you a nice bath and then a lot of pretty curls, and you'll be just lovely."

"You don't understand. I'm in a hurry. I don't want a bath. I want to see the prince."

"You can't see the prince like that," she said determinedly. "I'm not letting you out of here until you're cleaned up."

"All right," I said, starting to run water in the sink. "I'll wash my face and comb my hair, but that's it."

"And I'll take your clothes to freshen them." She held out her hand insistently.

"I keep telling you, there isn't time for that."

Her hand was still out, and her expression was more like an evac warden's than ever. I handed over my blue challis. She draped it over her arm, handed me a robe that seemed to be mostly pink ribbons, and disappeared with the challis. I gave myself a quick sponge bath and dragged a comb through my hair. I heard a knock and opened the door for the maid.

A guard was standing there. "I've come to take you up to the prince, my lady."

"I can't . . . ." I started to say, and then thought better of it. There was no telling when the maid would be back, if ever, and I couldn't afford to waste any more time. I went with him.

The guard took me up to what had to be the top floor of the Empress, went through a complicated ident process, and then opened the door for me. I turned to ask him how long it would be before I could see the prince, but this time he was ready. The door shut, and at the same time I caught a glimpse of myself in the mirror.

It wasn't hard to do. Except for the bed, which seemed to fill the entire room, the place was solid mirrors. And there I was. Sure enough, the robe was mostly ribbons and some airy pink chiffon stuff that could only have come off the same bolt as that misbegotten dress of mine.

The last time I had seen the prince had been in Mother's offices. I had been trying to make him believe I wanted to seduce him so I could get to Mother's thermos. I had succeeded, so well that Joss had had to rescue me. And this time Joss wasn't here. I'll just have to be firm with him, I told myself. I was going to have to talk awfully fast, and as I now recalled in sickening detail, the prince wasn't a good listener.

I sat down on the bed. Mistake. It was covered in the Empress's idea of royal purple, with a royal crest hastily embroidered on for the occasion. I sank in a foot when I sat down, and a smell of roses wafted from its wavering surface. I had read about beds like this. I glanced up. Of course. Mirrors on the ceiling, too.

I stood up and walked around the bed, hoping I could find a lamp or something I could use as a weapon, but there wasn't a thing in the room except that obscene bed. The door opened, and I spun around, pink ribbons flying everywhere, but it was only the guard again with a tray of champagne and a narrow table to set it on. He set it down next to me and left again. I picked up the champagne bottle, thinking if that didn't work, there was always the ice bucket, and then the glasses. And the table.

The door started to open. I backed up to the far wall, gripping the bottle by its neck. The door opened.

"Why is it," Joss said, "that whenever I find you, you are always about to hop in bed with my employer?"

I sat down on the bed before my knees could give way, still clutching the champagne bottle. "You have no idea how glad I am to see you!"

"Really?" he said. "I thought you were here for a romp with the prince. I'm afraid he's not here, but I, the devoted equerry, of course, am ever willing to serve." He took the champagne bottle away from me and put it back in the ice bucket. If he was trying to look sternly disapproving, he was failing, and what had happened to that accursed poker face of his? He looked more than a little pleased with himself, which under the circumstances was hardly appropriate.

I stood up again. "Clare's here. In Victoria. She knows the biots are here. She grabbed me on the ferry and tried to get me to take her to them, but . . ."

"But you were saved by a roving band of reporters who brought you here to be ravished by their gypsy king."

"Yes, but she got away, and that means she's still out there. We've got to find the biots before she does." I started for the door in a cloud of ribbons.

"Do you think it's a good idea to go out in that? Conspicuous. The reporters are still down there. They'll expect you to be with the prince for at least a couple of hours. He does have his reputation to preserve." He took hold of one of the ribbons and brushed it delicately against my bare arm. "The way the tabloids tell it, you might be here a couple of days. After all, it's your honeymoon." He sat down on the bed and began pulling his boots off. Roses filled the room. "What do you want to do? Computer chess, two-handed bridge, an old-fashioned game of Trivial Pursuit?"

"Will you be serious?" I said. "Clare is here in Victoria, and with or without me she's going to find Skids. We've got to get to him before she does. We've got to find out where Beejum is."

"I know where he is," he said. He lay back on the purple bedspread, his hands behind his head. "Min and I figured it out yesterday. Her intuitives are really something, do you realize that? Working with nothing more than your letters and a few facts about the redoubtable Mrs. Ponsonby, she came up with the theory that if the baby had been burned, Mrs. Ponsonby would most certainly have kept the children because the evacuee medical benefits are an even better racket than evac checks, but she couldn't because her house was gone, and if the authorities took the children they'd assign them to somebody else who'd get the checks. Also, if she let go of them she might lose her chance at a hefty lawsuit, whereas with the bandaged-up twins, she could probably collect a bundle, so she'd get a friend or relative to take them till she could find a place to live."

"Her sister," I said.

"In Yellowknife. Righto. That's what Min said. And that's where they were."

He propped himself up on his elbows. "Chilkie, Verity Ann, and Beejum are on their way here. Two of the most capable agents I've got are bringing them here, posing as Verity Ann's parents. They'll be here within the hour."

"Is it safe? With Clare?"

"Clare is on her way to Yellowknife at this very moment. She's just figured out that's where the children are, thanks to Skids, the mailboy, who should be on his way here, too, after giving her the information I told him to. He was waiting on the dock for her. Min is responsible for finding Skids, too, and he's proved very useful. When Clare gets to Yellowknife Mrs. Ponsonby's sister will tell her the children have been taken to a refugee center in High Prairie. And by the time she gets there, we'll have the biots."

"What if Mrs. Ponsonby's sister tells her where the kids really are?"

"She won't. Because Mrs. Ponsonby is presently in custody for fraud and misuse of Red Cross funds, and her sister is anxious to get her out before Mrs. Ponsonby attempts to save herself by incriminating her sister. Min's idea. If, by chance, Clare would get hold of Mrs. Ponsonby, she thinks the children are in Calgary. Also Min's idea. Her intuitives are quite good, actually. We've nothing to do but wait, my dear, and entertain the media."

"But what if something goes wrong and she runs into them on the way?"

"She won't run into them, Ari."

"She's dangerous, Joss! On the ferry she put a bracelet on me that was really a bomb."

"She did?" he said. He stood up.

"Yes, and she might have put some other kind of bug on me or on one of the reporters who came here with me." He was fiddling with the ribbons that held the robe together. "She's very smart and dangerous and she'll do anything to find those biots and . . . what are you doing?"

"You said the bug might be anywhere. We're going to have to look for it." He grinned. "She might have bugged this ridiculous ribbon thing. If so, we've got to get you out of it."

"Joss! This isn't funny!" I stepped back, the backs of my knees pushed up against the bed and ready to topple me backward at any minute.

His tone changed. "I know it isn't funny. I'm here alone with you, we're shut in this room for at least an hour while we wait for Beejum to get here, and we can't leave because a whole army of tabloid reporters is out there waiting to report on the prince's latest romantic escapade and neither of us can step outside this room without ruining an entirely necessary cover. Meanwhile, those reporters' imaginations are running wild, and you're in here in that ridiculous nightgown, looking rather devastatingly beautiful. As usual. No, it definitely is not funny."

"Oh," I said. "You sent the reporters, didn't you?"

"No," he said. He took another step that brought him up against me. "I sent an *Hourly Province* reporter who had instructions not to let go of you under any circumstances."

"She didn't."

"And a Yard agent."

"Who dived into the Strait."

"Who dived into the Strait." Joss was having trouble with the ribbons. They were almost impossible to untie. "I gave you as much protection as I could without coming to get you myself, which is the one thing I couldn't do without ruining the prince's cover."

He had the top ribbon untied. "Where is the prince?"

"He's here. He's not quite the amorous playboy of the tabloids, although he is a bit of a ladies' man. He's also one of my best men in the Yard. As soon as we get the GEM biots, he's taking them to Yellowknife." He had the last knot practically undone. "Any other loose ends you want tied up, Ari?"

"What about Min?" I said breathlessly. "If her intuitives are as good as you say they are, how did you get past her security systems?"

"I told her something she'd already figured out. She's quite good, actually. We may have to hire her on at the Yard." He pulled the last loop of ribbon free. "I told her I was in love with you."

# ESSEX ELOPES: MARRIES ARI!

---

"We were married the night of the Fete," the prince's new bride, formerly Hellene Ariadne, said in an exclusive interview with the *Victoria Hourly Province*. "We slipped away as soon as the dancing started."

Perched on a velvet chair at the Empress Hotel, seventeen-year-old Ariadne seemed unaware of the speculation that has swirled around her disappearance from Hydra Corp. "I was buying my trousseau," the dark-haired beauty said when questioned about her three-day absence following the explosions at Hydra Corp. "A girl needs some frilly things for her honeymoon, doesn't she?"

Although the elopement was sudden, Ariadne denied that it was a whirlwind romance. "We've been in love with each other since Essex first came to Hydra Corp," she said. "My mother sent me away to Victoria to keep us apart, but it didn't work. We were meeting secretly at the Empress Hotel every chance we got. That's why we decided to come here for our honeymoon."

News of the prince's surprise marriage has rocked the Commonwealth. The prince's grandfather, King Peter, was unavailable for comment. "He doesn't approve of me, of course," the new princess said, "but the old boy will come around eventually. He'll have to."

# CHAPTER SIXTEEN

Someone knocked at the door. They seemed to have been knocking for a long time while I kissed Joss. He didn't act like he heard it either. I was just wondering whether I should say something when Joss let go of me and began pulling his boots on.

"It appears you are saved by the bell," he said, stamping down hard on his boot. "Again."

"I don't want to be saved by the bell," I said. "I love you."

"I love you, too," he said, and kissed me on the forehead. "But there's somebody at the door."

"Maybe it's a tabloid reporter," I said hopefully.

"If it is, I shall be right back," he said, and kissed me lightly again, but it was the inside door he'd come through earlier that he opened, and I could hear Joss say, "How the bloody hell did that happen? I thought they were supposed to be watching her," before the door shut.

I felt a thrill of fear go through me. Was Clare in Victoria after all, with Chilkie and Beejum and the baby coming in on the ferry? What if she met them as they boarded the ferry the way she'd met me? Cover or no cover, we'd have to go get them ourselves. We couldn't risk Clare finding them and . . . I caught a sudden multiple glimpse of myself in the mirrors, barefoot and wearing a see-through nightgown. I wasn't going anyplace dressed like this.

I felt along the sides of the mirrored panels for the switch that had opened the door into the inner room where Joss had gone, found a keypad, pressed it without any hope of having it open, and was surprised when it did. But it wasn't a door. It was a closet, and Miles must have had it keyed to open to anybody female so all his sweeties could open it. At least I hoped that was the case. I didn't like to think he'd entered my thumbprint for future reference.

The closet was crammed full of clothes, but none of them were going to do me any good. There was a long row of filmy nightgowns on pink padded hangers, which was a feat in itself since hardly any of them had enough fabric in them to stay on a hanger, or on the sweeties, for that matter.

At one end of the closet was a small fashion holo, presumably so the sweeties could conjure up whatever their fantasies (or Essex's) desired, but there wasn't time to order up something, and the holo probably wasn't programmed for anything but chiffon and feathers anyway. I riffled hastily through the rack, knocking half the so-called nightgowns on the carpeted floor as I went, and feeling more frustrated by the minute. Joss was going to come in and say that he had to go out and for me to stay here, and I wasn't going to be in any position to demand that I go with him unless I wrapped myself in the purple bedspread.

Finally, nearly at the end of the rack, I found a pair of jams and a jacket. I pulled them on, glad that they were opaque in my underwearless state. They were a little big, which was also good.

Joss opened the door again. "Oh, good," he said, "you found some clothes. We've got to go meet the children at the ferry."

"Why? Is Clare in Victoria?"

"No. Skids delivered our message to Clare and then doubled back and watched her get on the ferry. One of my agents watched her get off and followed her to the landport. She's on her way to Yellowknife. Clare's not the problem. Your mother is. She's on her way to Victoria. Can you find something to cover your hair? Your picture's been on all the tabloids. The children are safely on the ferry, not the one Clare was on, and it's due to land in thirty-five minutes. The original plan was for my agents to bring them here to the Empress, but that's too risky when we don't know where your mother is. We'll take them somewhere else. My man will get the address of a safehouse for us to use."

"My mother's coming to Victoria?" I said, a little blankly.

Joss nodded. He opened another closet which must have been Miles's, pulled out a blue felt cap from a shelf full of hats. He pulled it down over my hair.

One of the hats had a broad brim and a plume, and there appeared to be a set of armor standing against the wall of the closet. "What does Miles Essex do up here?" I said.

Joss tucked a few stray curls under the cap. "When this is all over, we shall book this suite for the weekend and attempt to puzzle it out." He pulled the brim of the cap down a little more, rummaged in his pockets, and handed me a notebook and stylus. "There will be reporters at every exit. Including us. Ready?"

I nodded, and he put his hand on one of the mirrors. The door of the suite opened, and Joss put his head out cautiously, looked both ways, and motioned me to follow him.

There was a man in ordinary clothes and one in Joss's equerry uniform who looked enough like him to maybe fool the reporters waiting outside the suite, both Yard men, I gathered. We went down two empty corridors and into a service elevator. On the way down, the plainclothes agent put on a press fedora and pulled out a mike.

"Stay close to me and keep moving back," Joss said when the elevator opened onto another corridor. "Hang on if you have to, and don't say anything." He paused at a door, nodded to the two men, and then opened it, shouting, "My source says they're secretly married. Do you deny that?"

"No comment," Joss's look-alike said, or I guess that was what he said, because we were suddenly outside and surrounded by reporters who were shouting questions in my ear, Joss along with them. The agent with the mike crammed it practically down the throat of Joss's look-alike and bellowed, "Is it true Prince Essex charged his new bride's mother with treason?" And I lost sight of Joss in the jumble of reporters.

"Keep moving back," Joss had said, and I tried, but it was almost impossible. The reporters kept pushing toward the door. Joss's look-alike was trying to shut the door, but the *Hourly Province* reporter who'd brought me to the Empress had her foot jammed firmly in it.

I stopped, afraid she might look over and see me, and that accomplished what my struggling hadn't. Reporters surged past me, I lost my pad and stylus and almost lost my cap, and was all of a sudden nearly at the rear of the shouting mass. I glanced back, saw Joss at the very edge of the crowd, and then pushed back between two women who didn't even spare me a glance.

"Come on," Joss said, and we backed around a corner and into an alley.

The other agent was leaning against a wall, looking at his wrist terminal. "The ferry's in," he said. "Let's get going."

We took off running. We ran down an alley, over two blocks, and then circled back to the harbor. The light raid sirens started to wail.

"Bloody hell," Joss said. "What damnable luck!"

"Is it a real raid or do we keep going?" I said.

"It's real," the Yard man said. "They got us twice yesterday afternoon in Port Townsend and once on the docks. They got a ferry, too, as it was coming in."

"Where's the nearest shelter?" Joss said.

"The Empress has one, but we can't go there," the agent said. "The reporters will all have—"

"This way," I said, starting to run toward the harbor. There was a shelter in the basement of the old Parliament building. I'd gotten caught in it once during a practice drill when I went down to meet the ferry for Mrs. Ponsonby and bring her some more of her poor little profitable orphans.

We saw the first lights hit the northern edge of the city just as we ducked down the narrow stairwell. I must have stopped to stare. I was shocked to see lasers actually striking right here in neutral Victoria. Joss pushed me inside the dim basement.

The basement must have been three hundred years old. It was a large stone room with a high, vaulted ceiling and massive pillars. A dozen people were already in the shelter, most of them dockhands who smelled like fish. They didn't pay any attention to us as we came down the steps or to the raids either. Several of the men were playing cards on an upended packing crate. Another one had put his coat under his head and was sound asleep.

I could hear fire engines racing north. "It's not the ships," one of the men said in the same tone of voice he would have used for "I'll see your ten and raise you."

There were more sirens, either fire engines or ambulances, and they sounded close. "Chilkie and Beejum," I said. "What if the ferry got hit?"

Joss put his arm around me. "They'll be all right," he said. "We can't go out in this."

I knew that, but it didn't help. The Yard man had told Joss they'd gotten one of the ferries yesterday. I kept thinking of Chilkie and Beejum standing by the rail, looking toward the shore. Chilkie would be holding Verity Ann up and pointing at the sea gulls. They wouldn't even know what had hit them.

I heard the dull sound of an explosion. "Oil tank, up Malahat way," one of the card players said without looking up. He threw his cards on the packing case, and two of the cards fell through the slats onto the damp floor. "I'm out."

It took forever for the all-clear to sound. I dashed for the door, Joss and the other Yard man close on my heels. I ran all the way to the ferry slip and then came to a screeching halt when I saw the ferry bobbing safely in its moorings. The gullwings and landrollers hadn't been unloaded, but obviously the passengers had abandoned ship when they'd docked during a light raid.

"Is there another shelter where they could have gone?" Joss asked, taking in the empty ferry.

"Yes," I said. "This way."

I led them to the ferry office. People were coming up the stone steps. I recognized Skids.

"They're not here," Skids said frantically, talking as much to Joss as to me. "This is everyone from the ferry, and they're not here!"

"You were supposed to stay put," Joss said, looking annoyed.

"Look, I done what you asked, and now I want to see Chilkie. You owe me," Skids said. He probably hadn't trusted Joss any more than he would have trusted Mrs. Ponsonby where an evacuee was concerned. He had taken matters into his own hands and come down to the docks to meet her.

Joss didn't answer Skids. He was looking over his head at the people coming up the staircase, watching, I assumed, for his agents.

"They're not here," Skids said again. "I got here a few minutes after the light raid started, saw the ferry was empty, and went down in the shelter. They didn't come here."

Just then a man and a woman, both wearing rain slickers, came walking rapidly up the street. Joss stared and frowned, then hurried to meet them. They stopped in the middle of the street, talked a moment, then the man ran for the ferry office, and Joss and the woman hurried back to where we were waiting.

"The children gave them the slip during the confusion of getting to the shelter," Joss said. "Chilkie was carrying Verity Ann and holding Beejum's hand. As soon as my people realized they were missing, they came out to look. They haven't found them. I sent Edwards to phone for more people to search."

But Edwards was already running from the ferry office. "The comm lines are out because of the raid," he said breathlessly.

"They can't have gotten far," the woman who had been posing as Verity Ann's mother said.

"All right, here's what we're going to do," Joss said. "Skids, I want you and Ariadne to go back to the post office, tell my man there what's happened."

"I'd like to stay with you," I protested.

"I'm not your messenger boy," Skids said.

"Listen, lad. You do what I tell you, or I'll have you up on charges faster than you can blink an eye. I want you safely at the post office with my people so I don't have to worry about you while I'm getting this search for the children organized."

Which wouldn't be easy to do with the comm lines out. And it wasn't Skids he was worrying about. It was me.

"When you get there, you stay put," Joss said. "This isn't a game, lad. There are people on the loose who know who you are and who just might kill you."

I bit my lip. Clare was on her way to Yellowknife, so he had to mean my mother, who was on her way here. "Come on, Skids," I said. I took his arm, but he jerked free. I thought he was going to argue, but instead he abruptly turned away and sauntered toward his scooter. Even when I got on behind him, he didn't protest.

He drove the scooter two blocks toward the post office and then looked back over his shoulder at the harbor. "Good," he said. "They're gone." Abruptly he turned up the hill.

"Where are we going?" I said.

"To my place," he said. "Chilkie probably went there."

"You should have told Joss," I said.

"He wouldn't have listened," Skids said. "And if he had, he wouldn't have let us go. I want to see my girl."

"What if she's not there?"

"Then you and me can spend some time together. My place is lots nicer than the post office." He swerved across lanes and onto the bridge.

"I knew all that talk about Chilkie being your girl was a lie," I said disgustedly. "You're still a two-timing Romeo!"

"Me?!" he said, sounding genuinely shocked. "What about you? I read about you on the tabloids. Messing around with the prince and Captain Liddell. Talk about two-timing!"

He drove over the bridge and turned off the pavement. It was getting dark, and for a moment I thought Skids had made a wrong turn. He followed a dirt trail leading down to the water and then turned under the bridge. He stopped the scooter and put down the kickstand.

Under the bridge was a shack of sorts, just boards nailed up against the vee of the bridge and the cement. Skids pushed aside three boards on a shaky hinge. "Welcome to my apartment," he said, and stepped inside.

"Skids!" It was Chilkie's voice. I ducked inside. "Ariadne!"

She was glad to see me, but more glad to see Skids. She shoved Verity Ann in my arms and fell into his. Verity Ann needed her dipes changed, and she had been bawling so long she was hoarse. I hugged her against my chest and felt like crying, too. Chilkie held on to Skids, blubbering, while I took in the fact that there was nowhere to hide in the heap of torn, dirty blankets and old cans and bottles that Skids called his apartment.

"Where's Beejum?" I said, so loudly that Verity Ann started to bawl again.

"You have to help me find him," Chilkie said. "When the raids started, he scooted around the corner ahead of me, and I started after him, but Verity Ann threw her bottle down. I had to go back for it. It was the last one. By the time I found it and went after Beejum, he was gone. The sky was a mess with lasers and he was crying and so was Verity Ann and . . ."

"Don't worry," Skids said. "We'll find him, and if we don't there are plenty of other people out looking for him who will. How far can a little kid go?"

"All the way back to Yellowknife," I said, thinking of Pete, who had only been a couple of years older than Beejum and yet had managed to get away from the evac wardens and get all the way to Denver Springs. "Was he running back toward the ferry when he took off?"

"No, he was running toward the shelter, and that's where I thought he'd be," Chilkie said, sniffling. "Oh, Ariadne, if anything happens to him, I'll just . . ."

"He's probably in one of the shelters," Skids said. "They've probably found him already, and we're worried for nothing."

"Where would he go?" I said. "Did he say anything?"

"No, he . . . I don't know," Chilkie said, and started crying again. Skids picked a filthy rag out of the mess on the floor and handed it to her. "He kept talking about running away the whole way to Victoria," she said, blowing her nose. "He kept saying the people who came to get us weren't Verity Ann's parents at all, that they were spies and he was going to run away the first chance he got."

"They were spies," I said grimly, "and Joss and I should have known better than to think agents could just bring you to Victoria without any explanations. Of course Beejum would turn it into some spy story."

"Who's Joss?" Chilkie said, looking up from her filthy handkerchief, her eyes bright with interest, and, for the moment at least, forgetting all about crying.

"It doesn't matter," I said. "What matters is where Beejum is. Did he say what he was going to do when he got away from these spies?"

"He said he knew what they were after, and they weren't going to get it. Because he'd hidden it."

Unbidden, the thought of Pete came back to me, saying he'd hidden some stuff in his house after the light raid. "I hid there for two weeks before the evac guards got me. I'm going back there as soon as I run away from here."

"The house," I said. "I bet he went to Mrs. Ponsonby's. It's the only place he could have hidden the biots."

"But it blew up," Chilkie said.

"I know," I said, shifting the snuffling Verity Ann in my arms, "but I'll bet that's where he is. I say we go look for him at the house."

"An excellent idea, Ariadne," Clare's voice said from behind me.

Verity Ann abruptly stopped crying. I turned, still clutching her to me, and Clare stepped through the door. Skids let go of Chilkie and started for something in his boot, but thought better of it when he saw the clip pistol she was holding.

"We'll go look for him at Mrs. Ponsonby's," Clare said. "Him and the biots. Of course the biots are there. I can see it in your face. Thank you, my dear niece, for being so very transparent."

from the *Victoria Hourly Province*

## Mona's Light Raid Predictions True!

---

You saw it first in the *Victoria Hourly Province*. Neutral Victoria's sirens screamed at 0400 hours and for the first time, it wasn't a drill. Lapping batellites took aim and seared the Victorian buildings and antique shops in Port Townsend, then, leaving the unique shopping district in flames, moved on to the Provincial Museum in Victoria. Though the museum had been coated with aluminum only days earlier, the batellite was able to keep on target for the needed forty seconds because, amazingly, Victoria has no GTAs! It was a Western States GTA that finally deflected the beam, but not before the old museum burst into flames.

"We've lost a segment of history that isn't replaceable," Provincial Museum curator Hannah Klipsh lamented. "I don't see how we can remain neutral under fire like this. Are our officials crazy?"

Officials refuse official comment, but sources inside the Parliament say the danger is not over yet. Residents of Victoria are unofficially warned to stay close to light raid cover, and to prepare for the worst.

(Port Townsend bed-and-breakfast after lasing, Screen 7.)

# CHAPTER SEVENTEEN

"**O**h, dear. You don't seem happy to see me at all," Clare said. "What's the matter, Ariadne? No reporters around to rescue you this time? Tell me, did you enjoy your little tryst with the prince? I rather expected you two to meet Skids at the ferry, but it was Liddell you brought. Thanks for leaving him behind this time."

I looked at Skids and Chilkie. She was peeking out from around his shoulder, looking more surprised than frightened. But Skids kept holding her, keeping his body between Clare's clip pistol and Chilkie. There was no doubt he understood the danger, even if Chilkie didn't.

Hold her still, Skids, I said silently to myself while I thought of what to do. The shack was tiny, Clare no more than two feet from me. But she barred the way to the door, and with Verity Ann in my arms, what could I do?

"And you, lover boy. I didn't believe for one minute your story about Chilkie and the children being in Yellowknife. Not with Joss Liddell's people fumbling around the post all day. If you were in Victoria, so was Chilkie, or—as it turns out—she was on her way."

"Liddell will be here in just a few minutes," Skids said. "He was right behind us."

Clare laughed, and the sound of it chilled me. "I was right behind the bomb shelter door. I heard every word. Liddell is searching the harbor for the children, and he thinks you and Ariadne are back at the post office with his agents." She laughed again. "I had plenty of time to duck out the back door and get my gullwing. I didn't even have to use the follow I'd put on your scooter this time. I had you in sight the whole time."

"Look," I said. "Skids and Chilkie have nothing to do with this. Let them go."

"You're wasting your breath. Of course they're involved. Even this sweet helpless little baby." She reached forward to chuck Verity Ann under the chin. I pulled her back out of Clare's reach. "I want the biots, Ariadne."

"But I don't have the biots," I said. "I don't even know where they are."

"But Beejum does. And he's back at Mrs. Ponsonby's house, or so you were saying when I came in."

"I was just guessing," I said frantically. "Who knows where he'd really go? Someone may have seen him wandering around. A little kid alone like that during a light raid would attract someone's attention. By now the constables have him, and Joss will know about it."

But Clare was shaking her head, wearing a bemused smile. "Orphans in war are far too resourceful to be picked up, even when they're frightened. I know from firsthand experience. Medea wasn't much older than Beejum when we were found. What they never knew was that we'd been on our own for over a year." She wore a look of pride on her face that looked like Mother's. "Don't try to tell me what orphans are capable of doing, Ariadne. That boy won't be found until he wants to be. Unless, of course, a friend happens along. A friend he trusts, like you." She smiled again, chillingly. "But first . . ." She looked at Skids and Chilkie, her knuckles white as she aimed the tiny-barreled pistol more carefully.

"No!" I said. "Don't kill them. If you do, you'll have to kill me, too, and then you'll never find Beejum."

She hesitated, but I didn't think it was my threat that stopped her. A clipshot, even one from under a bridge, might be heard and investigated. "Tie them up, Ariadne. See that you do a good job of it, for of course I shall check."

I handed Verity Ann to Clare, hoping she would take her without thinking, and that in reaching out to hold the squirmy baby she would lose control of the pistol for a minute, but she stepped back, still leveling the pistol at me.

"You didn't think that would work, did you, Ari? Put the baby down."

"I can't just put her on the floor. It's filthy," I said, unwilling to let go of her. As long as I was holding on to her, Clare couldn't shoot her without shooting me, and she didn't dare do that yet, but I knew she'd have no qualms about silencing a baby who might cry and let people know where we were.

"Put her down," Clare said.

Verity Ann started to cry again. "Shh," I said, cradling her head against the hollow of my throat, "don't cry. Shhh." I took the few steps to the cement stanchion of the bridge that formed the back wall of Skids's shack and put her down on an impossibly oily, dirt-caked blanket behind a jumble of pots and pans that might at least deflect the clip's projectile. Then I stepped back over the pans and bent down, looking for something to tie Skids and Chilkie up with and hoping I would find a knife or even a broken bottle in the junk on the floor. Skids was looking at a white plastic spacer's trunk in the corner. I ignored it for the moment, picked up a tattered sleeping bag to look underneath, then dug into a wicker basket, but it was full of rags.

"The spacer's trunk," Clare said coldly.

I sighed and went to the trunk, tried to open it. It was locked. I fiddled with it, hoping it would stay locked until I could think of something. But it flew open on its own before I had hardly touched it. Inside were aluminum paint, chocolate bars, and an assortment of other things probably all stolen from the post office, even two cans of salmon and a roll of packing tape. So the war hadn't accounted for all the mail's unreliability. I looked at Skids.

"I didn't steal any of it," Skids said. "It's all packages for people who aren't at their addresses anymore."

"There's no rope," I said to Clare.

"The tape, Ariadne," Clare said. "Use the packing tape."

It was thick plastic tape with twine reinforcements. It probably would hold better than rope. I took it out and closed the trunk.

Clare had moved over to the pile of pots and pans. "Sit back-to-back," I told Chilkie and Skids. I pulled a length of tape off the roll.

"Tie them up separately," Clare said. She set the pistol and pointed it at Verity Ann's head. I taped Skids to his only chair, and Chilkie to a sturdy-looking beam. She made me gag them, too. I looked at Verity Ann. She'd picked up a corner of the oily blanket and was sucking vigorously on who knew what horrible germs. If I gagged her, she might choke, but I was certain Clare wouldn't except her from the procedure.

"We'll take the baby with us," Clare said.

I wasn't sure I was relieved, but at least I wouldn't worry about the gag. Chilkie and Skids would be terribly uncomfortable, but they wouldn't choke like Verity Ann would.

Clare checked the bindings on Chilkie and Skids, then gestured for me to get Verity Ann. "You lead the way," she said. "My gullwing is tethered to a tree up by the road."

I picked up Verity Ann and took the blanket out of her fingers. She opened her mouth to scream. I gave it back to her. "We should walk," I said, pushing open the door. I was hoping Joss or someone would be waiting outside, was ready for him to push me aside and rush in after Clare. But there was no one. It was completely dark under the bridge, and silent.

I could only hope Joss would somehow find out that Skids and I had never showed up at the post office and that he'd try to find us. But so far as I knew he had no reason to check up on us. He'd trusted me to make sure we went where we were supposed to.

Victoria was almost completely blacked out. The laser raid must have spooked everybody into heading for shelters because there were no vehicles on the street except the gullwing that must be Clare's, and no trace of light in any of the houses.

"You pilot it," Clare said. "Keep the baby in your lap and go slowly."

The clip pistol was in her coat now, but I knew her finger was on the rocker. I opened the door and got in the front seat, Verity Ann on my lap. Clare got into the back seat.

"No lights," Clare said, and I stopped looking around for the light switch.

I headed the gullwing back toward the wharves.

"Turn around," Clare said coldly. "You're going the wrong way."

"I think it's this way," I said, my heart beating furiously.

"Stop," she said. "Stop right now." In the darkness I felt her hand grasp my hair. She yanked my head back and I felt the barrel of the pistol on my neck. "Ariadne, I need you to get my sister to come with me later tonight. She's here, you know, waiting on a private boat. She expects me to bring you; she seems to think there's hope you'll become a true Quebecker if we give you half the chance. I don't agree. I think you're Hellene through and through, but I didn't have time to argue. So I agreed, and with my sister, I like to keep my word. But if I must, I'll bring her your dead body, which I tell you honestly, dear niece, is my preference. It would save a lot of grief later on, for you'll never be a

Quebecker. My sister is young enough to have another child, one untainted by Hellene genes and Hellene conditioning. So be certain you don't misjudge anything else tonight, for I have no more patience left. Do you understand?"

"Yes," I said.

She let go and I turned the gullwing around.

When we got to Mrs. Ponsonby's, we got out of the gullwing and walked across the lawn. I shifted Verity Ann to my other hip and looked hopefully at the house next door. It was dark, no trace of light. We walked right past the front porch, but no one was sitting in the rocking chair or standing looking at the sky, watching for laser flashes. Then I noticed the door was wide open. There's no one in this neighborhood at all, I thought desperately. They've all been evacuated.

In the dark, Mrs. Ponsonby's house didn't look much different from when I'd last seen it. The hinges on the gate had rusted through years ago and the gate lay half-rotted in the weeds behind the fence. The sidewalk was cracked, but that wasn't new either. Clare gestured for me to walk down the gangway to the back of the house. I opened the back screen door, and it fell down. There wasn't a door behind it. I looked inside. The stairwell was still there, but it was cluttered with bricks and plaster. There was a trace of moonlight coming through the ceiling. I started up the stairs, picking my way over the rubble. My heart was beating rapidly. The house was only a shell with pieces of plaster and sheeting clinging to rafters and support beams. It was a wonder they hadn't been killed when it blew.

"Call him," Clare hissed behind me.

Please don't let him be here, I prayed. Please let him be in one of the shelters down on the wharf. Please let Joss have found him. "Beejum," I said softly. "It's me, Ariadne."

No answer. I didn't expect one. Frightened as he had to be, Beejum was quite likely to be curled up in a ball somewhere sucking his thumb. He wouldn't take that thumb out of his mouth to reply right away.

"Go upstairs," Clare said.

Half the second story had fallen through, exposing the stairwell. But as our eyes adjusted, it was plain to see that the front side where the bedrooms had been was still there, even though the walls were gone. We crept up the stairs, me testing every one. They didn't feel steady, but they held.

On the upstairs landing I looked across to the bedrooms. One beam had held, the others had broken off, leaving a hole in the second floor that ran from one outside wall to the other. What had been our bedrooms sloped, but not so steeply that someone would just roll off. My bedroom was completely gone.

"Call him," Clare said again, this time poking me in the ribs with the pistol, just to remind me she had it, as if I'd forgotten about it because it was dark.

"Beejum. Beejum. It's Ariadne. Where are you, Beejum?"

As we waited in the darkness, I was beginning to think Beejum wasn't there after all and starting to wonder what Clare would do if he wasn't. Whatever it was, finding Beejum was the key, and if he wasn't here, he could be anywhere. I felt a surge of hope. He wasn't here. He had been in one of the shelters after all and Joss had found him and taken him to the Empress. They were there right now, having cocoa and toast.

"Ariadne?" a little voice, a frightened voice, called out. "Where are you? *Ariadne!*"

"Answer him," Clare said.

"It's all right. I'm here."

"I can't see him," Clare said. She shifted the pistol, took a flashlight out of her pocket, and risked a quick sweep of the bedrooms.

"*Ariadne!*" he wailed. Definitely from the bedrooms, but Clare couldn't find him with her light.

"He's in the closet," I said to her. "He always hides in the closet."

"Well, get him to come out and you find out where those biots are," she said, snapping off the light.

"Honey, I'm right over here by the stairs. Come on out."

"I can't," he said.

"Why not?" I said, wondering if the door was stuck.

"I'm scared," he said, and he started to cry.

"He won't come out when he's this scared," I said. "I'll have to go get him." I was wondering if I could get across to him with Verity Ann in my arms. If I could, there'd be considerable distance between us and Clare, and maybe a chance to get away.

"Yes, you will," Clare said. "And be certain to bring back the biots, too. But before you go, we're going back downstairs."

"What? Why?"

"Ariadne?" It was Beejum, still crying softly. It was an embarrassed kind of cry. I wished it were the loud, angry kind. Someone just might hear it.

"Move," Clare said sharply, so I stepped past her and picked my way carefully down the stairs.

I was mystified, but I wasn't going to argue. Once downstairs, she stepped up onto the rubble of what had been the floor of my bedroom, now in the kitchen. In the center of it was my bed, almost untouched, the bedspread still neatly pulled over the pillows, though the top of it was level with the rubble and there was a fine powdery dust on everything.

"Put the baby on the bed," Clare said. "You'll need both hands free to get across that beam."

"She'll cry if I leave her alone," I said. If I didn't take Verity Ann with me, I knew I couldn't try to run. No doubt Clare knew it, too, but I didn't want her to think running had even occurred to me. "Someone might hear her, but as long as I hold her, she won't cry."

"Put her down," Clare said, "right now!"

I hesitated, and Clare reset the pistol again. I didn't want to find out if she was still worried about using it before she had the biots, so I pulled the bedspread back and set Verity Ann down in the middle of the sheet.

The baby looked around, still clutching that filthy blanket and looking bewildered. She was wet, maybe getting hungry, but not yet tired. Still, she looked up at me with the look that precedes a wail. "She's going to cry," I said.

Clare leaned over and snapped a bracelet over Verity Ann's fat wrist, like the one she'd put on me on the ferry. It didn't fit, of course, but it sure got the baby's attention. She stared at it, fascinated.

"I've set the dead man's switch on the detonator. It won't be a matter of choice this time. If the baby gets more than twenty-five feet away, the bracelet goes off."

Verity Ann felt the bracelet on her wrist and grabbed hold of it with her other hand. It slipped off her wrist, but she held tight, and promptly put it in her mouth. I gasped and Clare laughed.

"You'd better hurry, Ariadne. Beejum's waiting. And I'll be waiting over there, behind the stairs. If I don't hear you coming back in five minutes . . ." She was holding the pistol in one hand and her other hand was on her belt where she'd hooked the little control box. "I'll put the detonator back on manual and I'll blow that baby to smithereens."

For a second I stood there staring, judging my chances for getting Verity Ann and throwing the bracelet into the basement stairwell before

Clare could activate it. Not good, I decided, and it just might bring down what was left of the second story and get Beejum, too. Nor could I jump Clare, who was already safely behind the brick and mortar half-wall by the stairs, and besides, hand-to-hand combat with a fully trained Quebecker spy couldn't have good odds for someone like me. I walked up the stairs and stared at the beam.

Beejum had probably crawled across it on all fours, but I doubted I could do the same. I didn't think I could walk all the way to the other side tightrope style either, so finally I sat down and started to scoot across on my bottomside. Halfway across, the beam lurched, making a screeching noise before it settled an inch or two lower. I sat still, waiting for it to finish falling or for my heart to stop pounding so hard, whichever came first, before I moved again. The beam must have caught securely, but my heart was awash with adrenaline and wouldn't slow down. I started scooting along again, moving toward the sound of Beejum's soft cries.

Below me I could just barely make out Verity Ann sitting on the bed in the middle of the rubble and could hear her cooing over the bracelet. It would be full of drool by now, and maybe have two little teeth marks in it. Eventually she'd tire of it or it would fall out of her hand. Then she'd start crawling, and that would be even more dangerous than playing with the bracelet. Beyond the bed were gaping holes to the basement, which was full of water. I worked my way to the beam and crawled onto the sloping bedroom floor.

"I'm coming, Beejum," I said.

"You didn't bring that lady, did you?" he said. He sounded really close.

"What lady?"

"The lady that came and got us in Yellowknife. She said she was Verity Ann's mother, but she wasn't. She was a spy."

"No," I said, wishing with all my heart that I had brought that lady instead of this one.

"I heard you talking to somebody. Before."

"That was . . ." What exactly was I supposed to tell him? Oh, that's a nice lady who's going to blow all our brains out once she gets your biots? "That's a lady who came with me to help find you."

"But it's not the lady that came and got us in Yellowknife?" he said, and his voice seemed to retreat as if he were huddling back in the corner of the closet.

"No, it's not that lady," I said firmly.

I was still on my hands and knees because of the slope of the floor, almost close enough to put my hand on the doorknob. I reached up. The knob was gone.

"What are you doing?" It was Clare calling from below.

"The doorknob is gone," I said. "I can't get him out."

"Just find out where the biots are," Clare said.

"He won't tell me anything unless I get the door open," I said, hoping she hadn't been able to hear our conversation about ladies who were spies. I looked around frantically for something to pry open the door, but almost everything had slipped off into the pile of rubble below, and anyhow bedrooms didn't usually have crowbars even when they haven't been blown apart. I picked up a jagged splinter of wood, thinking I might be able to wedge the sharp end into the mechanism and turn it that way. But when I turned to go back to the closet, the door was open and Beejum was standing in front of it, his face a smear of dirty tears, but trying to look as if he hadn't been crying at all. Before he could say anything, I dropped the piece of wood and clamped my hand over his mouth.

"Beejum," I whispered. "The lady downstairs is a spy, too. She's got Verity Ann and she's got a clip pistol and she's going to try to kill us."

Beejum tried to squirm loose and get my hand off his mouth. Just as he clamped his teeth down on my finger, Clare called from below.

"Ariadne, bring him down here now. And be quick about it."

"I've almost got the door open," I said through tears of pain caused by Beejum's teeth in my finger. But he let up instantly when he heard Clare's voice and his eyes grew wide. "She's very dangerous," I whispered to Beejum.

"Is she going to kill Verity Ann?" he whispered back.

"Yes. And you and me, too, if we let her."

"What are we going to do?" Beejum said.

"I don't know," I told him, and that was the truth of it. I just didn't know what to do. Find out where the biots were and shove him back in the closet? Maybe he'd be safe enough there even if she decided to blow up me and Verity Ann. But I doubted it; the sag of the floor suggested any more explosions would send it crashing through to the basement. There was no way out. There was nothing to do except take Beejum down with me. "Come on, Beejum. We're going to get Verity Ann."

I took hold of Beejum's outstretched hand and he crawled over to me.

"Does he have the biots?" Clare asked.

"Of course he doesn't have the biots," I shouted. "He doesn't even know what biots are. I have to explain.

"Beejum," I said softly, "do you remember my little dishes that I kept on the windowsill?"

"Your garden?"

"Yes, my garden. Do you know where those little dishes are?"

He nodded and let go of my hand and dived to the back of the closet. He came back with a single cracked petri dish. "I didn't break it," he said.

"I know you didn't," I said. I wondered how long the dish had been cracked. With the seal broken, the biots were probably all dead. I peered at it through the cloudy cover. There was only a dry, greenish residue on the curved sides of the dish. Good, I thought, they're dead, and she won't get the biots after all. If they were dead, we were, too, and if they weren't, I was handing the war over to her.

"Ariadne, the baby seems to have lost interest in her toy," Clare called. "She's crawling over to the edge of the bed."

"Beejum doesn't know what I'm talking about," I shouted down at her, putting my finger to my lips so Beejum wouldn't contradict me. He stared at me wide-eyed. "I'm trying to explain it to him."

I looked frantically around the bedroom, trying to see if there was some other way down. "Beejum," I whispered, "how did you get up here?"

"The back stairs," he said, and pointed back behind a tangle of half-fallen beams and part of the wallpapered wall.

"They're still there?" I whispered.

"Yeah," he said, and began to pick his way up the sloping floor to the beams. I jammed the petri dish in my pocket and started after him. "He says he left the petri dishes on the windowsill," I called down to Clare as I walked, hoping the floor wouldn't give way with my next step.

Beejum had disappeared behind the wallpaper. I climbed over the unsteady beams, and there he was, standing proudly at the top of the narrow back stairs. They were completely intact, even though the banister leaned out over nothing.

"See?" Beejum said.

I saw, all right. For the first time since Clare had walked into Skids's shack, I saw a way out. The back stairs led down into the pantry, which opened onto the kitchen, where Verity Ann was. And Clare wasn't. She was in the hall, standing under the front stairs, waiting for me. If Beejum and I could get down the stairs and into the kitchen, we could get the bracelet away from Verity Ann and escape out the back way. Clare would still think we were upstairs. I motioned to Beejum to stay where he was and backtracked a few steps.

"There's a lot of rubble here by the window," I shouted, scrabbling loudly in the loose plaster. "I think they might be under here. I just found a flowerpot of Mrs. Ponsonby's." I knocked a board over and scrabbled some more and then tiptoed as soundlessly as I could over to the stairs.

"We've got to be perfectly quiet," I said, taking hold of Beejum's hand. We started down. I held my breath, thinking the whole thing might collapse at any minute and trying to resist the urge to grab for the precarious banister, but nothing happened. The second step from the bottom, which had always squeaked and which I put my foot gingerly on, didn't even make a sound.

The door to the pantry was wedged open by one of the beams from the bedroom. I lifted Beejum over it and crawled over it myself. And looked up into Clare's pistol.

She had Verity Ann in her arms. The bracelet was back on the baby's arm, jammed above her elbow where it couldn't slip off. "Were the biots on the windowsill?" Clare said.

"No," I said.

"Give them to me or I'll kill you all right now." Verity Ann started to wail, as if she understood what Clare had said.

"I'll give them to my mother," I said, pulling out the dish so Clare could see that I had it and then putting it back in my pocket, "but not to you."

"Give me the biots," she said.

Beejum stepped behind me and grabbed my legs. I managed to grab his hand so I could control him.

"I told my mother that you tried to kill me. Before I left Denver Springs. I called her from the landport. If you kill me now, she'll know it wasn't an accident."

I watched her consider the possibility, knowing that if she had been with my mother after the explosion at Hydra Corp she'd know there hadn't been any call, but I was hoping against hope she had been busy setting up the alibi that would have her burned and in the hospital. Apparently she had been.

She put Verity Ann back down on the bed. "Pick her up," she said harshly, pushing Beejum out the door ahead of her. "We're going down to the harbor to meet your mother. You can give her the biots. And then she can give them to me."

from the *Christian Science Enquirer*

# Victoria Blacked Out

The only thing aglow in neutral Victoria tonight is Parliament—with indignation. In its attempt to preserve its peaceful charm and beauty, the one time capital of British Columbia had declared itself a neutral province and bowed out of the war between Quebec and the Commonwealth. But Quebeckers, long of the opinion that "if you aren't with us, you're against us," gave their answer to the neutrality question on this dark night by lasing Victoria itself.

With its fishing industry being one of the few reliable sources of protein left in the Northern Hemisphere, did Victorian Parliamentarians really believe they could remain neutral? They did. They continued to have trade relations with both the Commonwealth and the Quebeckers, and provided refuge for many draft dodgers from the Western States. But it seems the Quebeckers viewed every tin of salmon traded to the Commonwealth as that much less desperately needed food for Quebeckers. Tonight they put a stop to Victoria's trade with the Commonwealth by lasing the fishing fleet at their moorings. Will hundreds of beautiful trees and masses of colorful flowers at Butchart Gardens have to be sacrificed before Victorian Parliamentarians realize neutrality is a luxury the Quebeckers cannot permit?

(Winding paths and rolling lawns at Butchart Gardens, Screen 4.)

# CHAPTER EIGHTEEN

**B**ack in the gullwing I had to contend with both Beejum and Verity Ann on my lap. It was difficult to stay straight and level, but I don't think Clare cared.

"Standoffs aren't all they're cracked up to be, are they, Ariadne?" she said. "Someone always has a little more to lose, like you."

Yes, two little lives, aside from my own. But if I could hold on to them until we reached my mother, we might all be safe. Mother wouldn't let Clare kill me, or Beejum and Verity Ann either. Or would she? She'd let a lot of people back at Hydra Corp get killed.

"Good," Clare said when we reached the harbor. "It looks like they've abandoned the search around here. Land the gullwing over there," she said, pointing to an open space at the edge of the docks. I set it down.

"Carry both the children, one in each arm." Clare's hands were in her pockets, one pocket bulging with the pistol. "Come along, my dear. There are no reporters here this time to help you."

I perched one child on each hip and walked slowly out onto the dock. The boats here were small private craft, most of them not in use because of the wartime fuel shortages. They were all painted silver, though that was the only work that had been done on them in years.

"Third one down," Clare said.

It was an old British shearwater bobbing in the water right next to the dock.

"Step aboard, Ariadne. Your mother is waiting."

I watched the hydrofoil bob, stepped over the gap between the dock and deck, stumbled and recovered. Clare was right next to me. She untied the lines and tossed them back to the dock. The shearwater started slowly drifting. I looked around, hoping to see Joss or anyone. After all, he and his people were supposed to be looking for Chilkie, Beejum, and Verity Ann around here. There was no one in sight.

"Into the cabin," she said, half shoving me.

I put Beejum down to pull open the cabin door. It was pitch-dark inside.

I felt my way down a few steps, then turned to help Beejum. Clare was pushing him in behind her, slamming the door. She must have reached for the light at the same time.

"Clare!"

It was a warning shout. With my eyes nearly blinded by the light I barely recognized my mother diving out of a chair and onto the deck. Behind her a man raised a stunner, saw me, and hesitated. Clare shot right through her pocket, and the man pitched over, his face only visible for a second before he fell facedown. Verity Ann and Beejum both started to cry.

"Oh, no," I said, trying to stop myself because Clare didn't know I loved Joss and if she did she'd shoot him again. Because it was Joss lying there, blood coming from somewhere under his head.

"Oh, Clare, praise the *bon Dieu* you're all right," my mother said, picking herself up off the floor. She'd reached over to take Joss's stunner out of his unresisting hand. "There are two more of them hiding on the next boat. I would have gotten away if Liddell hadn't recognized me. He figured you'd be coming and decided to wait. They probably saw you come on board."

"Then we need to hurry," Clare said, stepping over Joss to the wheel. She hit the starter panel. "Watch the door in case they've slipped aboard. And shut that baby up."

Verity Ann was still screaming, clawing her way up over my shoulder like a frightened kitten, but I was only faintly aware of her. I knelt down beside Joss.

There was a puddle of blood around his head, but I couldn't see where it was coming from. I put out my hand gingerly to turn his head. His eyelid fluttered. I pulled back a little, not even breathing.

"Is he dead?" Beejum said.

Clare looked around.

"Yes," I said. "He's dead."

Clare turned back to the wheel and guided the shearwater along the dock pads, then we were far enough away for Clare to add some power, and then we were shooting away from the docks.

"Did you get the biots?" my mother asked.

"Ariadne has them. Take them from her. Now. I wouldn't trust her not to throw them overboard if she gets the chance."

Mother looked at me for the first time, her face tense and preoccupied. I wasn't sure she even saw me.

"Give me the biots, Ariadne."

"I don't have them," I said, standing up so Mother wouldn't have a good view of Joss. He was breathing shallowly, and I didn't want her to notice. "I left them at the house. I took them out of my pocket when I picked up Verity Ann. They're on the bed at Mrs. Ponsonby's."

"She's lying," Clare said. "I told you she'd never make a Quebecker. Give your mother the biots, Ariadne. I don't have time to play games."

"I can't," I said to Mother. "They're the only thing that's kept Clare from killing me. If I give them to you, she'll see to it that I fall overboard. She already tried to kill me on the ferry."

Mother's hand on the stunner never even wavered. "Clare has had to be rough with you, but it was necessary. We have to get to Quebec with the biots."

Beejum was squatting down, looking interestedly at Joss. "Rough?" I said, the panic I was feeling coming through in my voice. "She put a detonation bracelet on me. She tried to blow me up. She would have blown all of us up!" I shouted, snatching Beejum up by the arm and thrusting him toward Mother. "That's what she wanted to do! She told me she was going to kill us and tell you there'd been an accident! Tell her, Beejum!"

Beejum started to cry, a helpless, whimpering cry that made me ashamed, and Mother's eyes almost seemed to focus on me.

"I had to frighten them into getting the biots," Clare said without even turning away from the wheel. "She wouldn't help me any other way."

There was a sudden deafeningly sharp crack of sound, and the shearwater lurched. Clare grabbed for the wheel as it started to spin. "What was that?" she shouted, stabbing violently at the buttons on the console.

Mother darted for the steps, stepping over Joss as she went. Another crack of sound, closer, with a hiss I couldn't identify, and the shearwater slewed sideways again. Mother appeared at the top of the steps, clutching the railing with both hands, but still managing to hang on to the stunner. "Get up here, Clare!" Mother said.

Clare jabbed at more buttons. A green light appeared above the wheel, and the shearwater seemed to steady. "Hurry, Clare!" Mother said.

"Is it a navy cruiser?" Clare shouted back, sounding shaken for the first time. She started up the stairs.

"You can't," I said. "Verity Ann . . ."

She snatched the baby out of my arms and ran up the stairs out on deck.

"Beejum, go close the door," I whispered, and knelt down next to Joss, feeling in his pockets for anther weapon.

"It's not a navy cruiser," Joss whispered. His eyes opened.

"Joss, are you all right?"

"No, but help me up. Maybe I can . . ."

"No, you can't, Liddell," said Clare from the hatch. "Whatever it was, don't. Just put your hands behind your head and get up."

Joss got as far as his knees and reeled. Now I could see where the blood was coming from. There was a wound on the side of his head. It was bleeding too much for me to tell how deep it was.

"He's hurt," I said.

"Not as much as he'll be hurting if he doesn't do as I say. Now, move, Liddell!" Clare stepped down the few steps, pushed Verity Ann at me, and stepped away from Joss herself. Joss lurched to his feet. "Get down here, Medea!"

My mother came down the stairs cautiously, her stunner also pointed at Joss.

"We're going to have to get rid of Liddell and these screaming brats!" Clare said.

Mother actually looked surprised, but Beejum didn't have any doubt about what Clare intended. He dived past Mother and up the stairs. Mother grabbed his arm and stopped him, and he struggled against her, kicking and yelling. Verity Ann was still crying in her sopping-wet dipe on the floor. I scooped her up and held her tight. "Mother, she wants you to throw them into the Strait. She wants you to kill babies. For Quebec. She'll do anything for Quebec. She would have killed Dad and me back at Hydra Corp if she thought she could get away with it. Do you love Quebec that much, Mother? Do you love it enough to kill me and a six-year-old boy and a helpless little baby?"

"Shut up, Ariadne. Now you step over to the hatch," Clare said.

"Clare, you aren't . . ." Mother began nervously.

"I'm not going to kill anybody," Clare said, and my mother immediately looked relieved. She apparently was going to believe anything Clare told her. Beejum wasn't, though. He continued to struggle against her, and I watched closely, hoping he would make her drop her stunner.

Clare took one swift step toward them and grabbed Beejum by the arm. She twisted it up and behind him, and he went absolutely rigid, like a mouse with a snake. "You can see how ridiculous this situation is, can't you, Medea?" she said, sounding calm and almost kind, and I wondered if I was seeing the same technique she had used to talk my mother into stealing the memories, into planting the biots in Morning Glory Pool. "A laser raid, screaming children, and a boyfriend who may try heroics at any moment. The biots are the important thing."

"I know," Mother said, but she was looking at Beejum, not Clare.

"I'm not going to hurt them. We'll put them over the side and let a navy cruiser pick them up. That way, if they are following us, they'll be slowed down and we can get away to Banks Island."

"But what if no one's following us? The light raid . . ." Mother said, still uncertainly, and I grabbed what little chance I had.

"Oh, don't worry about the light raid, Mother," I said. "If it doesn't blow them up, this will." I unlatched Verity Ann's arm from its death grip around my neck and held out her arm. "You see that bracelet? It's a detonation device. She put it on Verity Ann so I'd go find her biots for her. It goes off if you get more than a certain distance away from her. It blows her up, Mother," I said. "An innocent little baby."

"Shut up, Ariadne," Clare said.

"She put a bracelet on me, too, Mother. On the ferry. She told you she'd let you take me to Quebec with you, but she's lying. She's going to kill them as soon they're in the water. And as soon as she's got the biots, she's going to kill me. And you."

Mother's hand came up with the stunner in it, steadier than ever. "Get the life jackets, Ariadne," she said.

"Over there," Clare said, gesturing. "In the bulkhead."

I opened a cabinet and found it jammed with life jackets, all of them too large for Verity Ann and Beejum. "They won't fit," I said.

"Make them work, or they'll have to do without," Clare said sweetly, shoving Beejum toward me.

I put the second smallest life jacket on him and then draped the smallest one over Verity Ann's head, wrapped the Velcro straps around her twice, and put a strap between her legs, working as slowly as I dared and wishing for a laser beam to hit the hydrofoil and knock that pistol out of Clare's hand, just for an instant. Verity Ann stopped crying again, started chewing on one of the plastic straps. She looked like a beach ball with arms, and she'd roll like one in the water.

"One for the boyfriend," Clare said. "Hurry!"

Reluctantly I went over to Joss. He was slumped against the bulkhead, his eyes closed. "Joss," I whispered as I slipped the life jacket over his head, but he didn't answer.

I looped a life jacket over my arm, then picked up Verity Ann. If Joss and the two little ones were going into the Strait, I was going with them.

We stepped out onto the deck, me with Verity Ann first, then Mother and her stunner, then Joss half crawling up the stairs, and finally Clare with her clip pistol. The laser raid was too far away to help me. Beams slashed through the water on the far side of the Strait, lighting up the dark, choppy water like lightning flashes. The wind was rising, carrying with it a smell of ozone and acrid smoke.

We would never stay afloat in that water, but that wasn't going to stop Clare. She motioned us all over to the railing. Joss fell against the railing and collapsed against the deck, his head and arms hanging over the water. One more lurch like that last one, and Clare wouldn't have to throw him overboard. He'd fall into the water all by himself.

Beejum clung to my legs. Verity Ann was sobbing, snuffling, her nose running so hard in the sudden wind that she could hardly breathe. I reached in my pocket for a handkerchief and felt the petri dish.

The biots. I didn't have a weapon, and I didn't have Joss or a navy cruiser to help me out of this, but I had the biots. Someone always has a little more to lose, Clare had said, and she was right. I had the children and Joss to lose, but she had the biots to lose, and they were all she cared about. I closed my hand over the cracked petri dish and tried to think what to do.

It was as if Clare had read my mind. "Give me the biots, Ariadne," she said, and took a step not toward me, but toward Joss, deliberately increasing the distance she was from Verity Ann and the deadly bracelet on her arm.

I clenched my fist around the dish, and it snapped along the crack, though I couldn't hear it because of the wind and Verity Ann's crying. And neither could Clare. The dish seemed to be in two parts, a small pie-shaped piece and the other which might pass for the whole dish. Clare bent down toward Joss.

"Get away from him," I said, and pulled the larger piece out of my pocket. I held it up where she could see it in the intermittent flashes of the laser beams. "Or I'll throw the biots overboard!"

Clare straightened and looked at me and then at the petri dish in my upraised hand, gauging distances. She would have no qualms at all about shooting all three of us if she could be sure the biots would fall onto the deck. I tightened my grip on them and stretched my arm out behind me, over the water.

"Drop the pistol over the side!" I shouted, and my knees were all of a sudden no longer under me.

"No!" my mother shouted, and I thought, Now that Clare's shot me she'll see what kind of sister she has! and made a futile grab to keep Verity Ann from falling with me.

A great hissing splash of hot water hit me in the face. Clare didn't shoot me, I thought, it's a laser strike! and, too late, tried not to drop the biots. Clare had them before the petri dish even hit the deck. She straightened in one easy motion, braced herself against the boat's sudden pitch that sent me sprawling again, and was standing above Joss with the biots in her hand, leveling the pistol at me, before the light from the strike had faded.

I looked around desperately, unable to see because of the dazzling afterimage. Joss was still lying by the rail, unaware even of the close laser strike. Beejum had been knocked over to the hatch. He was clinging to the stair rail. Verity Ann was lying flat on the deck where I had flung her, crying in short, breath-knocked-out-of-her gasps. I picked her up and got slowly to my feet.

Mother and Clare were standing together, the lasers outlining their hair in red. I couldn't see their faces, but it didn't matter. I knew how Clare would look, satisfied and maybe even smiling because she had the two things she wanted most, the biots and an excuse to kill me.

"Throw the baby in the water and get your life jacket on, Ariadne," Clare said.

"You don't have the biots," I said, having an insane feeling that this was going to go on forever, attempt after attempt, and that none of them was going to work. "I have them. I gave you an empty petri dish I found at Mrs. Ponsonby's."

Mother turned to stare at the petri dish. "It won't work," Clare said, but she turned to look, just for an instant, and in that instant, Joss's hand shot up and slashed at her ankles. Clare's knees buckled, and then she steadied herself and stepped down hard on his hand. "And that won't work either, Mr. Liddell." She kicked at his side with her foot. "Throw the baby in the water, Ariadne," she said, and lightning hit the bow.

The silver-painted wood flashed, and the whole boat was flooded in light, as if somebody had turned a holocam on. Clare staggered back against the rail, the force of her fall knocking the petri dish up in a beautiful arc. Clare stretched far out over the railing, both hands cupped under it to catch the petri dish. There was another flash, and the shearwater yawed sharply. The dish came into her hands, and she went over.

"Clare!" Mother screamed, and I heard her, and I saw her dive into the wake after Clare. Only I didn't really. Because Clare was in the water, being dragged away by the wake and the speed of the shearwater, and Verity Ann still had the bracelet on. I didn't even think. I just grabbed the bracelet off her arm and flung it as far out into the water as I could. I could see the water and the bracelet and my mother's dark curly hair. The bracelet sliced into the water so close to her head I could see it splash water on her face, and then all the water in the Strait went up in a fountain and I was on my knees again.

But Verity Ann was in my arms, and Joss was trying to get up, using the railing for support. "Get the wheel," he said. "We'll circle back and try to find them."

"Are they gone?" Beejum said, peering out the door of the hatch.

"Yes, they're gone," I said, my voice choking on a sob.

Somehow, even with Verity Ann under one arm, I got Joss to the stairs, Beejum trying to help. I left them there and went down into the cabin.

I sat down at the console and tried to turn the wheel, but it didn't respond.

"It's still on automatic pilot," Joss said. He was still sitting on the top step when I turned around to look, his hand pressed against his head. I punched the pilot control and tried again.

"Cut the throttle back," Joss said.

"Where . . ." But then I found the throttle and pulled it back all the way. The engine sputtered and died. "Oh, no," I said. I hit the starter panel again, pushed the throttle a little, and the engine caught.

"Good girl," Joss said, and fell face-forward down the steps.

Oh, no, Joss, not now. I peered at the screens, trying to see which direction the laser raid seemed to be moving, turned the hydrofoil in what I hoped was the opposite direction, punched in automatic pilot again, and went over to Joss.

His head was bleeding profusely, but not pulsing and squirting as it would if an artery were cut. I felt his chest; his heart was beating strongly, but he didn't stir.

"Ariadne, are *you* crying?" Beejum said, his wide brown eyes looking at me.

I wanted to say yes and just sit down and do it, but with Joss lying there unconscious again, Verity Ann screaming her head off, and Beejum looking more frightened now than he ever had, even when Clare had the pistol on him, I knew I couldn't. "No, honey. It's just seawater," I said. I rummaged in the life jacket cabinet again, found a halfway-clean rag, and tied it around Joss's forehead. I covered him up with a blanket, got Beejum to get a life jacket to put under his feet, and went back to the wheel. "Somewhere there ought to be a comm link," I said, more to reassure myself than to explain to Beejum what I was doing. It was the old kind with a switch on the mike. I pulled it off the hook, depressed the hook, and said, "Hello? Can anyone hear me? This is Hellene Ariadne and I'm lost somewhere in the Strait. Can anyone hear me?"

"You have to turn on that thing first," Beejum said, pointing to a button on the console.

"Right," I said, and pressed it. Again I asked for help, but no one answered.

"What if the bad lady comes back?" Beejum said.

"She won't," I said, not letting myself think about what that meant. The light from the laser flashes seemed to be getting closer instead of farther away and to be lasting longer. I handed the mike to Beejum. "Talk," I said. "Press that button and talk. I've got to steer."

"What should I say?"

"Anything . . . S.O.S." I took the shearwater off automatic pilot so I could turn it out of the path of the light raid. The engine promptly died.

"S.O.S.," Beejum said. "This is Beejum calling, S.O.S. There is a spy after us and we want a constable to please help us. S.O.S. . . . ."

A light blinded me, and I braced myself for the flash and the following shock, but neither one came.

"Ahoy, there! I say, is anyone there? Joss, my good man. Are you there?"

"Essex?" I said. "Essex!" I pulled the throttle back for the third time and the engine stopped again. I stared into the lights, finally made out the coast guard lettering on the side of a huge black cutter. I scooped up the baby, took Beejum's hand, and went up the stairs.

They had pulled the coast guard cutter alongside, thrown lines, and two men had already leaped aboard. One of them was Miles Essex. He was wearing a postal uniform, the other man was in Royal Navy fatigues.

"Joss is below," I said. "He's hurt."

Miles took only one solid glance at me, as if to check me over from head to foot. Then satisfied that I was all right, he leaped through the hatch. I handed the baby to the surprised man behind him and followed. Essex was on the comm link.

"Head wound," he was saying. "I want the medic over here right away." He hung up the mike. "You look fit enough," he said to me. He went back over to Joss, kneeling beside him.

"I'm all right."

"Can you tell me what happened?"

"Clare shot Joss," I said.

"I didn't think you'd done it," he said. He was checking Joss's pulse again.

"I did . . . in a way. He hesitated shooting her because I was in the way."

Essex shook his head. "Where are they? Clare and Medea?"

"In the water somewhere," I said. "They went over the side after the biots, and I . . ."

"Bloody hell!" He got up and went back to the comm link. "Our two duckies are in the water somewhere." He snapped off the mike. "How long ago?" he asked me.

"I don't know. Maybe a few minutes ago. I threw a detonator in after them."

He snapped on the mike again. "Get the searchlights going and start retracing the minute the medic gets over here. They may have been hit with a detonator. Check for bodies."

"Roger, sir. What about Captain Liddell?"

"I'll take him back to Victoria on this craft."

Just then a white-clad medic stepped through the hatch. She knelt at Joss's side, and immediately hooked up an IV pack, starting the feed's motor . "He's lost a lot of blood," she said, looking up at Essex. "I've got generic with me, but I'd like to get him back to shore as soon as possible." She pulled the bandage back slightly, barely peeked at it, then turned back to her bag.

"Is it bad?" I said.

"He'll get over it," she said, efficiently pulling out a blood pack and fastening it onto his arm. "The projectile just grazed him." She finished pulling off my makeshift bandage, but Joss turned uneasily and half-opened his eyes. She stopped, rummaged in her bag again, and peeled off a plasmostat patch. She stuck it on his neck, and then started on the bandage again.

Miles Essex hit the starter panel, and the engine turned over . . . and over and over. I got up and looked.

"It started a couple of times for me," I said.

"Hope you haven't used up all your luck," he said. "Give it a try."

I tried. The engine caught. Miles Essex smiled at me.

"Miles?"

Miles Essex turned around. "Joss! Nice of you to join us, old chap."

"If you thought I'd leave her alone with you again, you've slipped a cog," Joss said. He was holding the plasmostat patch in his hand.

I went over and sat down next to him. The medic glared at him and went on applying antiseptic to his wound. Joss winced.

"Ariadne," Joss said. "Did Clare get the biots?"

"Yes," I said, "she had them in her hands when she went overboard. But she doesn't have all of them." I reached into my pocket and pulled out the remaining wedge of the petri dish.

"Good girl," Essex said.

The petri dish had gotten wet. I took it over to the light and looked at the greenish residue. "These are the ones I gave to Chilkie to put over her evac tattoo. She doesn't have the biots after all." I turned to Beejum, who was sitting on the knee of the uniformed navy man. "What happened to the rest of my garden?" I asked him.

"You won't be mad if I tell you?"

"I won't be mad."

"They're in the toilet. They fell in and I couldn't get them out."

"All of them? There were three or four petri dishes full of hydra stuff."

"All of them."

"You mean this was all for nothing?" Miles Essex said. He sounded vexed. "There were no mature biots after all?"

"There are mature ones," I said, "and we can recover them, too.

Mrs. Ponsonby's pipes blew up from the ones she put down the sink. I bet the septic tank is getting ready to do the same thing." I laughed. "I can't think of a better place to incubate them, except maybe in the Morning Glory Pool."

"You're not mad at me?" Beejum asked.

"No, honey, I'm not mad."

"I am," Essex said, and I frowned at him. "Well, who do you think he's going to send to fetch them up? You?" Essex shook his head. "I think he gets a sadistic pleasure in sending me on demeaning assignments."

"Miles?" Joss said.

"Sir?"

"See to it," Joss said, and he closed his eyes again.

# VICTORIA'S IN!

Victoria has declared war on Quebec. Mayor Begbie made the momentous announcement this morning.

"We have just declared war on Quebec," Mayor Begbie said, speaking from his office in the new Parliament building. "We have notified our allies, the Commonwealth and the Western States, and have received a promise of immediate GTA support."

Loud cheering greeted the announcement, which has been expected since the raids on Duncan and the Inner Harbor. Mayor Begbie called an emergency session of the Privy Council yesterday following the lasing of Malahat. Debate was heated, with several council members arguing for Victoria's continued neutrality.

At 7:05 P.M., sirens signaled the beginning of another raid. The Privy Council adjourned to the shelter located in the basement of the new Parliament building, where the meeting was continued. Although the declaration of war was not issued until this morning, sources inside the Privy Council revealed that the actual vote to declare war was taken last night at 7:13. The vote was unanimous.

# CHAPTER NINETEEN

Getting the boat into shore seemed to take forever. Miles went at a crawl, the engine set so low it didn't make any noise at all, and I knew he was listening for my mother and Clare.

I listened, too, holding on to Joss's hand and peering into the darkness. The light raid was almost over, the batellite moving out of effective range so that most of the strikes were out over open water. When they hit, they lit up the black, choppy waves for a moment, and I strained to see a dark head bobbing in the water. My hand tightened on Joss's, but he didn't respond.

I looked at him. At some point the medic had managed to get another patch on, this one larger than the other, and he was sleeping deeply, his breathing even and untroubled. He looked terribly pale, though, and there was still blood seeping through the bandage. The medic had taken Verity Ann and Beejum below, and I half-stood to go and get her when she emerged from the cabin with the baby in her arms. Beejum was at her heels, looking tired but no longer quite so frightened.

"Is Joss all right?" I said. "He looks so pale."

"He's lost a lot of blood," she said, handing Verity Ann to me and moving to check the IV pack, "but he's going to be fine. He just needs to rest. I'm sorry about the makeshift diaper. It's the best I could do."

I had hardly been aware I had Verity Ann in my arms. Now I saw that the medic had cleaned her up and put her in a square of woollen blanket for a diaper, wrapped the rest of the blanket around her, and pinned it with a large Velcro pin. She had wiped away the tearstains on her face, too, but Verity Ann was busy making new ones. She still clutched the filthy, oil-stained rag she had had since Skids's shack.

"What about Chilkie and Skids?" I called to Essex. "Clare tied them up and left them in Skids's shack."

"We found them," Essex said. "How did you think we found you? They're out in one of the other boats, helping with the search."

"Search?" I said blankly. "For the biots, you mean?"

"For the bodies, I bet," Beejum said. He went over and sat down by Essex. "Can I help look for the bodies, too?"

I held Verity Ann tightly against me. "You don't know for sure they're dead."

"No," he said, "we don't know for sure. They may still be alive, and if they are, we'll find them. We've got two boats out looking for them now, and as soon as we get Joss back into shore, we'll send this one out, too."

"Good," I said, but I knew it wouldn't do any good. I went back over to Joss and sat down.

"Raid's over," Essex said, and kicked the shearwater up to full speed. We took off rapidly for shore. In the far distance, I could hear the steady wail of the all-clear. Verity Ann started to wail, too, as if she knew it was safe to cry again, that no one would shoot her if she did. I held her against my shoulder, patting her to quiet her sobs. My mother was dead, and I had killed her.

Clare had dived in, and I had thought, "The bracelet!" and flung it into the water. And then the flash from the laser raid, lighting up my mother's dark, curly hair as she struggled through the water screaming, "Clare!" and the bracelet slicing into the water so close the splash from it hit her hair, and then the explosion.

Verity Ann was choking herself, sobbing and trying to get her whole hand in her mouth at the same time. I pulled her little hand out. There was a bandage on it that the medic must have applied. I must have scraped her hand when I tried to pull the bracelet off. I peeled the Velcro edges apart to look at it, and Verity Ann screamed and tried to pull her hand away. Poor baby! I had completely taken the skin on her knuckles off. I refastened the bandage, and she promptly jammed her fist back in her mouth.

I hadn't even realized I'd hurt Verity Ann. All I had been able to think about right then was that Clare had gone into the water and I had to get rid of the bracelet. It hadn't even been a rational thought. It was an instinct. The bandage on Verity Ann's hand was testimony to that. I didn't even remember getting the bracelet off of her.

It wasn't that I didn't love Mother, or that I could ever, even to save the children, have done anything to hurt her, but in that instant, Clare going over the side and the baby in my arms, my mother hadn't even existed. Somehow that thought was comforting now. Maybe Mother's thoughts had been so fixed on her loyalty to her sister and to Quebec that I hadn't existed for her either, and what she had done to Dad and me wasn't intentional but was just the equivalent of my hurting Verity Ann.

Essex punched a lot of buttons in rapid succession and then left the wheel and came back to look at Joss. "How's he doing?" he asked the medic.

"Okay, but I'd like to get him on genetically matched blood as soon as possible. I've given him two generic packs."

"Can he walk?" he said.

"No," the medic said after a minute, as if she had seriously considered the possibility.

"That's what I was afraid of," Essex said, shaking his head. "If I send for an ambulance, the press will find out about it. Oh, well, it can't be helped."

He went back to the wheel and pushed some more buttons, with Beejum avidly watching every move he made, and the boat picked up speed. The blackout made it impossible to gauge how close we were to shore, but suddenly a few feet ahead I saw a cluster of flashlights.

Essex had seen it, too. He abruptly cut the engine and began to maneuver us in toward the lights. The medic unhooked the IV pack from its support and taped it to Joss's shoulder. She shut her medical bag and stood up. Essex put on our hooded running lights and guided the boat into the slip. The dock was covered with people. A holocam light came on right in our faces.

"Put that light out," Essex shouted, "or I'll hit you with a blackout violation. And give me a hand. We've got an injured man on board."

While the reporter handed the cam to the man next to him, Essex bent down to Beejum and whispered, "Do you want to be a spy? Then you can't say a word to those people. No matter what they say to you." He glanced at me. "We'll come up with some kind of cover story tomorrow, but for tonight, it's 'no comment.'" He turned back to Beejum. "You got that, Beejum?"

Beejum nodded breathlessly. Essex took off the postman's cap he'd been wearing and put it on Beejum. The reporter jumped lightly onto the deck, followed by two ambulance attendants with a stretcher. I hefted Verity Ann into a more secure position in my arms and gripped Beejum's hand. "Don't let go of me, no matter what. Okay, Beejum?" He looked up at me seriously. "No comment," he said.

The reporter and Essex lifted Joss onto the stretcher and handed him up to the attendants on the dock. The crowd parted for them to get through and then closed again before I even set foot on the dock.

"What happened, Ariadne?"

"Was the boat hit in the light raid? How bad is he?"

I pushed determinedly through them, clutching Beejum's hand so hard I was probably taking the skin off his knuckles, too. He was holding his hat down tightly with his other hand. Verity Ann was bellowing, which was good because it meant I couldn't hear half their questions.

They had Joss in the ambulance and already hooked up to a matched blood pack by the time the children and I made it to the doors. Miles Essex, repeating, "No comment," over and over, herded us in and got the doors shut.

Verity Ann cried all the way to the Empress and up to the prince's suite. She stopped cold at the sight of the mirrored room with its garish purple bed and draperies, and I took advantage of the momentary silence to hand her to the Yard agent who'd opened the door for us, tell Beejum to wait for me, and follow Miles into the inner room.

It was filled with terminals and screens, and people I assumed were agents of the Yard. Miles Essex motioned me past them toward a farther door. "He's in there," he said, and stopped to look at one of the screens. I caught a glimpse of a picture of cruisers and water taken by infrared sensors.

"Have they found anything yet?" Essex said to the woman in front of the screen, and she shook her head.

Joss was in a small room that had been hastily rearranged to accommodate a body-scan bed and two monitors. He was getting blood and an IV from a regulated feed, though he still looked about the color of the sheets, and he had two large medication patches on his neck.

The doctor and the medic both assured me that he was fine and they would let me know if there was any change. I went back out into the computer room. The image of the cruiser on the computer screen had been replaced by one of the ferry at the dock with reporters everywhere.

"Have they found something?" I said.

"No," Miles said, taking me by the arm and leading me back into the mirrored bedroom. Verity Ann was asleep in the agent's arms, and Beejum was leaning against his legs, his eyes only half open. "We've got rooms for each of you down on sixth. Jenkins here will take you down."

"No!" Beejum let out a yelp that woke up Verity Ann. She began to whimper. "I want to stay with Ari," Beejum wailed.

"Shh," Miles said. "Now, is that how an agent of the Yard would act? No, an agent will follow orders and go where he's told," he said sternly, which would have worked an hour ago, but now Beejum only repeated, clinging to my hand with such force I thought he was going to break it, "I want to stay with Ari."

"It's all right," I said quietly. "The children can stay with me. They've been through a lot tonight even for agents of the Yard. If you could just have them send up a collapsible crib for the baby."

"Righto," Miles said, and disappeared back into the computer room.

Jenkins took us down to sixth and let us into the room. "This one's the largest, I think," he said. He handed me a fixed doorkeep with the room number on it. "I'll just check the other two rooms and see if they've left a crib." He went back out into the hall.

I put Verity Ann down on the bed and pulled the bedspread over her. She was instantly asleep. I looked around the room. This looked more like what I had expected a hotel room at the Empress to look like than the prince's rococo boudoir. It had high plastered ceilings and a plush but subdued-looking carpet. The furniture was obviously twentieth-century antique, a mattressed bed, two comfortable chairs and a little table in one corner that gave it a sitting room effect, a large tiled bathroom with an inviting-looking tub, even though I knew they were probably on water rationing. There was a terminal on the wall by the chairs and a holo platform above the bed.

The agent came back in. "I've found these," he said, carrying a neat pile of clothes and dipes and an old duffel bag that had one broken strap and looked like it had been through a light raid or two.

"My stuff!" Beejum said, and made a dive for it.

The agent's wrist terminal began beeping. He glanced at it, said hastily, "I'll have the front desk send a crib up," and went out before I could ask him what they'd found. But it didn't really matter. I knew what they were going to find. I just hoped I'd managed to kill Clare with her murderous bracelet, too. I suddenly felt so tired I could hardly stand.

"Boy, this is great!" Beejum said. He had dumped his bag upside down on the floor and was looking through the mess. It was mostly odds and ends I recognized from Mrs. Ponsonby's: a table knife, a flashlight, and a mangled box of coloring styluses. The remains of an ancient carob bar were mixed in with the toys and wadded-up clothes, and there were carob smears all over the none-too-clean pajamas.

I looked through the pile of clothes the agent had brought us. They were mostly baby clothes, though there was a large soft shirt I could use as a nightgown and some underwear. There was nothing that would fit Beejum. I looked back at him, thinking we'd have to make do with the carob-stained pajamas. He was sound asleep sitting up, his head lopped forward on his open duffel bag.

I picked him up and put him on the bed, pulled off his shoes and socks, and worked the blankets and bedspread out from under him. He stirred a little when I put covers over him, then stuck his thumb in his mouth and went back to sleep.

I pushed the bed over against the wall so he wouldn't fall off and looked at Verity Ann. The agent had apparently forgotten the collapsible crib. I could call Housekeeping, but I wasn't sure I could stay awake till they came with it. I also couldn't have Verity Ann share a bed with us with only a scrap of gray wool for a diaper. I knelt on the bed and changed her into a real dipe and a too-big nightgown, hoping she wouldn't wake up. I needn't have worried.

I pulled my clothes off, put on the shirt, and lay down next to her, envying her her baby's ability to fall asleep instantly no matter what the circumstances, and was instantly asleep myself.

## "I KNEW HER WHEN!" EVAC MOTHER WAS MUM TO ARIADNE

"Ariadne was like a daughter to me," Victoria resident Ella Ponsonby said in an exclusive interview with the *Hourly Province*. "I remember the first time I ever saw her. Poor, frightened little thing. I already had more evacuated children than I knew what to do with, but I took her in anyway, out of the goodness of my heart."

Mrs. Ponsonby played mother to war heroine Hellene Ariadne and five other children for over a year in her now-destroyed Victoria home. "I volunteered to help out with the kiddies the day the war started. I thought it was my patriotic duty to our allies, the Western States."

She has paid a heavy price for that patriotism. Last week her house suffered an explosion that Mrs. Ponsonby is convinced was an act of sabotage. "Those Quebeckers wanted to get back at me for helping the Western States," she said.

When asked what her famous charge was like, Mrs. Ponsonby commented, "A sweet girl, but flighty. When she run off that way without a by-your-leave, I was worried sick. Of course I never for a moment dreamed she was involved in all this espionage stuff, and now here's her mother killed and her an orphan. Ah, well, at least she still has me."

# CHAPTER TWENTY

**B**abies and six-year-olds pop awake at six in the morning, bright-eyed and impossibly cheerful, too, in spite of the circumstances. I ordered up a big breakfast and then tried to get through to the prince's suite on the room terminal. While I was still trying, Essex knocked.

He was still wearing the clothes he'd had on in the boat, and he looked exhausted. "I asked the kitchen to notify me as soon as you'd arisen. I have something to tell you."

"Is Joss all right?" I said. I had set Verity Ann and Beejum to drawing on the hotel stationery with Beejum's coloring styluses, but both of them looked up when I said that, and Verity Ann looked as if she were about to cry.

"Joss is fine. The doctor's had to plaster him with sedative patches to keep him from getting up." He stopped talking and made a circuit of the room twice before saying anything else. "I wish he weren't so sedated, actually. I rather need his help on this." He stopped, looked unhappily at the children as if he wished he could ask them to leave the room, and then said, "We've found your mother's body."

I had known it all along, of course, but that didn't make it any easier to hear. I sat down on the bed. "What killed her?" I said, even though I knew that, too.

"She appears to have drowned," he said, and looked at me kindly as if to say, "So you see, you didn't kill her after all," but of course it only meant that the blast from the bracelet had knocked her uncon-scious. In the water.

"You didn't find Clare's body?"

"We found Clare," he said slowly. "She was still in the water, quite close to where they went over, actually. We found her an hour before dawn."

"She's still alive," I said, and wished again that I'd gotten her with the bracelet. Instead of my mother.

"No," he said, and there was no emotion in his tone at all. "It was quite clear that she had not been able to make contact with her people to give them any information about the biots."

Someone tapped on the door, but neither of us made a move to answer it. Essex's handsome face wasn't showing any emotion at all, and I saw for the first time what he would look like when he was king. "It was essential that we keep the biots secret," he said.

"Room service," a voice called through the door, followed by more knocking. I went and let the waiter in, watched him spread a tablecloth on the little table and take the stainless-steel covers off the eggs and oatmeal, trying to take in the fact that they had killed her, executed her as a spy out there in the boat, an hour before dawn. The waiter set a pot of camomile on the table and left. I shut the door behind him.

"She had not been able to contact other agents to tell them the biots were in Victoria," he said. "We made sure of that before we executed her. We intend to leak the news that she got away and is hiding out. We've got to have as much time as possible to get the biots out of Victoria and into production before Quebec realizes their agent is not in possession of the biots."

While he was talking, I had been mechanically getting Beejum settled at the table. I poured him some cocoa and dished him up scrambled eggs and toast. I put Verity Ann in a chair, tied a napkin around her neck and one around her middle, and started spooning oatmeal into her.

"Did you have to execute my mother, too?" I said.

"No, Ariadne," he said gently. "I told you, she drowned. Her body washed up on shore before we could find it with the sub-waterline detectors."

This was somehow the bad news he had been trying to find a way to tell me, though what had happened to my mother's body didn't seem to be having any effect on me, at least right now. I wondered how they had executed Clare, and it occurred to me that no matter what method they had used, she deserved it.

He was waiting for me to respond to this news, and I didn't have any idea what he wanted me to say. "On shore? In Victoria?" I said vaguely.

He nodded grimly. "The body was spotted by the passengers of the early ferry, including a reporter for the *Post-Gazette*."

Now I understood. The press had seen my mother's body, and now what little hope we had had for keeping the biots secret had disappeared. "What are you going to do?" I said.

"I don't know. We'd come up with a cover story that accounted for us being out in the boat and Joss getting injured. You were trying to find the children, who'd run away from the evac center."

"You didn't tell the press that?"

"No, thank God. We were going to release it this morning. Now we've had to come up with another one. It wasn't easy to devise a plausible story."

"No," I said, thinking of Clare defecting, the explosion at Hydra Corp, my supposed romantic rendezvous with the prince, and now this, Joss injured and my mother dead and the press determined to find out what was really going on. I wasn't sure any story but the truth would satisfy them.

"The thing is," he said, and I could tell by his face that this was the bad news he'd been working his way around to this whole time, "we need your cooperation on the cover story."

I took a sip of Beejum's cocoa to fortify myself and wished it were madderblend.

"We've got to have a story that will fool not only the press but the Quebeckers, and that means your mother's got to be a hero."

"A hero?" I said shakily, and took another swallow of the cocoa. Beejum yelped, and I poured him another cup.

"If you're alive and your mother's dead and Clare's missing, what's the obvious conclusion the Quebeckers are going to draw?"

"That Clare's dead, too, and we've got the biots," I said, and then thought of something else. "They're going to know you and Joss are Scotland Yard."

"Or at least spies." He shrugged that aside. "It can't be helped. No matter what story we come up with, they're still going to know that. The only thing we can hope for is that Quebec will believe Clare got away with the biots. Clare tried to get the biots from Medea, but she refused to cooperate, so Clare kidnaped you, hoping to use you as bait. Medea appeared to go along with the plan, but at the last minute made a heroic attempt to rescue you. She succeeded in getting you safely onto a boat and sent you for help, but by the time you returned with us, it was too late."

I sipped at the lukewarm cocoa, trying to gauge how the press might take the story. They had all believed the story about Clare's escape and my mother suffering silently in jail, and they might be even more willing to believe she was a hero now that she was dead, but the story left too many things out.

For starters, why had I left my mother to be killed? Going for help was hardly a good enough answer, although I supposed we could claim that I had to protect the children, but what were they doing on the boat? And what about my well-publicized rendezvous with the prince? If he was really a Scotland Yard agent, then why had I come to Victoria in the first place? Just to be convenient kidnap material? The story seemed full of pitfalls which would become all too apparent as soon as one of us started talking to the press, and by then it would be too late.

"Are you sure . . ." I started to say, but Essex had already stood up and was leaving.

"The computers are completing the story now," he said. "I would imagine it will involve your accompanying your mother's body back to Hydra Corp. Please don't say anything to the press until you've checked with our office."

He turned at the door, looking completely done in. "We've notified your father, of course. We didn't want him to read of your mother's death in the tabloids, but he'll want to hear from you." He pointed at the wall terminal. "We've hooked up a direct comm line to your computer at Hydra Corp. Just type in MINERVA for access."

"All right," I said, wishing there were something I could say to make him feel better. To make me feel better. To make Joss feel better when he woke up and found out his cover had been destroyed. "Look, Min is really a smart computer. Maybe she can come up with a story that wouldn't involve you and Joss."

"You are welcome to try, of course," he said without enthusiasm, and took his leave, promising to let me know as soon as Joss woke up.

I finished feeding the kids breakfast and gave Verity Ann a quick bath to get the oatmeal off. I stuck them on the bed with the holo platform turned to cartoons, called Min on the comm link, and asked her if the line was secure.

"I've added my own safeties to the Yard's comm link hardening," Min said. "In-transit Navajo scramble. What's so important?"

I obviously didn't have to ask whether she had her intuitives engaged. "We've got a terrible problem, Min," I said, and told her what had happened, taking my time and not leaving anything out because I knew the details were what were likely to trip us up. What I didn't remember to tell her, she asked, and as the conversation went on I felt better and better, as if I were talking to a sympathetic friend instead of a computer.

When I had finished telling her the cover story Essex had come up with, she said, "Beejum could make up a better story than that."

"I know," I said. "And so can you, but you need to do it before the Yard computer releases it to the press. You can hook into the Yard computer directly, can't you?"

"I can hook into any computer directly, " Min said. "Your father wants to talk to you."

I had been dreading this. "Just a minute," I said, and went and got Verity Ann. I set her on my lap in front of the screen. She stared as raptly at it as she had at the cartoons. "Put him on," I said.

"I've put a page on him," Min said, which meant *she* had decided he wanted to talk to me, but I didn't rebuke her. I did need to talk to him.

Dad came on, a ragged voice asking if I was all right, and I found myself close to tears. "Mother's dead," I said.

"I know," he said. "The prince called me this morning." I wished I could see his face. He sounded so frail and worn out. "When I asked him how she died, he said she was trying to save your life. Is that true, Ariadne?"

Because I couldn't see him, the image that kept coming to mind was of him sitting in his chair that first afternoon I got to Hydra Corp, with the setting sun on his face as he stared bleakly at me and told me to go away. "No, Dad," I said sadly. "She was trying to save Clare."

There was a pause, and then he said, "I knew that. I knew it that first day, when the house got lased, but I just refused to see it. I almost got you killed before I saw it, Ariadne."

"I'm coming home, Dad," I said feeling like Essex handing out the bad news one item at a time. "I'm bringing Mother's body home. We have to pretend she was a hero to protect the biots." He didn't say anything, and after a minute I said, "I know it's hard, Dad."

"It isn't, you know, " he said, and there was an echo of my old father in his voice. "Now that she's gone, it's all so easy. I know exactly what to do. I've resigned as head of Security. I've asked for work rebuilding Hydra Corp. Not war work, nothing requiring a security clearance, just construction."

"You don't have to do that, Dad," I said, and it struck me for the first time that Essex's insistence on the impossible cover story might have been partly to protect us, so we wouldn't have to leave Hydra Corp, the suspect husband and daughter of a traitor.

"I do have to," he said, sounding more than ever like his old self. "I can't be trusted, Ari. You can. For some reason, in spite of your parents, you never seem to lose sight of the essentials. I did. I completely lost sight of everything except keeping your mother. I lost sight of everything else. Can you understand that, Ariadne?"

I traced the line of the bandage on Verity Ann's hand, the bandage that was there because I had lost sight of everything but the necessity of getting that bracelet off. "Yes, Dad," I said.

We talked a little while longer, making arrangements for me to come home with the body, and then Min came back on the line. "What about the children?" she said without preamble.

"I'm bringing them back to Hydra Corp with me," I said. "I don't want them to have to put up with any more Mrs. Ponsonbys."

"Do you want to bring Joss Liddell back to Hydra Corp with you, too?"

I wish I could, I thought, but that was clearly impossible, at least until the war was over. Even Min couldn't come up with a story that would let him go with me when I took my mother's body back to Hydra Corp. The fewer connections between us, the less suspicious it would be. Which meant I might never see him again. "The important thing is that no one find out he and Miles Essex are agents of Scotland Yard so they can go on being agents," I said, and wished I could sound more convincing.

As soon as Min broke the connection, I called up to the prince's suite and was told that Joss's condition was "good" but that he was still sleeping. I wanted to see for myself, but Beejum was still in his pajamas, and Verity Ann looked like she might take her morning nap any minute.

If Chilkie had come back I might be able to leave the children for a minute and run up to see him. But she wasn't there. The Yard agent of the night before told me she was out at Mrs. Ponsonby's house, helping locate the septic tank, and offered to watch the children for me, but Beejum said loudly, "I want to go with you," which made Verity Ann start to whimper all over again, so I told him no.

I called Housekeeping and demanded a whole list of things, starting with the portable crib that had never arrived and including clothes for all of us and toys for the children.

It was noon before the clothes arrived. By then we had taken a walk down the hall and back and played two games of old maid with cards I made out of the hotel's comm link blanks. Min had called back to ask me several more questions about what the press did and didn't know, which made me feel at least mildly useful, and the Yard agent had dropped by to ask me if there was anything he could get us.

I told him we were all getting shelter fever and asked if we were confined to the sixth floor. He said no, but to stay in the hotel, so when the clothes finally arrived—a passable set of jams for Beejum and a subdued navy skirt and jacket for me—I announced that we were going out to lunch.

And to see Joss, though I didn't tell the children that since Verity Ann was already cranky with hunger. I simply took them up to the prince's suite, dumped them on the agent who had watched them the night before, and went in. Joss looked about the same, though his color was a little better and some of the hookups had been removed.

"He's doing very well. He woke up earlier," the medic said. She saw me glance at the patches on his neck. "When he's awake, he insists on getting up."

"How long will he be out?" I asked.

"The doctor wants him in bed till tomorrow," she said, and shrugged, and I assumed that meant he would be sedated until then. I wouldn't even get to talk to him before I had to leave.

I took his limp hand. "Joss," I said, "they want me to go back to Hydra Corp with my mother's body, and I don't know when I'll get to see you again."

"You give that back!" Beejum yowled from the next room, followed by an ungodly shriek that could only be Verity Ann.

"I love you," I said. I let go of his hand and stood up. "Goodbye, Joss," I said softly, and kissed him on the forehead.

"It's mine!" Beejum howled. I went hastily back out to the royal bedroom, where the agent and Beejum were trying to pry Essex's postman's cap out of Verity Ann's iron grip.

"Are you hungry, Verity Ann?" I said brightly. "Do you want some lunch?"

She immediately held out her arms to me. Beejum dived for the cap and mashed it onto his head. "It's my spying hat," he said defensively. "She's not a spy."

"They're both hungry," I apologized to the agent, and swept them both out of the suite and down the hall before he could order me not to bring them back. "We'll go have a nice lunch in a restaurant," I said gaily, getting them into the elevator. "It's called the Garden Cafe, and they have wonderful things to eat."

"What?" Beejum demanded.

The elevator opened onto the lobby. "We'll have to read the menu to find out. All kinds of things."

"Is that it?" Beejum said, letting go of my hand to point in the direction of the Bengal Bar.

"No," I said. "It's over . . ." and was suddenly swamped by reporters.

"Is it really your mother that was killed, Ariadne?"

"What was she doing in Victoria?"

"Is it true she was a spy on her way to Quebec?"

"I . . . please . . ." I said, trying to get to Beejum. When the agent had said not to leave the hotel, I had assumed it was off limits to reporters. I should have known better.

Beejum was being led toward the Bengal Bar by two reporters who were bending over him with mikes. "Where'd you get that great hat?" one of them was saying.

Oh, no, there was no telling what he might say. The house, the biots, Clare. "Beejum!" I shouted, but he didn't even look up.

The rest of the reporters did, though, and seemed to realize all at the same time that Beejum was more likely to tell them something than I was. They surrounded him so that there was no way I could get to him, holocams ready, mikes stuck in his face, and the reporter who had asked him about his cap said clearly, "What happened last night?"

Beejum adjusted his hat to a jaunty, spylike angle and folded his arms across his chest. "No comment," he said.

The tabloiders roared. I decided not to press my luck. I pushed forward, got a firm grip on Beejum's hand, and said, "My mother has just died. I'll be glad to have a press conference this afternoon, but right now I'd like to take the children to lunch. They've been through a lot," I said, and suddenly found my voice breaking. "We've all been through a lot."

I would never have believed it, but the entire assemblage stood back silently and let us walk across the lobby and into the cafe. It was only when we were seated at a table for four, with Verity Ann put into a high chair, and handed our menus, that I realized tears were streaming down my face.

"How'd I do, Ari?" Beejum said anxiously.

"You did great, honey," I said, wiping away the tears with my napkin. "Just great."

He looked relieved. "The prince said to say, 'No comment,' and I did."

"You certainly did," I said, "and I intend to tell the prince that when I see him." I opened my menu. "We've got to have something special to celebrate. They have fish and chips and . . ." The menu was even sparser than when I had been here before. With Clare. I pushed that thought out of my mind. "How does fish and chips sound?"

I ordered fish and chips for Beejum, the day's special for me, and a poached egg and toast for Verity Ann, and asked if she could have some crackers to chew on while we waited. "We'll have dessert," I told Beejum brightly, "in honor of your being such a good spy. They bring the desserts to your table on a cart here, and you can pick out your own. They have raspberry torte and . . ."

Raspberry torte. I had ordered that the day I had lunch with Clare. The day I had been convinced my father was dead and had taken off for home. And he hadn't been dead, but things had been even worse than I'd imagined. I remembered standing in the lased-out rubble of our house and Joss finding me and . . .

"Is this seat taken?" Joss said, brushing cracker crumbs off the empty chair. His head was still bandaged, but he was smiling at me.

"Are you supposed to be up?" I said, trying to ignore the joy that washed over me at seeing him. I bent toward him and whispered, "And down here? There are reporters everywhere."

"I know," he said unconcernedly. "They caught me in the lobby or I would have been here in time to order."

The waiter reappeared with our orders. "Fish and chips, eh, mate?" Joss said to Beejum. "I'll have an order of that. And some camomile. I'm still a bit woozy." He put his hand to his head.

"Are you all right?" I said.

"I'm fine." He mashed up Verity Ann's poached egg. "That damned medic had me on enough sedatives to bring down a batellite. I think she intended me to sleep a year, and I would have, too, only I heard an angel say, 'I love you, Joss,' and then this appalling caterwauling." He pointed at Beejum with his fork.

"She took my spy hat," Beejum said defiantly. "I have to have it if I'm going to be a spy."

"Quite right, old man, and I'm grateful to you for awakening me. I managed to come to enough to get the patches off, and here I am." He spooned poached egg into Verity Ann's mouth.

I looked down at the specialty of the day. It was canned salmon on a lettuce leaf, the same thing I had had the day I had lunch with Clare, the day I had thought my father was dead. And now my mother really was dead.

Joss put his hand over mine. "I know it's rough, Ari. I'm sorry I haven't been around."

"I killed her," I said. "I threw the bracelet in the water."

"Did you know the original plan was for Clare to kidnap you here in Victoria? Medea and Clare were going to pull their escaping scientist number, get the biots, and then the three of you were going to Quebec. And your father was going to be set up as the traitor for the sabotage and the missing memory. Only you turned up and stopped them."

"Wow!" Beejum said with a mouthful of fried potatoes. "I didn't know you were a spy, too, Ari."

"She was a great spy. She saved your life. And Verity Ann's. And I'm not talking just about the bracelet. After Clare'd kidnapped you, she intended to blow up Mrs. Ponsonby's house and everybody in it to cover up your disappearance. She told Miles and the Victoria government that last night. As a result, Victoria's finally decided to come into the war on our side." He patted my hand. "I know this doesn't make it any easier right now, but maybe later on, when it doesn't hurt so much, it will."

The waiter came with Joss's fish and chips and a pot of camomile. Joss asked for the pastry cart, poured me a cup of tea, and made me drink it. "We've got a good deal to do this afternoon," he said as the waiter wheeled the pastry cart over. "Min's come up with a devastatingly good cover story, and all of you must help me implement it."

"Can I have some camomile, too?" Beejum said.

"No, what you need is a piece of raspberry torte." He had the waiter cut a huge piece for Beejum and a little one for Verity Ann, and I didn't protest even though I knew she would be solid raspberries from head to foot. Joss had appeared and suddenly the painful memories weren't half as painful. The next time I ate at the Garden Cafe I wouldn't remember Clare. I would remember this, Beejum holding on to his hat with one hand and shoveling cake in with the other, Verity Ann's face a red smear, and Joss somehow managing never to take his hand off mine.

"Ready?" he said, taking an ineffective swipe at the baby's face and lifting her out of her high chair. "You'd best get packed. We're leaving for Hydra Corp this afternoon."

"We?" I said.

"I'll tell you the cover story Min came up with when we get upstairs," he said, putting his hand on Beejum's shoulder. "Until then, just follow my lead."

The reporters were waiting in the lobby again. I tightened my grip on Beejum's hand, but they didn't even try to ask him any questions. Or me.

"When did all this happen?" the reporter from the *Enquirer* said to Joss, and I wondered what she was talking about.

"The minute I saw her," Joss said.

"I suppose this means you're leaving the prince's employ."

"Left," Joss said, grinning, "and that's a polite way of putting it."

"Did he give you that bandage you're wearing?"

"No. That was courtesy of your enemy and mine, Quebec."

He had been moving effortlessly toward the elevators this whole time with a fascinated Verity Ann in his arms. He palmed the handset, and we stepped in. I started to state our floor, but Joss shook his head. "Beejum," he whispered, "when I tell you to, say six as loud as ever you can." He put Verity Ann down on the floor at the back of the elevator.

"You stole the prince's girlfriend," the *Enquirer* reporter said. "Aren't you worried about him stealing her back?"

"What?" I said blankly.

"Now," Joss whispered, and took me in his arms.

Beejum screamed out, "Six."

"I told you Min came up with a good cover story," he said, and kissed me.

The reporters practically killed themselves getting their cams up before the door closed. At least, I suppose they did. I wasn't paying much attention. I didn't even know the door had shut and then opened again until I heard Beejum say, "This is our floor. I did pretty good, huh?"

"How'd I do?" Joss murmured.

"What exactly is this cover story of Min's?" I said, unable to keep from smiling at him. Verity Ann was crawling out of the elevator by herself. Beejum tried to heave her up into his arms, using his knee to support her diped bottom.

"You did jolly well, old man," Joss said, taking Verity Ann from him. "You saw Clare set the bomb that blew up Morning Glory Pool and realized Clare was a spy. You tried to tell your mother, but she didn't believe you. You fled to Victoria to tell the prince, with her in hot pursuit. He, being the decadent woman-chaser that he is, wasn't interested in hearing your story. All he wanted to do was get you into bed. I, on the other hand, listened sympathetically. I called Scotland Yard to tell them you were in danger, but before they could get here, Clare had gotten hold of you."

"How did she do that?" I said, opening the door to our room.

"She kidnapped Verity Ann and Beejum and used them as bait. Beejum, you're going to have to tell the tabloiders that you called Ariadne and told her you'd run away from the evac center. Can you do that?" Beejum nodded. "So she's got you, and now that she's got you, she realizes that instead of killing you, she can use you as bait to get war secrets out of your mother. Not biots. There will be no mention of biots to the press." Beejum nodded seriously again. In another minute he'd be saluting. "Your mother came, handed over the secrets, and attempted to rescue you."

"An attempt in which she was killed," I said. "Why didn't Clare kill all of us?"

"Because I arrived in time to save you, and Miles Essex, furious that I'd taken off with his girlfriend, arrived in time to rescue both of us, a purely amateurish rescue done by an obvious civilian and not a seasoned Yard agent. Clare fled and is at large with the war secrets in her possession. If all goes as planned, Quebec will interpret war secrets to mean biots, and they will wait for Clare to turn up."

"What about all that stuff in the elevator about you stealing the prince's girlfriend?"

"Ask Min," he said, handing Verity Ann over to me. "I've got to go have a fistfight with Miles."

"A fistfight?" I said, and he smiled that melting smile again. "Are you really coming back to Hydra Corp with us?"

"Thanks to the redoubtable Minerva, I really am," he said, and kissed me again. "That kiss was not part of the cover story." He shut the door firmly in my face.

I washed cake off of Verity Ann's face, hands, and legs, and put her down for a nap in the portable crib. Beejum went in the bathroom to admire himself in his spy hat. I turned on the screen. "All right, Min," I said, "what's this cover story you've come up with?"

She told me the same story Joss had, adding a few details and at the same time showing a timetable on the screen that showed how all the story could be made to fit the events the press already knew about.

"The prince's equerry, Joss Liddell, was injured in the rescue attempt, and this injury made Hellene Ariadne realize her true feelings for the first time," Min recited.

"What?" I said. "Min, you sound like one of the tabloids."

"You wanted him to come back to Hydra Corp with you, didn't you?" she said, and didn't even wait for an answer. "When Liddell informed the prince of his intention to marry Hellene Ariadne, the prince fired Liddell."

"Intention to marry?"

"Liddell punched the prince in the nose and accompanied Hellene Ariadne to Hydra Corp, where he was employed as an assistant to Hellene Ariadne's father. Later, the prince regretted having alienated his friend and servant and agreed to be best man at a lavish postwar wedding. The couple adopted two war orphans and lived happily ever after."

"Min!" I said. "You were just supposed to come up with a story that would keep the tabloids from finding out Joss and the prince work for the Yard." And she had done just that, I realized. The prince would keep his image as an effete ladies' man, and Joss would look like a bungling amateur. Nobody would suspect the two of them were still working together. "Min, my father has resigned as head of Security. What good will it do for Joss to be his assistant?"

"Your father won't just be helping rebuild Hydra Corp after you get here, and even if he were, Liddell would still have access to me. I have access to everything at Hydra Corp, including the biot tanks."

"Min, does it ever occur to you that you're getting entirely too intuitive for a computer?"

The screen went blank. "Light raid interference makes it impossible to complete your call at this time," Min said in a flat voice.

"I'll bet," I said.

Joss knocked on the door. "Old Miles has a hard nose," he said, nursing his hand, when I let him in. "So, what do you think of the cover story?"

I got a wet washcloth from the bathroom for his hand. "What does Essex's nose look like?"

"Bloody," he said with satisfaction. "But not broken. Just what Min ordered. The blood will look suitably garish on the tabloids."

I wrapped the washcloth around his bruised knuckles. "Did you really have to hit him? Couldn't you have used stage blood or something? I mean, he saved your life last night."

"There wasn't time to set it up. At any rate, I've owed him a pop on the nose ever since the night of the Fete. It was terribly thoughtful of Min to arrange it." He grabbed my hand. "You still haven't told me what you think of Min's cover story."

"I think maybe Dad and I had better shut her down and pull her intuitives before she takes over Hydra Corp."

"She is starting to play rather the Delphic oracle, isn't she?" he said. "But she doesn't know everything. For one thing, the war's not going to last nearly as long as she thinks it is. We've found your biots, and they're nearly fully grown. For another, there's not going to be any lavish postwar wedding."

"Oh, I knew that," I said, trying to sound as if I didn't care. "Her intuitives have given her some kind of matchmaking tendencies, but you don't have to—"

"If Min thinks I'd wait until after this war or any war to marry you, she's got no intuitives at all. I intend to marry you as soon as we return to Hydra Corp. Otherwise, I shall never be able to concentrate on winning this war."

"Light raid interference has subsided," Min said, and her screen lit up. "I've made wedding arrangements for the fourteenth, the day after your arrival, Captain Liddell."

"I told you she was getting entirely too smart for her own good," I said.

Joss went over to the screen. "Min, how would you like to be an agent for Scotland Yard?"

"I should love it, sir," she said in a patriotic tone of voice I didn't even know she had programmed into her.

"Very good. Your first order is to report for duty to the Yard computer."

"Yes, sir."

"Your second is to stop eavesdropping on us. I'm going to kiss Ariadne, and I should like a little privacy."

"Righto, sir." Her screen went blank.

"Are you sure this is a good idea?" I said.

"What? Kissing you? I thought it a first-rate idea."

"I mean making Min a Yard agent. She might take over the Western States. And the Commonwealth."

"Ah, but I'll be her superior officer. She'll be taking orders from me." He put his arms around me.

"I don't know," I said. "That 'Righto, sir' didn't sound much like taking orders to me."

"She's got spunk. I like spunk in my people. Perhaps I should hire you as well. Then I could order you to stop fretting and kiss me."

"Righto, sir," I said.